The Leda

TITLES BY BILL LEFURGY

Sarah Kennecott and Jack Harden Mystery Series

INTO THE SUFFERING CITY: A NOVEL OF BALTIMORE

MURDER IN THE HAUNTED CHAMBER

Non-Fiction

CRIMINAL SLANG: ANNOTATED EDITION OF THE 1908 DICTIONARY OF THE VERNACULAR OF THE UNDERWORLD

PROSTITUTION AND ILLICIT SEX IN BALTIMORE: COMMERCIALIZED VICE, REPORT OF THE MARYLAND VICE COMMISSION, 1916

Back cover images (paperback): "'Spirit' photograph, supposedly taken during a seance, actually a double exposure or composite of superimposed cut-outs, showing woman with portraits of men and women around her head," Library of Congress, Prints and Photograph Division, https://www.loc.gov/pictures/item/91732576/ .

ISBN (Paperback): 978-1-7345678-3-0

ISBN (Kindle): 978-1-7345678-4-7

LCCN (Paperback): 2021907328

This novel's story and characters are either products of the author's imagination or used fictitiously. Baltimore is, of course, a real city, and the author has worked to frame the novel in an accurate physical and historical context. Any resemblance to actual events, organizations, or persons, living or dead, is entirely coincidental.

First edition: July 1, 2021

High Kicker Books

Takoma Park, MD

www.billlefurgy.com

The Leda

– the geological obsession of
Dr. Argile –

E.K. Wicher

Catastrophic landslides in the Leda Clay may come once in a thousand years. For a small village in Quebec, Canada, that's tomorrow.

A predatory pastor and a new ager, a harassed mayor and a biker gang meet on a landscape moulded by Leda Clay, quick and deadly.

Meet Dr. Argile as the village of St. Petraphile stands on the brink of collapse.

EKWicherbooks
1400 rue Archambault
Sainte-Adèle
Quebec J8B 2X6
Canada

ISBN 978-1-7774547-0-8

To LG, VCM and FRM with Love

The Leda Clay is a geological formation widespread in eastern Ontario and parts of Quebec. It is young as geology goes; deposited as the glaciers began their last retreat some ten thousand years ago. It is relatively soft—barely qualifying as rock—and notoriously prone to landslides. Clay is non-sentient: it has no agency, but to those whose lives are crossed by the Leda, it must seem a capricious malignity.—E.K.

PART I
OBSESSION

Chapter 1

THE VILLAGE OF St. Petraphile de Crewe lies at the edge of the Canadian Shield, where rugged hills descend to the flat farmlands of western Quebec and eastern Ontario. The inhabitants call it 'St. Pet', or Crewe, depending on whether they are speaking French or English.

Dr. Chester Argile and his partner Marie-Marie—known as 'Ems' by Anglo friends and Marie by everyone else—bought their country cabin in the hills above Crewe six years ago; the result of a down-sizing project which left them, after the dust settled, with a two-bedroom apartment in the city and the cabin as a weekend escape. As it turned out, the weekends had stretched at the expense of time spent in town. In this late-winter-almost-spring, Argile found more reasons to go up to the cabin. The heavy snows over the past winter meant some damage was inevitable and had to be repaired. Feeders needed to be filled with sunflower seeds for ravenous birds. On the list was sanding and staining the hardwood floor, and thinking about painting the kitchen. For Ems, March meant visiting relatives in Montreal.

The cabin was built seventy years ago on high ground, before watersports became a priority and the lakes and rivers of the region were besieged by summer cottagers. The summer cabins were listed by realtors as non-winterized, but Argile and Em's was made in the tradition of the logging camps; uncompromising log-on-log building with white pine, walls and roof maybe two hundred years thick. With the wood stove going, Argile wore tee-shirts even when it was twenty below outside.

The cabin stands on rock of the Canadian Shield. This is hard and ancient rock; melted, folded, up-lifted, eroded over millennia, and finally scoured by glaciers. Close by the cabin is a handsome outcrop, polished to a mosaic of red, ochre and pale grey.

A veranda stretches along the rear of the building. As soon as the snow melted, Argile had set out the two Adirondack chairs on this veranda, retrieved from their winter huddle beneath a tarpaulin. He had pictured himself with Ems sitting in these chairs, gazing across the wide valley of the Akonaga River to the flat lands of Ontario and the ridge of the Frontenac Arch in the blue haze of the far distance. It didn't happen: spring was blackfly season.

To the left of the front door is a stack of split wood, much diminished at this tag end of winter. To the right are the larger rock specimens Argile had collected over the years: pink granite, green apatite, brown micas and garnet-rich gneiss. Inside the cabin, on every free wall, Argile has built shelving, much of it loaded with smaller rocks. Only once in a long while does Ems insist that he dust.

One of these shelves displays fossils; shellfish from the ancient limestones of the region. Another shelf holds a tray of oval stones, like loaves of heavy grey bread. Cracks around the widest diameter of each stone reveal where Argile has split them with hammer and chisel. These, as Argile would explain to guests, are sedimentary nodules or 'concretions' from the Leda Clay.

"Baked with glacier flour," he would say. "And much, much younger than those other fossils."

Argile would then open the two halves to reveal shell fragments and the odd fish bone.

✦ ✦ ✦

ARGILE SAT UP, rolled slowly out of bed and walked the five steps to the bathroom, stepping over the cat stretched out on the floor. Keeping a dream coherent at four in the morning needs concentration. Otherwise, the dream disappears from the corner of the eye like a fleeing rat: all you glimpse is the tip of the tail.

Back in bed, Argile pulled the white duvet over his head: a security blanket of snow, thicker and thicker. It piled high above him, a world of not so long ago when the great Laurentian ice sheet crushed northern Canada, a thousand metres of blue glacier ice topped by white, wind-scoured desert. Beneath the bed, at the crushing, grinding base of the glacier, the rock-armored ice sculpted mountains into rounded billows. It was hot beneath the duvet. Was it hot beneath the glacier, where pressure melted the ice into lubricating streams? Did sand-laden water blast through channels? Was it a cold, quiet dark or a black, noisy hell? By this time, Argile is awake, his head in gear. These are good questions for the dog walk, the routine which started his days. But first, check the weather.

Argile reached across his wife and groped on the bedside table to find Em's Ayetech.

"Ayetech, give me the forecast for this morning," Argile held the device close and whispered so not to wake Ems.

"Certainly, Dr. Argile," Ayetech whispered back. "You can expect minus 3 degrees rising to zero at ten o'clock. Overcast but the pollen count is low." This Ayetech was a bit of a joker.

Ems was still sound asleep so Argile grabbed his clothes from the floor and tiptoed naked to the bathroom. He dressed quickly and went downstairs to be greeted by Jet, their Australian shepherd, eager for his morning walk.

Ten minutes later, Argile is following Jet along a trail which slants downhill into the forest. He has left his Ayetech smart phone on the kitchen table. He had really meant to take it, he had promised Ems he would, but he had been in a hurry to leave the house. There was fresh snow, and he wanted to be out early before the day turned sullen.

The snow is still a foot thick and a brief thaw the previous week had done little except glaze the surface. An incautious step broke through the ice crust. Snow trickled into the boot. Damn. Argile seldom wears snowshoes and usually stays on trails compacted by snowmobiles. Snowshoes are hard work.

Walking on, one sock damp against his skin, Argile passed a frozen cascade, a jagged curtain of blue icicles. Some were broken, leaving jagged stumps barring the mouth of a dark cave, like broken teeth.

Below the icefall the slope eases and the path emerged from the trees into sloping fields. In the morning mist, all is pale grey in the flat light. Argile picked his path with care, skirting the foot of the escarpment. Above are gaunt woods of oak and maple, bare in this season.

At this point, Argile is one hundred and twenty metres above sea level. Five thousand years before, the waves of the Champlain Sea would have lapped at his feet. This had been a coastline: the cabin would have been beachfront then. A sign at the lookout further along the escarpment informs the visitor that there had once been a kilometer of ice overhead. A diagram shows three Eiffel Towers stacked on top of one other. Thick ice indeed.

Argile followed the trail along the contour of the slope. It was easy going with little risk of falling. Ems really shouldn't worry so much.

The mist clears suddenly, and sun sparkles on the snow. Along the escarpment Argile has just descended, verglas gleams from slabs of bare granite. But here on the lower ground Argile is on the clay lands, once cleared for farmland but now abandoned.

Argile paused to take breath. The wind knifes across his cheek.

He clenched his fists inside his mitts, first one then the other. The temperature is minus twenty with the wind chill. His view is towards the village of Crewe, the spire of the Roman Catholic Church white against a fringe of trees bordering the partly frozen Akonaga River. On the near side of the river, cultivated land climbs in terraced steps. In contrast, the farther eastern shore is edged by low, hard hills shrouded in dark pine, spruce and hemlock. The north-facing slopes are still deeply frozen. To the southwest, the forest gives way to open fields, a patchwork of greys nibbled by partial thaw. The horizon is indistinct. Snatched by gusts of wind, snow devils rise from the open fields to meet the scudding clouds.

Argile sat on his snowshoes and watched Jet nose along the edge of the woods. Two turkey vultures skimmed the tree tops, side-slipping across the wind. The first of the spring migrants, the birds follow the snow line north, waiting for winter's corpses to emerge from the melting snow. Far from shy, the birds tilt to check Jet's health, before wheeling away downwind to look for carrion.

The dog huddled close to the ground and out of the wind. Once Argile's pulse had slowed, he stood and tramped through powder beside the edge of the woods towards a small ravine. Little more than a notch cut into the field, the ravine was carved by a stream tumbling from the escarpment above. The stream is still, frozen with only the occasional murmur to suggest the trickle of water beneath the ice.

On the ragged lip of the ravine, a small landslide has swept an ice-cream scoop of land downslope leaving a long smear of grey clay. The trees rooted in the slide are tilted backwards at wild angles, jack-strawed. Some are snapped in half, others bow so that their crowns meet the snow. Back from the edge is a deep crack a few centimeters wide. Across the gap, red roots are drawn tight as hawsers.

This is geological change in real time: impatient of millennia of gradual erosion—an interminable process—the land slides overnight. Catastrophic failure. This is a corner of the world uncomfortable in its skin. Argile's eye gleamed: the Leda Clay excited him, even in the depths of winter.

Chapter 2

THE SMALL TOWN of Schenedy Falls is in upper New York State, two hours due south of Crewe as the geese migrate, and a day by slow train from metropolitan New York. Like many close to the Canadian border, the town had seen better times. Along the banks of the fast-flowing Schenedy River, several mills had ensured the town's early prosperity. With the decline and eventual extinction of the textile industry, the town had struggled on as a minor centre for the surrounding agricultural area. Later, it was close enough to the new highway north to Canada to attract shoppers to its outlet malls. The town enjoyed a brief revival with the exploitation of natural gas from the shale underlying much of the region, but now that was exhausted and the jobs had followed the industry elsewhere. Recently, tightened controls on cross-border trade had depressed whatever industry might otherwise have flourished.

Marsha Teg, ex-marine and retired from the army on disability, had lived in Schenedy Falls since her discharge. Her house was overlarge for her needs; it had been built in the days when families of three or four children were the norm. It was clad in peeling wood with unnecessary ornament which passing motorists might think charming but was the devil to paint. There a large porch, shady in summer, which sagged alarmingly at one end where the ground had sunk beneath the downspout. The house was on a large lot which a contractor mowed weekly during the summer. A vegetable plot in the backyard had reverted to nature, but most years a few sunflowers would germinate from seeds which had fallen from the bird feeder.

Her neighbours in number twenty-four, an elderly couple, had preserved their white picket fence, but Marsha's had thoroughly rotted several years before and been removed. The Jacksons were now somewhere in Florida and would not return until the end of March. When they were home, a stars and stripes flew from the white flagpole in front of their house. Now the pole was bare, the Jacksons having politely declined Marsha's offer to raise and lower the flag in their absence. The couple in number twenty-eight to the right of the driveway were also away. They both did something in computers and used the place only on weekends.

Marsha was scrambling to print the research he had assigned her the previous week. Bible class started promptly at ten o'clock, and The Reverend Robert Harris—he insisted on 'Pastor Bob'—frowned on latecomers. The colour cartridge was running out of ink again so the copies were faint. The study group would have to live with it, she thought, with a flash of her old anger. She stapled the sheets together making sure the top copy was the sharpest and clearest. The image was a little pixelated because she had needed to zoom in for the screen capture but the label on the specimen could be read easily enough.

The temperature was getting up into the low forties these days and Marsha put on her lighter jacket. Thrusting her report into a satchel, she went out, allowing the screen door to slam behind her, and walked quickly to the corner of her road. Most mornings she would be launching into her daily run from this point—warm-up for a punishing workout—but that would have to wait for later. Instead, she swallowed meds to calm the symptoms which would otherwise be beaten into submission by exercise. Pastor Bob did not approve of running gear in study class. She slowed down to not break a sweat.

The 'Mission on Mill Street' was part of a redevelopment meant to rejuvenate the town. The project had been launched to conserve the character of downtown Schenedy Falls. Much of that character had proven too rotten to preserve, but the red brick buildings of the old mill works turned out to be sturdy and adaptable. Many had been converted into loft condominiums, which had attracted some buyers, but half remained unsold.

The Mission occupied what had been the manager's office, complete with its original dark mahogany panelling. The developers had even carefully conserved the old ticket window, where a clerk had sat to pass the weekly wages through the small opening to the mill workers lined up outside.

Harris looked up as Marsha entered the meeting room. He had already said his words of welcome to the dozen or so people who had arrived on time and was preparing to read from *The Guiding Hand*. This was a Mission publication which drew from biblical text to prescribe correct behaviour across a wide range of life situations, ranging from blogging to real estate. His audience, congregation if you like, was split between the taut-skinned and elderly, and listless youth. In her early thirties, only Marsha Teg bridged the age gap. Harris saw her as a potential magnet for more of her demographic. With his encouragement, she had passed through the Mission training camp, earning commendations from her instructors.

The 'Mission on Mill Street' was one of the dozen franchises in the northeastern states funded by the umbrella corporation known simply as "Mission". Harris had gradually extended his responsibilities as pastor to several of these, and his energy and ambition had been noted by the organization. He knew Mission's growth targets were ambitious, and that recruitment was key to advancement.

One way to achieve it was through online subscriptions to inspirational podcasts. Harris was alert to ways of improving the advertising with which Mission flooded social media. Successful religion was successful business, and he had always been secretly impressed by the marketing prowess of the opposition. Take the Old Religion, with its shrouds, bleeding statues, and the Virgin Mary manifesting in everything from tortillas chips to root vegetables. Something of the kind, but Protestant, would do nicely in Harris' opinion.

"Sorry, so sorry I'm late," said Marsha, and, in her eagerness, began to tell of her findings from her internet search. Harris quietly but firmly reminded her that the appropriate time would be at the end of the meeting. So with mounting impatience Marsha set quietly, listening to the reading from *The Guiding Hand* with helpful asides by Harris on how these should be interpreted for the every day.

Eventually, Harris snapped the book closed to signal that the time had come for group discussion. He turned to Marsha.

"Thank you, Pastor." Marsha looked around the small group in front of her. "You guys know that I have been searching the web for discoveries of biblical significance, especially in the Americas. The Pastor asked me because my Spanish is pretty good and you know, we thought stories on the web—if any—would come from the faithful in Catholic South and Central America."

Marsha knew that Harris wanted something here in the North. The face of Jesus, he had said, in a hamburger bun. Something of that sort.

"I have found something which I really hope will interest you, Pastor," continued Marsha, as she passed around her slim report.

"It's from a website folks use to sell stuff online." She was pointing to the image she had printed from the screenshot. It showed a dark grey rock shaped like an oval loaf, about a hand's width in breadth. It had been split in two to expose the pale skeletons of three tiny fish. The label said "Crewe Stone from Quebec, Canada". It was being auctioned with a reserve price of fifty dollars, from a site called Molly's Rocks.

"Yes," said Harris slowly. "Why are we looking at this exactly?"

"Well," explained Marsha. "The web site called these fish proof of the biblical flood and there was a hot exchange on social media. The bids went up into the hundreds of dollars. I thought this might be what you were looking for."

✧ ✧ ✧

THE REVEREND ROBERT Harris considered himself a modest man. Admittedly, his car was spacious and a lustrous black, but this was required by his calling. His constant travelling between Mission franchises meant it served as his private office, and respect for the grieving was an inevitable part of the job. He bought from Detroit and, as a man of the cloth, was exempt from state-wide all-electric requirements. It was a simple Lincoln; he had eschewed several of the extras the dealership had suggested.

But, on matters of the Old Testament, Harris admitted to some pride in his expertise. He was a big fan of Genesis. It had marketing appeal. Harris reflected that encased within the small round rock, the fish in the Crewe Stone came in a convenient size and packaging.

"So these fish were witness to the Great Flood?" he said. "Where exactly are they finding these creations?"

Marsha explained. "They are from a place call 'Saint Petraphile'. That's spelled 'P-E-T-R-A-P-H-I-L-E.' Weird name for a saint, I guess. Google says that's near a village called Crewe in Quebec, Canada."

She had checked: it was a four-hour drive from Schenedy Falls. "You have to cross the border, of course. So add an extra hour."

Harris knew that what most impressed senior management was finding new pastures for growing Mission, specifically by founding franchises embedded within new residential subdivisions. Mission invested where land was cheap and the people starved for spiritual guidance. Harris was privy to marketing research which confirmed that the new direction for expansion was clearly due north, into Canada. The market model projected a high rate of return.

"Thank you, Marsha. I think, people, a round of applause for Marsha. A worthy piece of research." The congregation clapped, a brief slapping that ended abruptly.

"Good, good. Well, that about wraps it up. You all have your reading for the week. Stay safe, and God bless."

Harris firmly closed *The Guiding Hand* on the lectern from which he had been reading aloud, and turned away. He was thinking quickly. It was a tried-and-true Mission practice to find a tangible, local connection when penetrating a new area. The organization found it economical to generate enthusiasm for Mission on social media using these associations. It was, frankly, click bait but of a wholesome variety.

Harris thought Marsha's discovery had potential to be such a local connection, provided there was an abundance of such stones. Surely there must be some quarry where Mission could mine these things? He resolved to propose the village of Crewe or St. Petraphile or whatever they called it as a prime candidate for expansion.

As people were leaving, Harris pulled Marsha to one side.

"Congratulations again on your research, Marsha. I think this Crewe Stone may indeed be of interest to Mission. I would like you to follow up and check out the source in person. I suggest you start with this Molly Rocks. The assignment would count as your annual contribution."

"Oh! Thank you, Pastor," said Marsha. "I can leave anytime. As soon as you want. My old camper should make it up to Canada."

Harris smiled and patted Marsha on the shoulder. He knew that a project like this beat tramping dreary streets and knocking on doors, which is what he required his flock to do when he could think of nothing better.

"You should take my nephew Priebus," he added, nodding towards the door where a pale young man was just leaving. "Travel abroad will do him a world of good."

Marsha's heart sank.

Chapter 3

DARA ODEK HAD four windows open. One was a French language news feed to keep in touch with the province, another CNN to learn the latest crazy news—fake or otherwise—from south of the border. The other two were the paper's Twitter account and its online edition.

At the interview, they had said that multitasking was a key competency for the job. No kidding. From her desk in a corner of the newsroom, Dara normally had a view of the river but yesterday morning during coffee break, the snow had slid off the south-facing metal roof with a whoosh. Now the front door to the newspaper offices was impassible and the view blocked. The three staff members had to struggle over the snowbank beside the parking lot to reach the back door. That could be a news story, thought Dara, but an avalanche of roof snow had killed no one in Quebec this year, at least not yet. Pity.

Reporting for a low-circulation weekly was the first step in Dara's journalism career and she had told herself that toiling in a provincial newsroom would soon punt her into serious writing. That was before all the main newspapers in Canada had shed staff like leaves in fall. Dara was grateful to find a reporting job here, in this corner of Quebec, for a beleaguered, English language weekly.

And a big 'Thank you' to Elsie Truelove, thought Dara. Elsie was the owner of *The Courier*, the last print newspaper still serving Crewe and the surrounding region. Also its editor and inspiration, Elsie was a type Dara thought had long gone extinct.

Dara had applied to the advert on Monster Board, and to her surprise *The Courier* had asked for an interview. As a journalism graduate fresh from Montreal, Dara didn't think she had a chance, but Elsie was persuaded by Dara's Algonquin roots. Born by the Akonaga on the reservation upriver, Dara realized that she could be the Aboriginal voice the paper lacked. She quickly discovered that Dave, the paper's lead reporter, and Lise the photo editor were reticent on Aboriginal subjects.

Dara looked up from her work to see Elsie sitting in her editorial swivel chair surveying the room. She pulled her focus back to trawling through the newspapers online in-basket.

"Any good posts this morning, Dave?" asked Dara. "I have nothing in the mail, just the usual bag of grumblers."

The online edition tried to publish more of the letters and comments received than made it into the print version. It was a way of keeping subscribers happy.

"Nope," said Dave. One of Dave's job titles was chief of social media but already by thirty-two a generation too late to connect with the post-millennials. David McClintock was also a great-great-grandson of a Scottish lumber baron who had made the Akonaga Valley his own in the last century. His company had felled the forest to bare the white bones of the land. Who had pushed my people off their land and upriver to the reservation, thought Dara.

David had inherited his ancestor's gruffness in speech. He was mulling tweets for the online page and was unreceptive.

The dream catcher spun slowly above Dara's keyboard. Dara had made one for each of her colleagues but hers was the only one doing its job in the office today. Catching daydreams, presumably so she could get down to work. The blue jay feathers woven into the web were from a bird that had crashed against the office window glass. Dara had found the corpse last week.

Dara scanned a draft of a piece she had begun yesterday. It was a feel-good story about a planned community event, an on-ice antique auction to support local charities. An annual event organized by the local historical society, it normally took place on dry land during the summer. This year, a fresh president of the society had proposed an 'on-ice' antique auction celebrating the coming end of winter. The other board members—volunteers all, and despite secret doubts—had acceded to the President's enthusiasm. The auction was to take place on the frozen bay beside Chemin de la Rivière. Naturally, owners of winter fishing huts scattered around the lower end of the bay opposed the plan. They said the banging of the auctioneer's gavel might scare the fish.

One detail caught Dara's eye. The organizers would leave the auctioneer's chair out on the ice at the end of the event. For ten dollars to support a local charity, you could place a bet on the date the chair would slip beneath the waters of the melting Akonaga. This would mark the official start of spring for Crewe, to be proclaimed by the Mayor and village dignitaries, bells ringing. It would mean local colour for the front page.

"For F's sake," thought Dara. "No wonder these local papers struggle."

The auction would take place in front of the Hotel les Draveurs, one of the older establishments along the Chemin de la Rivière. When Crewe was built, logging had been in full swing in the Akonaga Valley. *La drave*—the logging run—occurred every spring to drive the winter's cut downstream to the mills. The *draveurs* were the acrobats who danced across the rafts of logs to chivy them through the rapids. Younger patrons called the Hotel the 'Drafters' because of the wide selection of beers available on tap.

The Drafters was a popular destination pub for people driving up from the city, and the parking was usually full of Ontario plates on a sunny weekend. For some years, the Drafters had also been a rest stop for bikers out of Montreal: *les motards* known as the Blue Beards, or simply 'les Bleus', had been regular patrons. Now a large sign in the parking lot stated that the bar would not serve groups of bikers. Locals were surprised that this seemed to work. Some speculated that the hotel paid to preserve this tranquility.

The pub had a terrace overlooking the river. The auction would be relayed from the ice to a loudspeaker on the terrace. To add class, customers could make telephone bids from the hotel using a real, old-fashioned telephone, one with wires.

Dara muttered to herself as she typed 'In a break from tradition, this Sunday, the Akonaga Valley Association is holding their annual antique auction and craft fair on the ice in Crewe Bay. The auction will start promptly at two p.m. Organizers hope for good weather, but in the event of snow, rain or precipitation mixed with iceberg, the event will sink without trace. Tragedy on the Akonaga...' She started tapping the backspace repeatedly.

Dara looked across at the news board that hung on the wall beside the door. On good weeks, multi-coloured sticky notes proliferated, each with a hurried scribble about leads people were following. This week, a last yellow note had drifted to the floor, and the board was bare. Perhaps it was the damp grey weather.

"*J'ai quelquechose.*" Lise broke into Dara's reverie. "Maybe I have something for you. I'll send you the link."

Dara speed-read the text, a three-hundred-word submission for the inside section they ran for unsolicited contributions, dubbed 'Calls of the Akonaga'. At least, it differed from the usual carping. A Dr. Argile was proposing a geopark in Crewe to celebrate 'glacio-marine clays', whatever they were.

She googled 'geoparks'. There were several in Canada, mostly on the east coast and in the Rockies. It seemed there were none in western Quebec.

"*Merci* Lise. That ice auction was getting to me. Now, this guy talks a lot about the Leda Clay. That's a thing around here isn't it?"

"*Bien sûr que oui*," replied Lise. "People have died in Quebec, only last year there was this whole family gone, over in the Saguenay. The *maudit* Leda Clay. *C'était triste*".

Chapter 4

THE *DÉPANNEUR*, THE corner store at the crossing of Principale and La Rivière, 'downtown' Crewe, is called The Magnolia. It used to have a single pump with gas for sale at a steep markup. J-P, the proprietor, would explain, with impatient emphasis to motorists caught short in both gas and cash, this was because the nearest real gas station was ten miles down the road in Constance. Fuel-efficient cars had put paid to that racket. Still, you could pick up bundles of kindling, windshield washer fluid and bags of salt or grit stacked along the covered porch. A cage for propane cylinders past their due date leant against one wall of the building. J-P refilled and sold them to hurried barbecue chefs who hadn't thought to go to the discount store. Inside, it smelled of cigarettes and stale beer.

Sean Box pulled into a parking slot beside the 'dep'. He checked that the snowmobile in the back of his truck was still strapped firmly down. He grabbed his two cases of empties and pushed through the swing door, stamping more snow onto the sodden mat in the entrance.

"Salut J-P," he said. "Empties".

J-P looked up briefly and nodded to the back. "Put them on the trolley, Flatpack. Don't leave them in the cold room."

Flatpack was Sean's nickname since high school. Half the people living in Crewe were of Irish ancestry: the other half were 'real' Quebecois who traced their ancestors back to France. For youths like Sean, the common tongue was 'Franglish' with a twist of hip-hop. Box senior had strayed from the Irish to marry Marie-Lise Frippe and Sean was the product. Imperfectly bilingual, he learned French at school and English from the T.V. He could swear in both official languages. 'Box' became 'Flatpack' in the schoolyard. He was secretly pleased; he prided himself on his abs.

The beer fridge was in back. Sean pulled the door lever. Inside, frost-rimmed cases of beer in aluminium cans were stacked to the ceiling. Sean pulled out a tray of Bruno, a Quebec microbrew with Czech pretensions, labelled 'strong beer' at six-and-a-half-percent alcohol.

In summer, entering the cold room could be a relief from the heat outside. But in winter the smell of mouldering cardboard and the damp chill were unpleasant. Pushing the knob to escape the freezer, Sean wandered past the shelf holding the video library. A few years ago, there was even an adult section, but these days that business was exclusively online and in VR. The rack still held the usual disaster and action movies, Disney classics and yoga fitness tapes. For J-P it seemed to be a souvenir of better times—Sean had not seen anyone rent a movie from The Magnolia in years, this century even.

"That's twelve empties and a six of Bruno," said Sean, handing over a twenty. "And a *Courier*".

J-P gave Sean a toonie in return. "Have a nice day," he grunted.

Sean had been coming to the Magnolia since forever and buying beer since age fourteen, but that was all the change he ever got out of J-P.

Sean slid the beer behind the driver's seat and climbed into his truck with the newspaper folded in his coat pocket. He intended to scan the handful of casual jobs advertised in *The Courier*, but that could keep for later.

He was proud of his vintage Ford 150. The truck was twenty-five years old with only three-hundred-and-fifty-thousand kilometers. It was dark blue, mostly, and he supposed that the valuable parts of the vehicle were the winter tires, legally required for winter in Quebec. The engine was running well at the moment, after a long run down to Metro Laval and back the previous week. The big Ford had been fun for scattering the tiny, electric minicars which infested the city.

Reversing out from the parking beside the dep, Sean accelerated up Rue Principale, then took the left fork onto Chemin Crewe Lake, heading north. He slowed near the school. He smiled when he spotted the nose of a police cruiser poking out from behind a snowbank. He glimpsed blonde hair in a ponytail as he drove past and knew it must be Manon Patinaude: Sean had, on more than one occasion, been reprimanded by the officer. Which he had not minded because in Sean's view she was super fit. Sean supposed Manon was after drivers with Ontario plates on their way to the ski hills. She barely glanced at Sean.

The road followed a valley into the hills. At first, it ran through a forest of maple, oak and pine, a mix typical of this southern edge of the vast boreal forest which slants across Canada from the Rockies to Quebec. Further on, it passed frozen beaver ponds; white flats pierced by the sticks of drowned trees.

Too many beavers, thought Sean, as he drove past. He saw himself as a trapper in a previous life, or a *coureur du bois* perhaps. Nowadays, the Chinese fixed the price of beaver pelt and it was barely possible to make a living. The municipality gave the occasional contract to relocate stubborn beavers whose dams threatened to flood roads, but that business was sewn up by the Flemings at Brownfield. So Sean's winter income came mostly from blowing artificial snow at the local ski hill when the temperatures dropped. To supplement this, he cleared snow from roofs and driveways, strictly cash only. The past winter had seen unusually high snowfalls and the statistics on heart attacks from shoveling snow for those over sixty were encouraging. Thank you, climate change.

Sean slowed to turn onto an old fire road which climbed steeply through the forest. After nearly a kilometer, the gradient eased as Sean neared the top of the hill. The track abruptly emerged from the trees to peter out in a patch of rutted snow beside a dilapidated fire tower, long ago fallen into disuse. Sean let the truck roll to a halt.

In Sean's opinion, the crest of the escarpment had the best of views. The local youth frequented the viewpoint in summer, arriving two by two on motorbikes. But in late winter Sean knew he would be alone, which suited him fine. He sat in the truck, looking west across the descending treetops to the flat terraces of agricultural land below, gridded by the local roads; the *montées* running up from the river to the hills, tied together by the *rangs*, like rungs of a ladder which separate one row of farmsteads from the next.

Sean's gaze followed the straight arrow of a *montée* towards the white strip of the frozen river, then the dark line of trees along the Ontario shore. Flat lands stretched west to low blue hills in the far distance; the horizon fifty, sixty, perhaps a hundred clicks distant.

"Maybe next winter I'll drive to Whistler for the skiing," said Sean to himself. "Or maybe not." He imagined three days on the road and the truck dying in a Walmart parking lot near Winnipeg.

Sean reached into the glove compartment and pulled out the small bag of local weed and a pack of liquorice-flavoured rolling papers. The dope was from a friend who had a small plot in the bush. Called Akonaga Tea, the weed was good stuff, and entirely unregulated. Sean sat in the back of the truck, out of the wind, and lit up.

"Or I should have been a fire watcher," he thought, gazing up at the rusting metal derrick. The four steel legs of the fire tower were set in concrete blocks. On one of these, years ago, when he was a kid and into graffitti, he had sprayed his tag. The steel ladder to climb up to the lookout ended about fifteen feet from the ground. It could stay there as far as Sean was concerned after two drags. Those fifteen feet called for serious climbing skills.

After the smoke, Sean unhitched his tailgate and pulled the ramp down onto the snow. He undid the straps and climbed into the back of the truck to sit on the snowmobile. He pushed the electric starter. After whining briefly, the motor caught and settled down to a regular purr. Sean backed her slowly down the ramp. He zipped up his jacket, put on goggles and heavy-duty mittens.

Sean gunned the engine, pulled a steep turn which sent a shower of snow against the parked truck, and headed south along the crest of the escarpment. The first two kilometers were straight and Sean could build some speed. Other machines had left tracks earlier in the week, so the way was easy to follow. It was probably a club, he thought: riders with all the leather gear; perhaps a pair with headsets so the passengers on the back could chatter.

After getting air on one bump Sean throttled back and looked for a left fork in the trail which would take him towards the farm fields three hundred feet below.

The trail descended steeply through the trees to the foot of the escarpment. It was narrower here and less used by snowmobilers, and Sean took it slow. When he emerged from the woods, he was still on high ground relative to the church tower in Crewe which he could see in the distance. The field was rough pasture in summer but a blank sheet of ice-crusted snow in winter. It just asked to be tracked!

Late morning and the sun suddenly went behind clouds; the

day became dull with only the faintest of shadows on the snow to suggest the rise and fall of the ground beneath. Running along doing about fifty, Sean suddenly felt the machine tilt and slow. He tried to accelerate and turn out of what seemed to be a snow-filled gully. The engine screamed as he tried to drive the machine free, but he only succeeded in forcing it further into a deep groove in the snow. Finally, he gave up and switched off. He was wedged about three feet below the surface of the snow, the machine largely buried.

"Fuck it," said Sean.

✧　✧　✧

THE WHIFF OF gasoline was in the air as Argile plodded along the snowmobile track he had come across, trailed by Jet. Today, Argile carried his snowshoes, hooked over his shoulder on a stick. If you walked on the snow compacted by the machine, there was no need for them, but step off to one side and in you would go. They followed the track as it wound between rocks and trees to reach the fields at the foot of the escarpment. It now ran straight across the field in front of him, carving a white groove in the snow. But, after a hundred metres, the trail ended.

"Hey, over here!" Argile heard the shout. Jet was barking excitedly and circling a figure half buried in the snow. A minute later and Argile caught up with the dog and saw the end of a snowmobile just visible in the crevasse. Sitting awkwardly on the end of the seat was a young man, dressed in jeans and a heavy coat, looking rather sheepish.

"Fucker slipped into this *maudit* ditch," said the young man.

Argile assessed the situation. "You won't get this out without help," he said finally. I could go fetch a come-along and winch it out. I have a cabin up in the trees there."

"Great, man," said Sean, "I am kinda stuck. I guess I should wait for you here."

Argile grunted. "I don't think you have another option. What's your name?"

"Sean," said the young man.

"Mine's Argile. See you in fifteen." Argile turned and plodded back up to the tree line. The dog was already almost out of sight, lunging up the hill in the exaggerated slow motion gallop he used in deep snow.

Argile reached the cabin and collected the winch from the shed. It was awkward and heavy. Slung over his shoulder he realized that, with the extra weight, he would have to strap on his snowshoes after all. The morning walk with the dog was turning into an ordeal.

Back with the stranded snowmobiler, Argile attached the come-along to a rusted metal fencepost, the top eighteen inches protruding from the snow some distance from the machine. A single strand of barbed wire sagged beneath the snow on either side of the post.

"Lucky you didn't snag on these old field boundaries," he said, retracing his steps over to the young man. "Here. Latch on to this."

He pointed to the heavy-duty clip attached to the end of the thick strap. Sean grabbed the hook and clipped it to the bar at the back of the snowmobile, then stepped off the machine and immediately went knee deep into the snow. He stamped down a small area so he could stand aside from the machine.

"Ready?"

Argile began to work the lever back and forth and gradually the machine reappeared. When it was back on the surface, Sean jumped on and turned the ignition. The engine caught, Sean let in the clutch and drove a tight circle back to where Argile was winding up the cable.

"Hey thanks, man," said Sean. "Do you want a ride? I'm going back up to the road."

"No, that's okay," said Argile. "But you know that crack you just fell into? There are several along this slope, so best watch it next time. Oh, and maybe you could drop this winch back at my place." He gave brief directions.

"For sure," said Sean. "See ya, then."

Sean took off in a roar and a flurry of snow. After he disappeared through the trees, the whine of the engine faded and the blanketing, frozen silence returned.

Argile bent to struggle with the back buckles of his snowshoes.

"Come on, Jet," he sighed.

They retraced their steps uphill towards the cabin, the dog finally tired enough to follow in Argile's tracks.

Chapter 5

MOLLY LABERGE FOUND the spiritual energy of rock crystals calming. She was owner, manager and sole staff member of Molly's Rocks, at the unfashionable end of Rue Principale. Her small display window housed a large, blue crystal of fluorite, a geode artfully broken to show rings of agate lining hollow core, a large mass of quartz, and some perfect calcite crystal rhombs. A collection of dark grey nodules in a bowl, and some fine trilobites in black shale completed the grouping. She knew better than to clutter the window, and the blue light she used made the crystals pop against the velvet background.

Glass-covered cabinets walled the inside of the shop. Molly had selected silver rings and bracelets set with turquoise from the American southwest in the first cabinet. These caught the eye and led a visitor to the next which displayed an array of coloured semi-precious stones, along with Molly's written notes describing their healing powers. She had placed a collection of seashells in the third. These she had selected for their opaline sheen and had boosted their gleam with a carefully position spotlight. In one corner of the shop, a stack of trays full of rocks from various buying expeditions rose to the ceiling, partly concealed by exotic fabrics hanging from hooks in the ceiling—batik from Thailand where Molly had holidayed, it seemed an age ago. The scents of competing soaps permeated the air.

Molly's shop was in a small, wood-sided house dating from the early 1900s. It had originally stood on land about a mile away and later moved onto Rue Principale in the 1950s. House-moving seemed commonplace back then. People gravitated to the village as they aged, and they brought their houses with them. Molly lived in the front bedroom over the shop.

So far, the day could not be described as busy. Molly had spent the morning rummaging in her storage area looking for a box she was sure she had labelled 'Concretions and Nodules'. It contained her collection of those strange stones that formed in soft muds and sands as they turned to rock. They came in various forms, from flying saucers to grotesque nodules like balloon animals. She thought they might catch the eye of a customer.

Molly was also looking for specimens good enough to sell online. They had to photograph well. She finally found the box—the label had fallen off—and started removing each treasure from its wrapping of newspaper. As she half expected, she found nothing as dramatic as the one she had put up for online auction last month. It was a concretion from the Leda Clay that split to reveal the skeletons of three tiny fish. On an impulse she had withdrawn the specimen from auction, unnerved by the unexpectedly high bids. If there was such demand, then perhaps she should think of a marketing strategy. She hoped her friend Argile would find more good specimens on his next tramp through the Leda Clay: he always seemed to have success splitting concretions. Provided his wife let him out, that is. Molly felt sorry for Argile.

Although the till had remained firmly closed all morning, Molly was not one to dwell on the wisdom of trying to run a profitable shop in a town which had a track record of business failure. In the flush of springtime optimism new shops and restaurants opened, only to wither and die over the slow winter season, which often lasted into late April. Skiers heading for the hills rarely stopped in Crewe, except at the pub or coffee shop. It was only after the long weekend in May that tourists would start to explore and to buy.

The shop really did little to supplement Molly's income, which mainly comprised an early retirement pension. But she had paid off the mortgage on the building and let out an upstairs bedroom for extra cash. Dara, her lodger, had left for work an hour earlier and was unlikely to be back before evening, even though the office in which she worked was not more than a five-minute walk away along Chemin de la Rivière. A quiet, young woman, Dara seemed to enjoy the esoteric exhibits in the shop, had even contributed a dream catcher she had woven herself. It now competed with the cobwebs in the side window.

Given the tranquillity of the morning, the ringing of the cow bell on the screen door surprised Molly. She looked through the glass pane of the inner door—which she had left closed given the outside temperature—to see a young man struggling with the handle. Over his shoulder bobbed a woman's face.

"Turn the handle, Prieb, and push!" The man half turned, revealing a pale profile with a receding chin. He was wearing a baseball cap with the Chicago Cubs logo, a pale green shirt and blue jeans. The clothing looked light for the later stages of a northern winter.

"Oh. Hi," said the man as he turned to face Molly behind her counter. "I'm Priebus".

"And I'm Marsha, added the woman. "We saw your window as we were driving through and just had to stop," She scraped her boots on the rubber mat by the door. "We parked the camper on the street. Is that okay?"

"Well, yes, that's fine," said Molly. "Please look around. I'm here if you have questions."

While speaking, Molly checked that her Ayetech lying on the counter could get a clear view. The device monitored customers to check for potential shoplifters.

"Are you interested in anything in particular?"

While Priebus stayed by the door, Marsha examined the displays. Her eye lit upon the table where Molly had been unwrapping specimens.

Marsha pointed to a pale grey rock, rounded in the shape of a lentil. She looked at Molly enquiringly.

"I call those flying saucers," said Molly. "Sometimes they come in other shapes and forms which some say look like balloon animals".

"Yes," said Marsha, "I can see that. Is this a 'Crewe Stone'?"

"Oh," replied Molly, a little surprised. "Have you have been looking at my website? Yes, that box over there is full of our local rocks. The flying saucers are really 'concretions'. They grow around bits of shell or bone just under the seabed. Some sort of chemical deposit like you get in your kettle from hard water."

"Do you have any you have split?" asked Marsha. "I remember one on the website with fish."

Molly hesitated. She had put away the specimen with the three fish until she had spoken to Argile. She was getting a little uneasy with the directness of Marsha's questioning, and Priebus was still hovering near the cash.

"Well, no, that specimen is no longer for sale," she said and reached into the box. "But here's one I split which has a nice fossil snail. Or this one. It seems to have grown around, well, I can't quite make it out. Complete skeletons of fossil fish are rare."

"We can be in town for a few days and we would really like to get some of those fish," persisted Marsha.

Molly looked doubtful. "My friend Argile is a collector and I suppose I could ask him. I can't guarantee anything, mind."

While the women were talking, Priebus had moved over to look at a display of locally collected minerals. Suddenly he said, "I like the green crystals. Is that what folks collect around here?"

Molly turned to face Priebus. "You're holding a crystal called 'apatite'. It's pretty, isn't it? The locals mined it around here for over fifty years. Mostly, the farmers crushed it for fertilizer, the minerals being good for the crops. Nowadays, I think we have learned to focus its healing powers..."

"Yeah, well," interrupted the man, "it looks like kryptonite to me. Say, would you tell us where this Argile lives?" Priebus replaced the green crystal, picked up a rock labelled 'mica—for easing tension', hefted it in his hand and looked up expectantly.

"Er, yes," replied Molly, surprised. "Dr. Argile lives just out of town. He is the collector I was thinking of. He comes in now and again."

"Maybe we could drop by," said Marsha.

Molly hesitated but wanted to be helpful. She found a slip of paper and wrote down the address and directions. She hoped Argile wouldn't be mad at her.

"Thank you so much for your help," said Marsha. "You have a cute store here and..."

"I'll take this," said Priebus, placing the block of massive silvery brown mica on the counter by the till.

Marsha sighed and reached in her purse. Molly passed the proffered card over the reader and wrapped the rock in old newspaper.

"Great to meet you," said Marsha, clutching the parcel as she ushered Priebus out the door.

After her customers had left, Molly looked at the box that Marsha and been rifling through. There were several other concretions with suggestive shapes. It was a potential menagerie. She glanced nervously at the Ayetech. She found the device a little too independent for what—she reminded herself—should be basically a telephone. Ayetech had refolded itself and now appeared to be resting. In fact, it was digesting the conversation it had just heard and was sharing with its network the information it had gleaned about the recent customers.

✧ ✧ ✧

AFTER LEAVING THE shop, Marsha walked to the parked camper, Priebus trailing behind. They were both tired: it had been a long day driving up from northern New York. It was Marsha's van and Pastor Bob had assured her she would receive a decent mileage allowance from Mission, plus a per diem while in Canada. Paid in US dollars. The Mission drew on a diversified investment portfolio and could afford to be generous.

The highway was usually the quickest way to cross into Canada but Marsha and Priebus had driven on a day when the lineup at the border crossing was unusually long. It might have been quicker to drive through the country roads but in most border towns those crossings had been closed. Chain fences now ran down the centre of streets where Canadians faced their American neighbours.

Marsha unlocked the door to the camper. "Let's go park at the market we saw driving in and maybe pick up some fried chicken," she said quietly.

For the first time that day, Priebus smiled.

✧ ✧ ✧

OFFICER MANON PATINAUDE was scanning the plates of cars which passed her cruiser at the corner of Rue Principale and Chemin de la Rivière. The only vehicle which had been below the speed limit of fifty kilometers per hour had been a white camper van with a large 'Have U found Jesus yet?' sticker on the back and American plates. The others had been local.

"*On se souviens de lui, ben oui*" she thought. "I'll remember that one, for sure." Maybe she should have checked the tires. She doubted they were *pneus d'hiver*, as prescribed by Quebec law between December and March.

Chapter 6

I T WAS THE third of March, and the snowbank which lined the road in front of the coffee shop had partially melted and refrozen into iron-hard ice, crusted with dark grit from weeks of scraping and sanding by the municipal plow.

Jack Shawcross had to park with the near side wheels of his SUV in the snowbank. He cursed as he heard the ice scrape along the side of the vehicle. It would mean an expensive trip to the body shop in the spring. He had parked at such a tilt that his passenger had to exit from the driver's side. He let his door swing open and stood aside. Denisse Lafriche slipped her legs over the stick and eased herself out to stand beside him. Reaching past Denisse, he retrieved his black attaché case from the backseat.

"Let's see how he reacts to this proposal," said Jack. "He has had it for a couple of days. Say nothing unless I pass you a question on the numbers. Okay?"

"*Oui*, Jack, *ça va*," replied Denisse. "Let's go".

They walked a few metres up the road squeezing between the parked cars and an oncoming delivery truck, then picked their way through a gap in the snowbank to reach the sidewalk. Denisse was in her tall boots taking baby steps on the ice. She followed Jack to the door of the Café Pontiac. The Maple Leaf and the blue and white *Fleur-de-lis* of Quebec hung limply from poles above the door, both ragged after a hard winter.

Inside, the tables were empty except for one by the window where a man sat dressed for casual Friday, in an open shirt and blazer. The Flexfit jeans hugged his thighs and gave some relief to his expanding midriff. In his late forties, he had a ruddy complexion and was clutching a tall coffee.

"*Bonjour*, Bryce," said Jack. "You'll have a pastry to go with that?"

Bryce Desjardins, manager of public works for the municipality of Crewe, nodded.

"Three of those chocolate croissants," Jack called to the barista behind the counter. "One regular brew and a long espresso."

The café was empty and service swift for a change. Jack paid and carried the coffee over to the corner table.

Denisse slid along the bench beside Bryce. Jack took the chair opposite.

"You've seen these plans before Bryce, so do you think your department can recommend that minor zoning change and issue the permit? You know we have to get on the ground as soon as possible."

Jack took a rolled document from his case and spread it on the table, holding the corners down with their coffee mugs. He pointed to the slopes west of the town.

"As you see," continued Jack, "we have twenty hectares of river front for the hotel buildings and all the land right back to the foot of the hill. That is one hundred and fifty condos plus commercial. The question is whether we can get the parking and for that we need those five hectares right here, beside these houses. That will mean clearing the scrub over that so-called wetland and excavating along this hillside for the access road."

Denisse hated her boss in 'presentation' mode; when he exaggerated the laconic tones of Anglophone privilege. The family was from Toronto, having moved there from Montreal in the 1970s, together with their money. His father was in meat; the children in finance and real estate. Denisse sighed to herself: she had heard him run through the deck she had put together at least ten times, and could see the project map with her eyes closed. Beside her, she felt Bryce Desjardins stiffen.

"*Eh bien*, you know Jack, this goes by the planning committee and then to Council. That's plenty of time for objections," said Bryce "and there is the risk of a referendum if objectors get enough signatures."

"Yes," replied Jack, "and I know the committee chair. All I need from you is a briefing which makes mine the only option to make sense. Think you can manage that? Just make sure the breadcrumbs lead to the one conclusion. And no damn referendum. So make sure you nip that in the bud. By the way, how was the holiday? I never seem to get away over Christmas but I am glad to have the ski chalet used."

Jack paused, seeing that Bryce was now nodding.

"*Oui*. Okay, no problem, Jack. And looking forward to the golf this summer."

Signed, sealed and delivered, thought Denisse. She smiled sweetly at Bryce and passed him a chocolate croissant.

✧　✧　✧

THE WAY HIS strategy was falling into place pleased Jack Shaw-cross. He liked having his own way. Bryce Desjardins was a useful pawn in the real estate development he planned for Crewe.

Several hundred hectares now comprised the lands alongside the river where Jack wanted to build a large condo development and conference centre. He called it 'River View'. Jack had acquired the lands at the estate sale of two failed farms. They were the sole asset of his numbered company.

The old fields were quickly becoming overgrown from lack of grazing. The drainage was poor on the clay at the best of times and in one corner a swampy patch had developed which he feared might be classified as wetland. He felt he needed to act quickly before someone found a rare plant or animal and put the lands off limits to development. He had heard that the Mayor of Crewe had mentioned how nice it would be to see these lands protected from development as a 'natural area'.

Natural, my left foot, thought Jack. The lands had been farmed for fifty years and the wet bits were there because the culverts had silted up. Still, last fall he had encountered a group of greenies with binoculars wandering about and had warned them off. He had explained that their safety was his number one concern because the lands were being used for bow hunting. The following week he had posted signs all around the boundary warning trespassers of the danger. The graphic he had chosen needed no translation.

Much to his irritation, when he first proposed it two years previously, his scheme to develop River View had stalled. Although within the boundaries of the village of Crewe, and not subject to the strict limitations on the development of agricultural land, the area still required a zoning change. He had invested a significant sum in contracting a feasibility study, but he knew now that he had overpaid the consultant. The well-known name and string of qualifications had overly impressed him.

True, in over three hundred pages, the study had covered all aspects of the project. Shawcross had skimmed the executive summary. There was a compilation of research drawn from the web on environmental matters. The consultant had engaged local focus groups to determine social acceptability. There was an exhaustive list of scenarios run for financial viability. The last section focussed on the ground itself—the geotechnical aspects of the project. Here the contractor had, in Jack's opinion, gone into unnecessary detail by unearthing a report published by the provincial government. One paid for diligence, sure, but also for potential problems, once identified, to be dealt with. The map included in the report showed that three-quarters of the project was on Leda Clay, susceptible—as he discovered, after asking Denisse to translate from the French—to large, retrogressing landslides. The land was practically flat, for the love of God. Trust the Mayor to read the damn report to the end. Her cautious opposition had stopped approval of the project.

It was ridiculous that some public servant could at a stroke devalue his lands. Shawcross was sure he knew the type; some pasty-faced geek who never worked a minute beyond the thirty-five-hour week, if sitting at a desk looking at satellite imagery could be called 'work'. By now, the jerkoff had probably retired on an indexed pension. It was an arrogant overreach by government, and this tax payer for one would not suffer it. Even thinking about it now raised his blood pressure. His doctor had warned him not to get too worked up.

To be fair, awkward geology was not Mayor Beaubien's fault, but she still had a lot to answer for. The provincial map was old, and he was sure the Council could make zoning allowances in special cases such as River View.

As far as Jack was concerned, matters had improved since the recent election. The new government had run on a platform of less government and lower taxes. The ensuing cuts to the public service had rolled back many of the interfering edicts of the previous regime. Among the departments, Environment had suffered greatly. Many of its publications had been purged from the web, including—he noted with satisfaction—the offending map that had caused all the trouble in the first place.

Putting the project back on track had taken Jack most of the past year. His new proposal was due to come before the village planning committee in two weeks. After careful groundwork, which included his conversation with Bryce Desjardins, Jack was confident that the Mayor would not use her veto again.

✧ ✧ ✧

WHILE JACK SHAWCROSS was leading his meeting in the Café Pontiac, Argile was out on his cross-country skis. A sharp frost after a slight thaw had left an icy crust with enough strength to support his weight. He had prepared his skis with pink glide wax the previous day. With the temperature just below freezing, the ice crystals melted under the pressure of the ski and the friction was minimal.

By eleven in the morning, the sun would soften the snow, so Argile was out by eight-thirty and gliding across the fields below the escarpment, his skis hissing over the surface and the air sharp in his nostrils. Jet ranged a hundred yards to left and right, happy not to be plunging through deep snow. Argile was double-poling, effortlessly gliding thirty feet with each push.

He passed the groove carved by Sean's stuck snowmobile the day before and followed the line of the buried fence. To his left rose a tumble of fallen rocks, their angular forms softened by caps of snow. Boulders, some as large as houses, formed an apron of rocks at the base of the crag above. The gaps between the boulders formed an intricate maze, full of crevices for wildlife. Jet sniffed and lifted his leg beside a promising hole.

Somewhere under the snow, beneath the tumble of boulders, lay the hard granite of the Canadian Shield pressed against much younger limestones. Argile looked behind him along the twin track left by his skis. Beneath his feet, two ancient worlds touched; the rocks of the Shield twisted and forged in fire two billion years ago, give or take; and hard against them much younger limestones, a mere five-hundred million years old. In these limestones he had found the coiled remains of the country's oldest inhabitants, laid to rest in the down in the quiet of Cambrian seas.

The line Argile traced was a fault in the earth's crust where rocks had ruptured and foundered, creating the escarpment which defined the edge of the plateau. In his mind's eye, he saw the fault, neatly drawn. He had flown over it at thirty-thousand feet last year when returning from Europe and had seen the white streaks of the remaining snow, melting into dark, narrow lakes picked out the line of the fault. The fault ran north for a hundred kilometers, straight as a spear thrust.

To the south, Argile could follow the edge of the escarpment and its defining fault for a few kilometers to where the rock outcrops disappeared beneath fields where much younger clays hid all signs of this ancient convulsion. The fault continued, unseen at the surface, beneath Crewe and under the river to end somewhere beneath Ontario.

The route Argile chose dropped gently downhill towards the village. He would have to walk back home carrying his skis, although drivers sometimes stopped for hitchhikers. Plenty of downhillers would be heading up the valley to the hill at St. Marie, a modest and time-worn remnant of what was once a minor alp. Still, it would be a chance to buy groceries at the mini-market and collect a copy of *The Courier* which he had been buying every week since they had published his geoparks piece. He would stop at the Café Pontiac for a mid-morning coffee.

A short time later, Argile leant his skis and poles on the rack beside the coffee shop. He tied Jet to the metal bike rack, a reminder of the previous summer still half buried in the snow-bank. Dogs weren't allowed inside. Putting his shoulder against the heavy, winterized door, Argile pushed into the café and stood stamping his feet on the sodden rubber mat. Glancing around before his glasses fogged, he recognized Jack Shawcross, the developer, sitting at a corner table with two other people. He had read an article about Shawcross' River View project in *The Courier*. There had been a picture of a smiling Shawcross shaking hands with one of the village councillors. Argile doubted if Shawcross knew Argile's name: he was unlikely to figure highly on the man's list of people useful to know.

Argile ordered a latte. He looked at the girl, remembering Em's admonition to use people's first names, whenever possible. "It shows that you're human," she had said.

"Thank you, er, Candice," he said, after peering quickly at the name badge pinned to the apron of the barista. He carried the mug it to a window table far enough away to ignore the conversation on the other side of the room. He opened the paper to the editorial and letters pages. An activist group was calling for a ban on mineral exploration; a proposed adjustment to the schedule for garbage collection would utterly change the character of the village (according to the writer); and the community was invited to donate winter clothing for sponsored refugees from warmer climates.

The lead article in the paper concerned disaster relief to a community in the eastern part of the province. After a brief thaw, an ice jam had caused the local river to burst its banks, flooding the streets of a small town. Then the weather had turned cold again and, after hours of freezing rain, several electricity pylons had collapsed under the load of ice. The blackout was widespread and enduring. Several hundred people sought emergency accommodation. In a radio interview, the responsible Minister congratulated the emergency services, noting that all possible assistance was being offered. Responding to a reporter's question, the Minister acknowledged the importance of action to combat climate change, and that Quebec was at the forefront in this battle. He lamented the fact that federal funding was inadequate.

The Minister concluded by saying how heart-warming it was to see the community pulling together under these trying circumstances. It was the volunteers, *les bénévoles*, who showed the strength of our society.

Argile knew that a similar flood could easily happen here in Crewe although a downstream blockage of the Akonaga during spring thaw had not occurred in recent years Argile remembered reading tales of heroic actions to dynamite log and ice jams from the time when logging was still active on the river. It was a skill lost.

There was also another short article tucked away on an inside page about the River View project in Crewe. It seemed that the land proposed for development remained unceded by the local Ako Band, and that consultation with the band had been less than meaningful.

So Shawcross won't have it all his own way, thought Argile. The piece was by Dara Odek, a journalist at *The Courier*.

Chapter 7

T HE OLD COMPUTER was working through a barrage of new installs and patches. Argile had nursed this laptop for five years now and was still resisting Em's strong hint that he bought his own smart phone.

With its enhanced intelligence and iridescent green skin, the new Ayetech smart phones had overwhelmed their competition. Argile pretended to be unimpressed: Ayetechs may be everywhere, but they were not for him. He felt a bond with his old machine: old and getting slower, he felt they were well matched. Mind you, he did appreciate the flexibility of the Ayetech. The device could fold into different shapes, much like origami.

Argile decided on a second coffee. He had programmed himself to replenish the espresso machine in less than thirty seconds: flick on the heater, unscrew the basket, tap out the old coffee into the recycling bin, add the new coffee, tamp, twist and switch on.

The computer demanded a restart. Finally, the machine booted up and Argile connected his GPS watch.

Opening a file, Argile viewed the route he had taken the previous month. It criss-crossed the slopes along the base of the escarpment between the cabin and the woods overlooking the village of Crewe. The watch recorded the path he had taken to a fine resolution.

Today, Argile planned to revisit the survey points along this route. These he had flagged on large trees or rocks with spray paint. By repeatedly measuring the precise location of the survey points, he hoped to record ground movement; the creep of the soil downhill, or other signs of strain which might presage more dramatic movements.

In particular, Argile was watching the edge of a ravine which ran back towards the escarpment about halfway along the route. The stream running down the ravine had undermined the slope on the west side and unleashed a small slip. Argile had marked two way points, one high on the slope above the slide and another on the slip itself. It was only a matter of time before another slab of soil slid downhill, leaving a grey scar on the land and an acrid smell of rupture. He hoped his repeat surveys would allow him to measure the growth of the slide.

While waiting for his watch to charge, Argile printed a copy of the route he had taken last time, overlaid on a Google earth view of the whole escarpment above Crewe. He took the printout and inserted it into an old army surplus map case that he had picked up years ago. The map slid underneath a transparent overlay which he could mark with the pencil-crayon that Ems used for writing the names of her jams on mason jars. He made a mental note to put it back in the kitchen drawer.

Argile swallowed the dregs of his coffee and pulled his boots on. He shrugged into his coat, a process which had become more awkward since a shoulder tendon had played up. After a mild frost last night he hoped that the snow crust would support his weight, at least if he kept to existing tracks which had refrozen into solid ice. Better to be safe than sorry, he slung his snowshoes over his back on one of the poles, taking them just in case the snow was soft under the trees. He would not be caught out again and have to struggle home through the drifts.

As Argile was on the point of leaving, a blue pick-up skidded to a halt on the gravel in front of the cabin. A young man was driving; a face he recognized but damned if he could remember the name. The young man opened the door and waved.

"*Salut!*" called Sean. "I came to drop these by and to say thanks again for last week." He reached in behind the seat and pulled out a six pack. "I hope you like beer. I didn't know."

Argile gestured to the chair beside the logs on the veranda. Skidoo Sean. That was the name.

"Take a seat, Sean. I was just going out but it can wait five minutes. Thanks but I can't drink beer in the morning. You have one."

"Yeah, well, I think I will," said Sean, pulling the top of a can.

"So," said Argile, "what are you up to these days?"

"Not much doing," said Sean. "I am usually at St. Marie ski resort but they have stopped making snow and are laying off for the season. I might go up later if the sun warms up and softens the slopes: the boarding is best in the spring. Anyway thanks for pulling me out of the snow." He gestured towards the snowmobile in the back of the truck. "If you want to go for a ride, I could take you."

It occurred to Argile that he might get around the route much quicker on the snowmobile. And much easier on the knees.

"Are you interested in helping with something this morning, Sean? Seeing that you are not working? I have to go out and mark some trees along the base of the escarpment towards Crewe. I have to carry this pack, and it would be much faster if you gave me a ride."

"Sure. Are you tapping maples?" asked Sean. "My uncle has an *érablière* over towards Constance but he won't get going for a couple of weeks."

"No," replied Argile. "I don't make maple syrup. I am marking rocks and trees for a survey. I can explain on the way but it relates to that hole you fell into last week. It was a slump, and it wasn't there before Christmas."

Argile showed Sean a print of an aerial view of the escarpment and the slopes below the cabin. A drone flown by a friend of Argile had taken the shot the previous November. On the image, a carpet of maples, still vivid in rags of red, mingled with the dark green of pines. The leaf cover was thin enough to see through to see the forest floor where light glinted from wet rock. The bare fields below the woods were a uniform grey.

"Wow," said Sean. "That's a neat pic. So are you some kind of professor or something. Geo-stuff?"

"Well, yes. Geo-stuff. I am interested in landslides. Geomorphology."

Sean took a long pull on the beer can.

"So I wasn't such so stupid," said Sean, "I had ridden that way before, *pas de problemo*. Now you tell me that hole was new. I'd like to see that again. Why don't you get your stuff and show me where to go."

Sean went to the back of the truck, dropped the tailgate and walked the machine backwards onto the ground. Argile sat behind Sean and leaned over his shoulder.

"Follow the main trail down here past the icefall and then along the top of the fields where you got stuck."

"Right, hold on!"

Sean revved the motor, and let the machine lurch forward. They followed the track down through the trees. When they levelled out at the top of the field, Sean gunned the engine and they sped forwards, engine whining. A minute later, Argile tapped Sean who pulled left, throwing up a spray of snow and stopped.

"Here, right?" he asked.

Argile swung his leg over the back of the machine. He put his hand against a red mark on the side of a prominent boulder at the edge of the forest. There was a pale silhouette of his own hand outlined in a puff of spray paint. He had, much against his own rules, sprayed over his gloved hand when marking this rock last summer. This, however, was for science.

"This is the first point, what I call the 'key rock'. Argile pressed the button on his watch to record a way mark. Then he pointed down the slope, still covered with a blanket of snow.

"That's where you went in," said Argile. "You can just see the dip in the slope. Come back after the snow has melted if you want to see the crack. There should be a nice land slip there later in the spring."

Argile looked down at his route map.

"Ok, that's it," he said to Sean. "Let's move on to the next survey marker. Follow this line of trees."

Sean drove while Argile watched for the red blazes on the rocks and trees. He tapped on Sean's shoulder as they approached the next waypoint.

"Here," said Argile.

After an hour, they had checked at thirty-five survey points, all now logged on the GPS.

"Is that it?" said Sean. "Seems we have come a long way."

"Yes, that's it," replied Argile. "Usually I take a whole morning to do that route; today only an hour. Thanks very much. I owe you a coffee. Do you want to drive on into town? We could stop at the Café Pontiac."

"Sure thing. But you know, I used to work at that café when I was a kid. Got fired for smoking."

A few minutes later, Sean and Argile were entering the village. Sean drove along the snow-covered bike path, cyclists having abandoned the new path for the winter. He stopped the snow-mobile beside a municipal sign which prohibited skateboarding, electric bicycles and required owners of dogs were to keep them on leash. The parking of snowmobiles had so far escaped regulation. Sean turned off the ignition, and the two crossed the road to the Café Pontiac.

✧　✧　✧

"I'LL NEED A plug-in," said Argile as he took the laptop from his pack and looked around. Before the main window, a battered leather couch and two armchairs of similar vintage surrounded a low table covered in magazines. 'Free Wi-Fi' said a sign.

"Let's sit over there," said Argile. "What do you want Sean?"

But Sean was looking at the girl behind the counter.

"*Salut*, Candice!" Sean called to the girl, who was engrossed in her Ayetech. "Long time no see."

Sean and Candice had struggled through grades eight to twelve at the high school in Constance. They had been casual friends at school, and, most memorably from Sean's viewpoint, his date for the excellent bush party after graduation when the beer had flowed freely. Still, they had stayed on reasonable terms.

Candice dragged her attention away from the rapid fire texting she was having with a friend.

"Oh, Hi Flatpack, what's up? What are you working at now? Try the special, it comes with a free drink."

"Okay, whatever. And a coke," replied Sean. "I am driving this guy around looking at trees." Sean pointed to Argile, who sighed, reaching for his wallet.

"And a latte please. We are just over there." Argile indicated the couch.

Argile went back to the table, found the plugin and booted his computer. He connected to the Café's network and tapped in the password written in large caps on a card under the plate glass covering the table. Sean had sauntered back from chatting with Candice. He was sucking on his drink, and carrying coffee for Argile.

"Thanks," said Argile, removing his GPS watch and connecting it to the laptop. "Let's see if this works here."

Sean and Argile sat side by side on the couch and looked at a map of Crewe on the computer screen. Overlain on the background topography was the route they had followed that morning. It looked like a string of pearls, pale on a green background.

"The background is a summer image from Google," said Argile, "and each of those pear-shaped drops marks where we stopped".

Argile pressed the keyboard to add more overlays. The screen now showed twisted necklaces of strands which wound across the hillside east towards Crewe and then back to a starting point near Argile's cabin. Each strand was a different colour, and they mostly overlapped.

"Each colour is a different survey. I walked that route every month over the last two years."

"You can get a better sense of what is happening if I do this." Argile took the first and last survey layer and used the GIS software to subtract them. "There. That's the difference in centimetres, what we call the 'delta'. Now you can see the slope where you got stuck. Those survey points higher up the slope are showing what, maybe ten to fifteen centimetres? But look at the point downslope—it has moved nearly two-point-five metres! That's your fissure."

Sean slumped into the depths of the leather couch. He looked up gratefully when Candice arrived with a plate of *poutine du jour*, French fries with cheese curds.

"Poutine gourmand, with extra bacon," she said quietly to Sean, glancing back towards the service counter where the owner of the café had just appeared.

"Neat. Thanks Candy," said Sean. He said nothing more for a few minutes as he swallowed fries and gravy. Meanwhile, Argile fiddled with the laptop to adjust the display.

Then Sean said, "Do you need the snow cleared off your roof? I could do that. Only fifty dollars a shot."

"It's March," replied Argile. "You are four months of winter too late. But I could do with a hand to move some boxes to storage. I need a truck. Would you be on for some time next week?"

They arranged to meet the following Tuesday. Rock-filled boxes filled half the garage and Ems had made it clear to Argile that he should find alternative storage.

Chapter 8

E MS HAD RETURNED from the city late the previous evening and Argile got up carefully so not to wake her. He climbed carefully down the spiral staircase from the mezzanine. The cat, Lalique, was stretched on the bottom step.

Argile went into the kitchen. Jet was wagging his tail furiously.

Argile pushed open the sliding door to the veranda and watched the dog bound across grass stiff with frost. Argile stepped outside, wincing at the cold.

After completing ten minutes of leisurely stretches, vaguely Tai-chi, he went back inside and helped himself to cereal and orange juice. He glanced at his watch: definitely time for coffee. Argile started the espresso machine. It ran through its cycle of internal grindings and grunts before dribbling out coffee into a couple of cups. He knew the smell would waft up to the mezzanine.

Sure enough, Ems head appeared over the mezzanine bannister.

"*Merde*, buy a quieter machine, *pour l'amour du Dieu*," she grumbled.

"Oh, you're welcome," replied Argile. "It still makes good coffee, you know."

Ems came down the spiral stair wrapped in a dressing gown and sat down at the table. She turned on her Ayetech.

"What's up in the world today?" Argile asked after five

minutes of silence.

Ems needed information first thing in the morning. Before coffee. Even before a shower. Connecting to Ayetech—to Facebook and to the world—an essential part of her morning routine.

"Oh, the President is tweeting again," she said. A gap of two weeks between tweets had raised concerns about the President's health.

"And it's minus two degrees," she added. Minus five, thought Argile looking out of the window at the actual thermometer. "And your pension is in the account. Chester, are you listening?"

Argile nodded. He was trying to hear the radio but Ems kept the volume a fraction too low, as usual. RadioCanada was reporting traffic congestion on the bridges, suspected collusion in municipal contracting, and lengthening wait times at the local hospitals.

"There is a whole hoopla—*toutes sortes de niasserie*—about gas drilling in eastern Ontario," said Ems reading from her news feed. "It's the fracking again." She turned up the volume on the radio.

"You should really see the doctor about your hearing, you know."

An agitated voice issued from the radio. "...and, as I said before, the Province's partnership with TiteGas is going to be a catastrophe. We are spending eighty-million dollars of our own money to pay for these test drillings. Who is going to pay to clean up the mess? We are! We pay to murder our own environment and let the polluter go free. Public-private partnership? Pay, probe and pollute, more like."

The voice of the radio host came back on.

"To recap, the Province has just announced a partnership with Canadian TiteGas, a junior oil and gas company based in Calgary, to dig a number of test drillings on leases issued last year.

Local communities are opposing the drilling program, citing concerns over water pollution from proposed shale-fracking operations. Michel Monchagrin, our regular contributor on environmental matters, from EcoClub Canada. Thank you."

"*Merci*, Monsieur, and thanks for having me."

Argile reached across the table to switch to a station with a tranquil playlist and turned down the volume slightly.

"You know, Ems, the new tech greatly limits the impact of fracking. That won't satisfy those opposed, I guess. NGOs like EcoClub thrive on these fears."

"You could launch a second career as a professional cynic," said Ems, grimacing at the contents of her coffee cup. "But first maybe clean the filter screen. This tastes *de la merde*."

"Well, TiteGas is on to an interesting play," replied Argile. He visualized the black shale of the Ordovician Period, rich in vestiges of the life of ancient seas, lying deep beneath the eastern flatlands of Ontario. Over millennia, oil and natural gas was sweated from the shale, later to be trapped and sealed underground by impermeable salts.

"But I doubt if it's economic," he added. "Even with all the surplus equipment coming across from Alberta. My advice, Ems, is don't invest."

"*Très drôle, mon Chester*," said Ems.

Argile turned the espresso machine on its side and unscrewed the filter screen. This had been a major domestic discovery. There had been no mention in the instruction manual of this hidden screw or the need to clean out the screen from time to time. For months, he and Ems had been persuading themselves that the coffee was just fine. It was rancid: the screen was growing a black crust of moldering grounds.

'Play' was just the right term. Exploration had once been an adventure, a gamble. Its actors were the geologists and geophysicists competing to convince larger-than-life vice-presidents to commit their budgets in overlooked corners of the map. On the rigs were roustabouts and roughnecks, drillers and derrickmen. Global cowboys searching for black gold.

Today, there was little need for old-style exploration. Fracking had changed the exploration business to 'just in time' delivery from subterranean warehouses of shale, delivered by the brute force of monstrous pumps. Argile felt the romance had gone.

"You know, Ems, shales are like people. They each have their own character."

Ems did not tolerate geology lectures at breakfast.

"Really, Chester, you should pay more attention to the news. This TiteGas outfit seems serious about drilling near here."

But Argile was not listening. He was thinking about clays and their transformation into shales. Under the surface cover of Leda Clay, beneath the massive limestones of the Paleozoic era, lay the black shale called the Wendigo. It was once a soft clay, rich in dead micro-organisms that had sifted to the floor of a poisonous sea. Now, after three hundred million years of heat and compression the clay had hardened into shale; brittle, siliceous and eminently frackable.

"*Un autre café?*" said Ems. "The *météo* predicts rain for the weekend. And, for the rest of the month, cool and wet." She reached across to take the jug from the machine to refill the mugs.

"That should see the snowbanks melt, at any rate," replied Argile. "Given that the ground is already saturated with water, more rain on top of snow melt will mean flooding along Chemin de la Rivière."

"Did you finish that letter to *The Courier*?" asked Ems.

Argile nodded. He had finally decided, after some hesitation, to write a letter warning Crewe residents of the peril of Leda Clay. His earlier contribution to *The Courier* had not gained traction, merely a letter from Geoparks Canada thanking him for his suggestion. The reply noted that a geopark for clays might lack crowd appeal.

The Leda Clay was Argile's particular enthusiasm. The Leda is notorious across Quebec for its tendency to slip and slide unpredictably. It causes many problems; from the cracking of house foundations by uneven settlement, to major landslides. Leda Clay underlies much of Crewe.

A map, published by the Quebec Ministry of Public Security put Crewe on notice several years ago. It showed communities at risk from hazards such as landslide. Red hachuring on the map covered much of the municipality. This raised more indignation than alarm: implications for property values were unwelcome and people disbelieved what they regarded as a high-handed imposition by provincial bureaucrats.

"Experts being experts," said an editorial in *The Courier*. A quick Google search showed how wrong experts could be. The map gathered dust in the municipal library. After several uneventful years, many were convinced that modern engineering had tamed the capricious nature of the Leda.

Chapter 9

I T WAS THE third week of April. Rain was dripping from the corner of the gutter, the splashes boring a tunnel through the remaining snowbank. The melting of glaciers in miniature: like Greenland, that pallid ice-cap riddled with tunnels bored by meltwater. All the ice gone by mid-century, so say the experts.

Gone by noon at this rate, thought Argile.

It had been raining for much of the week, a driving rain, the product of a large depression which had stalled and was spinning over eastern Canada, sucking humidity north from the Gulf of Mexico. The system was taking its sweet time churning slowly towards the Atlantic. And the rain—while not torrential—was causing concern about flooding, not the flash variety but the inexorable drowning of flood plains inch by inch. The dam on the Akonaga below Crewe had already been opened in anticipation of the crest moving downstream.

Argile opened his computer. He logged into *The Courier Online* and clicked on the letters section. He saw that the paper had published his letter. No 'likes' so far. Just one angry emoticon. He wondered who could be so enraged about hearing the facts about Leda Clay.

On the front page was a picture of the river flowing strongly in front of the Hotel les Draveurs. The river ice had disappeared almost overnight, forced upwards and broken up by the rising waters, then tumbling and spinning downstream. The armchair on the ice in the bay had disappeared. One 'J.R.', a passing tourist, untraceable, had won the pool. The bar regulars shared the winnings. Now, despite the chill wind, the hotel management had decreed the start of patio season. Staff had dragged off the tarps and set out benches and tables for the lunchtime crowd.

Argile heard a car on the gravel in front of the cabin. Ems and Jet had gone to the food market in Crewe to pick up some essentials, and he was not expecting their return quite yet.

He heard the screen door swing open. "Hello? Are you Dr. Argile?"

Argile looked up to see a woman in green fatigues in the doorway. Behind her, leaning against a large, white camper was a younger man.

Argile nodded.

"Hi, my name is Marsha Teg. That's my partner Priebus." Marsha waved vaguely over her shoulder. "We have just driven up from New York. Molly, who runs the rock shop in town said you might help us."

"Oh, yes?" said Argile.

"Those are kinda pretty," said Priebus, before Marsha could continue.

Argile saw that Priebus was pointing to his doorstep collection, ranged beside the front door. This was the heavy stuff too big to bring inside. The rocks came from various road cuts in the region. The best piece was a schist, rich in garnets the size of quarters, but there was also a massive sheet of mica, and a twenty-pound block of feldspar-quartz vein, latticed with shiny veins of graphite. There was nothing here remotely semi-precious, but the specimens were there to be admired. It was rare that someone appreciated them.

"My wife will be back soon. Why don't you sit down?" Argile nodded to the bench beside the door. "Would you like coffee?"

Priebus nodded. "Thank you, Sir. Long, white and two sugars would be great."

"Just black for me, please," said Marsha.

When Argile returned with the coffees, Marsha was still standing while Priebus was hefting a large block he had selected from the collection.

"I know this one," said Priebus. "It's a mica".

"Yes, young man. It is indeed a mica. Or phlogopite to be precise. It was mined around here extensively and...,"

"We are interested in finding some good fish fossils, Dr. Argile" said Marsha firmly, casting a wilting look at Priebus. "We saw one on Molly's website. A 'Crewe Stone', she called it. Molly said you might have more you might sell us."

"Ah yes. The three fish. That was a nice specimen, wasn't it? I found it by cracking open a concretion from the Leda Clay."

"Did you find it here?" asked Marsha.

"Not just around here," said Argile, amused. "These rocks are much too old. No, the good collecting is along the river. But only when the water level is low." He did not elaborate; he was not about to share his favourite spots.

"Sir, may I use your washroom?" asked Priebus suddenly.

Argile nodded and gave the simple directions.

✧   ✧   ✧

MARSHA WATCHED PRIEBUS disappear inside. She turned back to Argile.

"Dr. Argile, we represent a community group back in Schenedy Falls. We all agree it would be a great attraction at our annual fund raiser. We are up here in Canada on vacation and thought to drop by. Perhaps we could buy some from you?"

As a cover story, this was weak, Marsha realized. But the subterfuge had been authorised by Mission: a little white lie. Pastor Bob had insisted that she not reveal his real objective in securing a supply of the fish fossils. And on no account was she to mention the Great Flood.

"I doubt that fossils from the Leda Clay would be of much interest," said Argile.

Priebus emerged from the cabin to overhear Argile's comment.

"Yessir," he said. "Folks will love them. They are proof of the Great..."

Priebus hesitated. Another vehicle had come down the driveway and stopped beside them. The woman driver rolled down the window and looked enquiringly at Argile. A dog hung it head out of the back window.

"These people are up from the States and are interested in the local geology," explained Argile. Turning to Marsha he added. "This is my wife Ems. She spends most of the week in the city at our apartment."

Ems got out and nodded to Marsha.

"*Bonjour*," she said, then walked back to the open the trunk. It was full of groceries. Jet bounded from the open door and rushed to inspect the strangers.

"Hi, Mrs. Argile. I see you have some unloading to do," said Marsha, patting down the dog. "We are just leaving. I am so sorry the camper is in your way. Good to meet you, Dr. Argile. Let's go Priebus!"

✧   ✧   ✧

AFTER THE CAMPER had disappeared down the drive, Ems turned to Argile.

"*Des États?*" What did they want with you, those Americans?"

Argile explained.

"*Bon*, but please Chester, no more boxes stored in the garage. They can collect those rocks by themselves!"

Chapter 10

Pumping up the tires on his mountain bike to a moderate pressure, Argile rehearsed the question he had prepared for Council on the risk of a landslide above Crewe. He had drafted it several times. Now, he felt, he had his points clear.

Council met on the first Monday of every month, starting at seven pm in the town hall on Rue Principale. It was now May, the evenings were getting longer, and for the past few days the temperature had struggled up into the low double digits. Argile decided to ride to the Council meeting on his mountain bike. Downhill almost all the way, it should not take more than twenty minutes.

On the swift ride, Argile had to concentrate to avoid potholes and treacherous patches of loose gravel. This took his mind from the prospect of facing Council. As he neared his destination, he felt the familiar queasiness at the prospect of speaking in public.

Argile dismounted and leaned his bicycle against the railing in front of the town hall. He attached the cable lock. An unguarded bike could tempt the likes of Sean's less reputable friends. Besides bicycles, Argile knew they lifted ski and snowboard equipment from the racks at the St. Marie ski hill while the owners were inside paying for expensive indigestion. There had been an upswing in this kind of crime, and the regional police in Constance had staked out the ski hill parking lot in response to the many complaints. The police made no arrests but had had a profitable time, ticketing many of the Ontario visitors who had forgotten to attach annual renewal stickers to their licence plates.

It was a few minutes before seven, so Argile sat on one of the limestone blocks which formed a retaining wall to the left of the entrance to the building. The light grey stone was from local quarries. The rough surface of each block was a snapshot of an ancient seabed. Argile recognized the coils of gastropod snails, a shell mash and the crinkled stalks of sea fans. The oblique evening light etched their skeletal traces in low relief.

People were already filing past him into the hall. After a few minutes, Argile dragged his mind back from his Silurian beach and followed them in.

Crewe's council chamber was a functional room. Decoration was minimal, furnishings sparse. There was a raised stage with a utilitarian desk and chair for the Mayor in the centre. Flanking the mayor, seats for the six councillors were arranged in a curve whose focal point was a wooden lectern on the floor of the hall. From here, members of the public addressed Council. Below the stage were desks for the clerk, assorted municipal staff and recorders. There was space in the room for perhaps sixty people on folding chairs. Twenty was a typical turnout.

Argile pushed open the door marked *Grande Salle* and went in. The councillors had yet to arrive, and only two members of municipal staff were present. A handful of citizens were selecting chairs.

'*Bonjour*, Good Evening," said the clerk, handing Argile a clip board. "Please sign the list if you want to address council." Argile read the name Jack Shawcross, first on the list. He wrote his name and address, then took a seat near the middle of the room.

Glancing left, he was familiar enough with local politics to recognize the 'group of four'; regulars at Council who opposed any proposal to raise taxes. A handful of petitioners sat to his right. Most looked grim and avoided eye contact. He thought that they must be first timers at a council meeting, here to seek variations to municipal zoning laws; a misplaced fence line perhaps, or inappropriate drainage. In the front row sat the developer Shawcross and his assistant.

At seven precisely, a door to the side of the stage opened and the council members filed in. None looked happy. The pre-meeting had gone badly and the Mayor's cheerfulness, nodding at staff and people she recognized in the audience, was forced. Once seated, those councillors who had not bothered to read the briefing notes prepared by staff reached for the large binders on the desks before them and began to flip through the pages. Those who had done their homework looked more relaxed, sitting back in the deep chairs and looking to see who they recognized in the room. Council meetings in Crewe were fairly intimate affairs.

Mayor Hilary Beaubien sat down and placed her Ayetech squarely in front of her on the desk. The device folded itself to angle the screen for easy reading. Protocol required she alternate between English and French and the Ayetech had highlighted the text in different colours according to language. The Mayor glanced down, hesitated and then called the meeting to order.

She moved quickly through the preliminaries, gave a brief report on the state of Crewe, and lamented the condition of municipal roads. There had been a heavy snowstorm—*une vraie tempête de neige*—followed by a rapid thaw. She feared Opera-tions would go over-budget. She noted her planned attendance at a conference of local mayors, and finished by complementing the organizers of fundraising to support the local seniors' home. Lifting her head to scan the room, and with an encouraging smile, the Mayor invited the public to address council. The town clerk rose to call the first name listed on his clipboard.

Jack Shawcross rose from his chair and walked to the podium.

"Thank you, Madame Mayor. *Merci*". The developer introduced himself, then begged a moment for his Ayetech to connect to the projector. "I have a short presentation relating to River View, if you will bear with me..."

The screen showed a simulated walk-through of the project. The route wound between gleaming condos, following a path which Shawcross insisted was an 'active transport' corridor. A large central block overlooked the river would house a hotel and offer commercial space along a 'human scale' riverfront. Smiling families wandered among species of tree which looked vaguely subtropical.

Argile knew that Leda Clay underlay much of the project. As he listened, he realized that Shawcross' patter was about spaces for living, through flow, lifestyle. Shawcross did not mention the Leda once but had used the word 'synergy' three times, by Argile's count.

How the man droned on! Perhaps the Mayor would cut him short. Or some other interruption; a heart attack perhaps? Argile mentally scolded himself for this uncharitable thought. The seat was hard and Argile recrossed his legs as he felt a slight cramp in his calve. God, the presentation was tedious.

Relief came sooner than expected. As Shawcross ran down his bulleted list of economic benefits on slide fifteen, the earthquake struck.

The first suggestion of imminent commotion was a faint rumbling which caused heads to swing towards the eastern wall. The noise rose rapidly like an onrushing train; the screen started to shake and tiny concentric ripples formed in the water jugs before each council member. Then the train receded just as rapidly in the opposite direction. Then silence: Jack Shawcross had stopped at the third bullet.

Argile knew it was a minor earthquake; unusual for the area, but not without precedent. He watched Mayor Beaubien take out a Kleenex and mop up the slight spill of water. She looked pale.

"Ladies and gentlemen, *Mesdames et Monsieurs*," said the Mayor after a few seconds. "I believe we have just felt a slight earth tremor."

People in the hall who had been ignoring their neighbours burst into excited discussion. The counsellors glanced sheepishly at each other.

"No harm done, I think," said the Mayor, calling for order. "Perhaps we can get back to business. Mr. Shawcross, did you have a question for council? I believe you had almost concluded your presentation before we were interrupted."

Argile had felt these tremors before—they occurred every few years—and he supposed that there were many more too small to be felt. He wondered briefly whether he had had a genuine premonition, but banished the thought. Still, it was some coincidence. He looked across the room, recognizing a young reporter from *The Courier* who he remembered was called Dara Odek. He supposed that she had drawn the short straw for the Monday night council meeting.

Shawcross was speaking again.

"And so, Madame Mayor, counsellors, River View is seeking a minor variance to the bylaws to allow this access road to be built. Without it, the economics of the project frankly will not fly, and I need not mention the knock-on effect our withdrawal from this development would have on local business. Thank you."

"*Merci*, Mr. Shawcross," said the Mayor. "Thank you for reminding us."

The Mayor glanced left and right to see if there were any questions from the councillors. "No? Let's move on. Dr. Argile?"

Argile stood and walked to the podium. He took a deep breath and addressed Mayor Beaubien directly, avoiding the glare from the counsellor at the end of the row. The previous year,

Argile had objected to an ill-considered regulation on municipal signage. By doing so, he had crossed Agnes Black, counsellor for the River Ward whose baby it had been. Agnes Black was not of a forgiving nature. That was the last time Argile had ventured into local politics. Crewe was a small arena, perhaps, but blood was often left on the sand.

"Madame Beaubien," he began. "The minor earthquake we have just felt reminds us that we build our town on uncertain foundations. We are at high risk from Leda Clay. You will, I hope, recall the map prepared by government experts which showed the zones at risk around Crewe. It is unfortunate that Council voted to remove this map from the municipal website. I find that regrettable. It was a useful reference for anyone planning to build. Madame Beaubien, how will the municipality minimize the landslide risk for new development around Crewe? For instance, will there be more building in the red zone on the provincial risk map, and..."

"Once in thousand years," came a call from behind him. Jack Shawcross had risen and was shouting across the room. "Once in a thousand years is what they said. You can't remove half the land from development just because of a slight chance. It's ridiculous."

Argile half-turned towards the interruption. He found himself short of breath, a tightening across his chest. "But it's a legitimate concern!"

"It is government overreach!" shouted Shawcross.

"Perhaps I could ask Dr. Argile a question, Madame Mayor?" Counsellor Black interrupted in a voice practised at quelling fractious meetings. She hunched forward on her forearms to speak into the microphone, fixing Argile with a baleful look.

"It is a comment really, Dr. Argile. I am not sure that we have a note of any engineering expertise on your part. I, for one, am assured that our new building codes fully mitigate any risk. We withdrew the map to which you refer to prevent alarming our citizens unnecessarily. Developers in this day and age can fully manage such issues. Mr. Shawcross here—she nodded across to the seated developer—has undertaken a thorough geotechnical investigation. Frankly, I am unclear why you consider yourself more expert in this field than the professionals?"

Argile felt his face flush but before he could reply, the Mayor intervened.

"I thank Dr. Argile for his question. The Leda Clay is certainly a concern for this community, but our budget for remedial work is small. As Madame Black notes, new projects have to undertake their own detailed analysis."

The Mayor paused, seeing Jack Shawcross nodding.

"And, to answer your question, Dr. Argile, I am not sure that we have any zone coloured red anymore." She looked down to the officials' desk for confirmation from her Director of Public Works. Bryce Desjardins gave a thumbs up.

"Yes, I believe that is correct. I would like to thank you, Dr. Argile for your question. Now, I think we should move on to the next item, the—she glanced at her Ayetech—variance to the by-law on collection of compost."

Argile sat down. He leaned back against the wall and closed his eyes. He was aware that his neighbours to either side had edged away.

The meeting settled into its administrative stride. The long-winded and slow reading of the relevant by-law clauses preceded each discussion. It would be a long evening. Motions were stated, seconded and voted. The most significant of these related to River View, which passed unanimously. At least Shawcross and his party had stayed for appearances' sake but the conclusion was foregone. The matter had been decided in committee.

The council meeting finally ended and Argile quickly slipped out of the door. It was gathering dusk and Argile fumbled to attach his rear light. As he was bending over, the reporter he had noticed earlier came over to speak to him.

"Hi, Dr. Argile. I'm Dara Odek from *The Courier*. Do you mind if I ask you some questions?"

Argile straightened.

"Well, I suppose so," he muttered.

"I was interested to read your article on Geoparks, Dr. Argile. I was sorry to see that your proposal didn't go anywhere."

"Oh, thank you," said Argile. "You are the first person I've met who has read it. I thought I had explained clearly about the superb local examples of instability in glacio-marine sediments."

"You did: I was most impressed," said Dara. "But if I may, I have a question about your comments on the River View development. What are your concerns?"

"I think the ground is unstable. No one should build there."

"The developer insists that he has done a thorough study," replied Dara.

"Woefully inadequate," said Argile. "There was not enough sampling, the rigour of the analysis was abysmal and the consultant was too keen to please his client."

"So what's wrong with the sampling?" said Dara.

"Not enough of it. Lots of copy/paste from other reports but little new data. Look, it's late and I need to get home..."

"Sure thing, Dr. Argile. I don't want to keep you but, please, one last question. I guess you also know about earthquakes. Was that a real quake we felt earlier this evening?"

"Yes, it was," replied Argile. "They are not unusual, even here in mid-continent where things should be quiet tectonically. The danger around Crewe is that even small earthquakes can shake the Leda Clay, and cause hillsides to collapse."

"Tecto what?" asked Dara.

Argile winced. "It means movement in the earth's crust. Look, I need to go before the light fails completely. If you want to understand what I am talking about, best you look at some evidence yourself. I can show you a landslide in the Leda Clay. After today's shake it may have slid again."

Argile straddled his bicycle, clipped in his left foot and buckled his helmet.

"Come up to the cabin around ten o'clock tomorrow morning," he said. "We are on Chemin Ridge, near the top of the hill. Watch for the sign. I expect to be there all morning."

Dara watched as Argile wobbled on to the cycle path, his red tail light blinking against the dark trees.

Chapter 11

D ARA HAD DRIVEN her small car, an ancient Honda Civic, pretty hard over the last few months. There was still plenty of loose gravel on the roads around Crewe scattered by the municipal gritters and several chips had appeared in her windscreen from stones flipped up by passing vehicles. Despite the seasonal blitz by auto glass and body shops in the media, repairs to her screen probably wouldn't happen. An oil change and swapping the snow tires for the just-legal tires she had used the previous summer was about all Dara wanted to spend on her automobile.

Over the winter, the cold had penetrated deeply, binding the road beds with solid ice. Now in March, the period of *degel* had begun as the ice thawed. On the highways, signs implored truckers to reduce their loads. On country roads, drivers could recognize *degel* by the rollercoaster ride as the ice melted unevenly, first over seepages of ground water and culverts, later over the drier sections. Only once the melt was complete would the asphalt relax back to a relatively flat surface.

Chemin Ridge—Ridge Road—road twisted up the hill from the turn-off two kilometres north of Crewe. After a few minutes Dara turned left onto a private gravel road, carefully picking a path between potholes. Artisanal wooden signs at the end of driveways announced the owners of the properties, the houses or cabins glimpsed through the screen of trees. Dara passed the entrances to 'Boucher-Gore' and 'Louise and Denis Chouinard'.

Finally, she saw 'Chester and Ems Argile—Bienvenue'. She turned into the driveway.

Dara rolled slowly to a halt in front of the Argile's cabin. Trees surrounded it on three sides but were stunted and wind-swept here close to the edge of the escarpment. Dara could see blue sky behind the building and guessed that the ground fell away quickly.

Three wooden steps led up to a covered porch and the front door. On either side of the steps, ornamental shrubs bound in protective sacking poked through remnants of snow. The wind tossed her hair across her face as she got out of her car. She pulled up her hood and stood still as a dog rushed around the side of the building and ran up to her, barking excitedly.

After a few seconds, the front door opened and Argile came out of the cabin.

"Hi, don't worry about the dog," said Argile. "He's friendly. Here Jet, find your toy!"

The dog disappeared into the cabin to emerge after thirty seconds with the remains of a soft toy which, after years of attention, was reduced to a mere rag dripping with saliva.

"Come on in. Jet loves visitors but it's best to keep your hands high unless you want a friend for life."

Dara mounted the steps onto the veranda, scraped her shoes on the mat, and followed Argile and the dog into the cabin. She was happy to get out of the wind.

Argile led the way through the hall into a room which ran the full width of the cabin. The morning sun angled in through the windows, making the hardwood floor shine as if wrought of bronze. At one end of the room, two comfortable-looking armchairs faced a soot-blackened stove. At the other end, papers and books were piled high on a table surrounding an old desk-top computer.

Dara walked to the nearest window and looked out.

"That is quite some view," she said. "Can you see Crewe from here?"

"No, not quite; the village is away to the left behind the trees."

Argile went to the table and pointed to a chair.

"Please, sit." Argile pushed some papers aside and switched on the computer.

"Since the mini earthquake which livened up the Council meeting, I thought I would look again at the seismic record for this region," he said. Argile's computer slowly connected to the Geological Institute.

"This is our best source of information about earthquakes," said Argile, pointing to the screen. "This map shows seismicity in western Quebec over the last five years. Each circle symbol represents an event."

Dara saw small circles in cool colours sprinkled across the map with no discernible pattern. Just southwest of Crewe she saw a slightly larger circle warmer in colour.

"What is that orangey symbol?"

"The larger the diameter and the warmer the colour, the greater the magnitude of the earthquake. The orange colour represents a magnitude of four. You would feel a tremor, like a big truck passing on the road. A magnitude five, on the other hand, is a pretty good shake. That orange circle nearly under Crewe is the minor quake we felt yesterday at the Council meeting."

Dara pulled out her Ayetech. "Huh. I can get the same directly from this data app. Look, this map seems the same."

Argile glanced over at the small screen that Dara was holding. He was curious to know how the device generated the map.

"May I?"

Dara handed her Ayetech to Argile who scrolled down. He soon found the explanation: the map was prepared from reports by people on social media.

"Oh, I see," said Argile. "People post after earthquakes about damage to property or to describe the strange behaviour of their pets. If enough do, you can estimate earthquake intensity. Algorithms can map the extent and severity of the event using these reports. You can see pattern without explanation—that's big data for you. It produces a pretty map, though."

"Dr. Argile, do you think with all this big data that we will ever be able to predict earthquakes?" asked Dara, retrieving her Ayetech from Argile.

"Exactly when? I doubt it," said Argile. "The earth gives us signs that an event like an earthquake or a landslide is likely to occur but one has to know what to look for and the timing is always vague. That earthquake surprised me as much as everyone."

"Would signs do you look for?"

"I would rather show you. Let's walk," replied Argile. He pressed the off-button on the computer and walked to the back door. "You might want to put on rubber boots."

Dara had a pair in the back of her Civic and went to change. She sensed that there was a story here. Dr. Argile seemed eccentric enough to make good copy and there was a strong local interest angle.

She came back around the side of the cabin to find Argile striding down a path towards the edge of the escarpment, followed by his dog. She hurried after them.

Argile called over his shoulder.

"After we get down through these trees, the trail runs out into abandoned fields. The grass is already high enough to soak your legs."

The temperature had climbed into the low teens over the first week of April. Here on the south facing slope, the snow had melted leaving damp brown earth. Bright green shoots were everywhere. White trillium lilies spangled the rocky, boulder-strewn slope above.

Argile and Dara emerged from the trees and stood at the top of a long field. Generations before, homesteaders had cut the forest for lumber and cleared the field of boulders for rough pasture. Argile pointed across the hillside.

"Over there," he replied. "You can see how the angle of the slope changes; that's where things get interesting."

They walked over the field. Hidden by the folds of the ground until the last moment, they reached the edge of a miniature cliff; a grey scar in the green grass. It was little more than a metre high and thinning to both left and right in the shape of a crescent. They were standing at the top of a small landslide. Dara saw bare clay at the foot of the cliff and the field below was no longer smooth but had a hummocky appearance where the ground had crept down the slope, wrinkling like old skin.

"I have been watching this slide," said Argile. "It started two years ago as a crack in the ground, only a few centimeters across when I first found it. After heavy rain last year, the ground began to slide, widening the fissure. It had grown enough by last winter to swallow a snowmobiler. No, no story there: I pulled him out."

"Do you think it moved during yesterday's quake?" said Dara.

"Hard to say. The scar is very fresh and the clay slick. Maybe a few centimetres: a slight reactivation. If the quake had lasted longer, the brakes might have come off and we would be looking at a major landslide. You can never be sure when these things let go."

Dara half slid down the slope and was about to walk across the slide.

"I wouldn't cross that!" called Argile. "See those flat patches where the clay is showing? Those are where the clay has liquefied and then set. It looks solid, but it's like quicksand; if you step on that you could go up to your knees. It has been wet lately, so I wouldn't rely on that crust supporting your weight."

Jet, with the benefit of four large paws, had ventured across the slide. He emerged with grey gaiters of mud on his legs.

"Okay," said Dara, backing slowly away. "I get it that this slope has some problems. But aren't we a long way from town here and nowhere near River View?"

"Let's go back," said Argile. As they climbed back up through the forest to the ridge, he explained that he counted five similar slips on satellite images between here and Crewe. Most seemed to be relics of earlier movements, perhaps from when the climate was wetter. The entire slope was adjusting to the land rising following the retreat of the glaciers. The streams along the base of the slope cut steep notches in the exposed terraces of clay which once formed the bed of the Champlain Sea.

"You know, you can find marine shells in the clay around here," said Argile. "The best places are undercut cliffs behind waterfalls where the exposed clay looks fresh and blue. It only turns grey when it dries out, like the smears on my trousers. When the clay is fresh, the shells look like the white hulls of tiny ships embedded in a frozen blue sea. Their scientific name is *Leda*. Hence, the Leda Clay."

Back at the cabin, they sat on the veranda steps, looking at the broad view across the valley.

"You have a beautiful place here," said Dara.

Argile scratched at the grey smears of clay which had dried on his boots. He spat on his hand and lifted his clay-smeared fingers to his nose, breathing deeply. "The Leda has a distinctive odour, you know. Do you want to smell?"

"Thanks, I'll take your word for it," Dara said hurriedly. "Do you think you could tell me more about the earthquake we felt yesterday?"

"Yes, indeed," said Argile, rubbing his hand on his trousers. "There have been more tremors in the last two years in this part of Quebec than over the previous decade. The tremors have all been small on the Richter scale, barely felt, but the occasional magnitude four gets noticed. If you plot the epicentres of these little quakes, they line up and the most recent quake is not far southwest of Crewe. If you extend the line, it points towards the village. I expect another shake, but when is impossible to predict. However, the reason I showed you the land slip was to make the link to yesterday's tremor. Around here, a landslide is the biggest danger from a quake."

"So," said Dara. "An earthquake shaking things up can trigger landslides. Can't they just happen on their own? I mean, do you really need an earthquake?"

"Any unusual stress will do," replied Argile. "It could be a heavy load, or a hillside undercut by a stream so the slope above becomes unstable. But shaking by an earthquake is widespread and you can get multiple slides. A swarm."

"I can use that!" Dara, quickly checking her Ayetech to make sure it had caught the conversation. "Great! Thank you, Dr. Argile."

"You are welcome. As you know, I am worried that people around here don't understand the danger. I suppose it's when I use terms like 'geo-hazard'. My wife Ems is always telling me to cut back on the jargon."

"Don't worry, Dr. Argile. Earthquakes, landslides and the Leda. I think I've got it."

Argile watched Dara get back into her car, wave and drive off. He wondered how their talk would appear in print.

Chapter 12

S EAN ARRIVED IN his truck while Argile was pulling couch
grass out of the front flower bed. After a wet week followed
by warmth, the weeds were getting the upper hand.

A riding tractor stood in front of the garage with the cutting
deck detached and upside down on the gravel. The long drive belt
which snaked through various pulleys to turn the blades, lay in
loops beside it. Sean knew that belts like that had minds of their
own, and could seldom be reattached without much swearing and
trial and error. At least, in Sean's experience.

"*Salut*, Professor," Sean called to Argile. "I can get that fixed
for you, if you like. Take it down to Freeman's in Constance for a
service?"

Sean saw the possibility for small jobs from Argile. He knew
how much Freeman would charge and planned to do the work
himself and pocket the difference. Anyways, in spring, Freeman
was overwhelmed with small engines being revived after their
winter sleep. Fat Phillipe at reception would be surly, even if Sean
could get him to answer the phone.

Argile, still on his knees, looked up at Sean. He really didn't
need the tractor serviced; he had done the job himself last fall. He
would reassemble the cutting deck in his own good time.

"Ah, Sean. Good morning." Argile climbed slowly to his feet.
"No, I think I can get the tractor going, but you can service the
snow blower if you like. The seasonal change-about; oil and filters,
greasing. Now, about those boxes of rocks. I want to take them

down to Molly Laberge in Crewe. Are you and your truck up for that? Fifty bucks."

Bingo, thought Sean.

Argile, after months of reminders from Ems, had agreed to thin his rock collection in the garage. Some specimens he decided he could bear to part with came from western Canada, where Argile had spent long days in the Cretaceous formations of the Drumheller badlands looking for dinosaurs. He had collected some fragments of bone and plenty of fossil wood encrusted with opal. It looked like crystallized fruit. Those should tingle Molly's aural senses, he thought.

Another large block of sandstone from the foothills of the Rocky Mountains contained a chain of vertebrae from an ichthyosaur, a Triassic marine lizard. That had been before the blanket ban on collecting. There were also many smaller fossils and minerals that he had amassed over a lifetime. As a child, he had stored them in an old, tin trunk. The companion of several family moves, it had faithfully carried his growing collection. Each specimen carried a payload of memories that did not speed Argile's wrapping and boxing process. Divesting a collection was far from easy.

And then there was the guilt about specimens whose labels had come adrift, and for which he could no longer quite remember where or when he had collected them. It didn't use to be a problem: each would conjure the image of a specific creek bed, an outcrop, or a shoreline. But time had shuffled his memories, as if the ordered layering of rock formations no longer mattered. Molly could classify the rocks by some arcane system of her own invention.

Argile and Sean went to the back of the garage and Argile pointed to two wooden crates filled with rocks to take down to Molly. "That block of magnetite is heavier than it looks," he said.

Sean lifted a crate with little effort, walked outside, and slung it onto the back of his truck. He returned for the second and slammed the tailgate shut.

Sean climbed into the cab and Argile sat beside him. They drove out of the driveway and turned down the hill towards Crewe. After four hundred metres, they passed a side road which climbed up to the old fire tower. Sean glimpsed a white camper van parked a short way up the side road, completely blocking it. He stopped the truck and reversed for a better look. He looked at the camper suspiciously.

"American plates," he said. "They might be hunters up from the States after turkey. Those birds can be a real pain."

Argile agreed that the proliferating population of wild turkeys had become a menace. Troops of the recently introduced birds were everywhere, marching across fields in lines like infantry. The birds looked over-sized in the landscape, even when seen from a distance; modern dinosaurs louting about. The growing population was hard on the local flora, too: platoons of the birds foraged with the ferocity of army ants stripping every green shoot in their path.

"No, that camper van looks familiar," said Argile. "I think it belongs to people who are looking for rocks. They turned up at the cabin last week."

"Oh, right then," replied Sean. He let the truck roll downhill and engaged the clutch.

A few minutes later, Sean was parking directly in front of Molly's Rocks, beside a new '*Stationnement interdit*'. These 'no parking' signs had sprouted like weeds since the spring thaw. Some replaced those flattened by errant snow plows during the winter but many were new, thanks to a village initiative to limit cars and boost cycling. Argile got out and walked over to open the door to the shop. Molly was sitting behind the counter and got up as the screen door swung open.

"Hi, Argile," she said, looking through the window. "Is that for me?"

She eyed Sean dropping his tailgate and lifting a large and evidently heavy box from the back of the truck.

"Yes. Ems made me clear out the garage. Some you might find saleable; the rest I suggest you chuck at the bottom of your garden."

Molly thought herself quite good at choosing what might sell. She had criteria: colour, brilliance, quirkiness. But, in the end, it usually came down to identifying an aura. If there was an aura to find, Molly was confident she would.

"You two want tea?" asked Molly after Sean had dumped both boxes in the back parlor-cum-store room. Sean was already excusing himself.

"I have things to do, places to be." He winked at Argile. "I'll catch up with you later Professor," he said, going out and letting the door swing closed behind him.

Argile accepted his tea. He carefully sniffed the rising steam. It had a familiar aroma which he could place.

Molly patted Argile's shoulder to reassure him. "It's an infusion of knotweed—you know, that plant sprouting though the asphalt beside the Magnolia. It's supposed to rejuvenate mind and body." She moved over to crouch beside one of the crates. "Now let's see what you've brought me."

She started to unwrap the contents.

"There is a note in the box which identifies each specimen and where it's from." Or my best guess, he thought to himself. Argile sipped his tea, mildly surprised to find it palatable.

"Wow, these are great. Thanks Argile!" She put aside several attractive blocks of mica and picked up a grey cobble. She recognized it as a concretion from the Leda, similar to one she had sold recently as a 'Crewe Stone'. She stared intently at the cobble which, frankly, wasn't much to look at. It was a hand's width in size, worn smooth and a mottled grey. Molly was sure that if she stared hard enough, she would surely know whether there was a fish skeleton inside.

She tried to focus on the stone, but all that appeared on the grey surface were vague swirls. Trying too hard, she said to herself. She gripped the stone and shut her eyes. In her imagination, she saw the surface of a vast lake rimmed with walls of ice, reflecting a vast sky. Approaching her from across the lake, steadily parting the waters was a white vessel, growing larger until its white sails filled her view. It was like an image out of Tolkien, she realized, having just re-read the Lord of the Rings. In a moment of clarity before the image dissolved, she saw that it was not a boat at all, but a giant swan. She opened her eyes to concentrate on what Argile was saying.

"...and it's from the Leda Clay, of course. You know the story of how Zeus, the chief god of the Greeks, changed into a swan to seduce the beauteous Leda. A story like that should sell some of these concretions. I left some intact to add to the mystery: buyers might want to try their hand at splitting them to see what's inside."

Molly started to weave the sales pitch in her head: 'Noah's Nodules, untamed' or 'Crewe's mystery stones'. She would fold some origami swans for a tableau in the cabinet beside the cash.

After Argile had left, Molly sat in thought. She usually classified men using a three-way system—empathic, pathetic or bastard. Most men plotted somewhere on the axis which ran from pathetic to bastard. This had certainly been true for her ex-partner, Ben Gold. As far as she knew, he was still in social work and living with his parents in Montreal West. The difficulty with the simple scheme arose when a man projected a strong aura. This trumped all other considerations. Molly curled up in her chair gazing at the tea leaves in the bottom of her mug. Argile's aura was a shining blue. 'Anything but gold!' she thought.

✧   ✧   ✧

ON THE SIDE road near Argile's cabin, Priebus had been fiddling with the switch for the camskin, a military-grade camouflage system which he had bought at the Hunting and Fishing outlet store just before crossing the border. It had been a cinch to install and now he switched on. To an observer the outline of the white vehicle began to flicker, and then melded into the background trees. Provided they kept the camper windows shut, only a close look would reveal some cracks in the camouflage.

"The camper is invisible now," said Priebus.

Marsha Teg was reading a text on her Ayetech.

"Okay," she replied distractedly. "It seems Pastor Bob has extended our mission. Good. We can move the camper to somewhere more comfortable. I hear there is an Allways supermarket in Constance. It's only about twenty minutes away. We can rent space in the parking lot by the month and the store allows campers to use its facilities, provided we do all our grocery shopping there. They even have showers, you will be happy to hear, Priebus."

"The Pastor wants a report," added Marsha Teg. "Finding out where this Argile collects his Crewe Stones is our priority. I'll think about that. Meanwhile, let's get down to the Allways. You drive, Priebus. It's straight through the village and follow the main road east towards Constance."

Priebus climbed behind the wheel. It's just 'do this' and 'do that', he thought to himself. Marsha's authority rankled. His uncle should have put him in charge.

Chapter 13

From mid-May to mid-June, the climate turns hot in west Quebec. Cool daytime walks through the woods where fresh sunlight dapples the forest floor are suddenly over. Now, the heat and humidity mounted to tropical levels by midday. Despite pacing himself, halfway around the circuit Argile broke into a sweat, which was attracting mosquitoes. He sprayed more repellent behind his ears and crammed his bush hat down on his brow.

Dense foliage obscured the markers that Argile had blazed on trees or painted on rocks in the spring. However, this was the fifth time he had made the circuit since his encounter with Sean in early March, and Argile had no difficulty finding the rock where he had spray-painted his hand. This was his starting point.

"Damn!" A low-hanging branch caught his hat and Argile felt a surge of frustration as he retrieved it. The lack of movement along the slope since winter annoyed him. Despite careful compilation of data and using statistical tricks, he had failed to show any significant change. That, he supposed, was a good thing. But why, after the small landslides in the spring, had the entire hillside between the cabin and Crewe gone to sleep? Perhaps it was the resurgent vegetation, the new growth gripping the soil more firmly by its roots. Maybe.

Argile decided this morning on a variation to his routine circuit. And he wanted to tackle this expedition alone. He left Ems nursing a large coffee and placated the dog with a large biscuit before heading out.

Starting from the key rock, Argile scrambled uphill between large blocks of rock that had tumbled from the cliffs above. The climb was strenuous. The view from above on Google gave a false impression of gentle topography; reality was dripping rock, ankle-twisting crevices and slippery hand holds.

Argile followed the twisting bed of a shallow stream. The trickle of water had winnowed the coarse sand leaving platelets of mica gleaming in the small pools, hinting at a mineralized vein higher up the slope. Argile knew he was on the right track.

After ten minutes of effort, Argile reached a narrow platform of rough stonework. Before him was a vertical cliff some thirty feet high. The overhang shaded the entrance to an abandoned mine, a drive hacked back into a mica-rich seam in the granite.

Test pits and shallow adits riddle the hills above Crewe. Most are now overgrown with fern and moss. At the end of the nineteenth and early twentieth centuries Crewe was an important mining area, but the veins of ore were small and quickly exhausted. Mica was one of the major exports until its industrial use became redundant with the invention of Bakelite plastic insulators.

A shallow pool barred the entrance to the mine. At Argile's appearance, frogs leapt into the water in a volley of plops. He shrugged off his backpack, took out a flashlight, holstered his geological hammer and scrambled around the edge of the pool into the shadows. The mine opening was not high enough for Argile to walk upright, and he stooped as he entered the mine. Fifteen metres from the entrance, the light faded. He waited until his eyes adjusted to the dimness and then moved on. Facets of mica in the irregular roof of the adit glinted in the light of his lamp. The temperature was about twelve degrees. When Argile had entered the mine, it had felt cool, but now after only a few minutes he was clammy with sweat.

Most mines in these hills were small family affairs. Farmers' sons prospected the lands in the fall after the leaves fell and before the first snow. They looked in the pits left by trees toppled in the summer storms; in streams and pools, in secret crevices and along the bare, exposed ribs of the ancient bedrock. In 1910, one Michael McClusky followed a lead amid the tumbled blocks and discovered a vein rich in mica. Digging operations had to respect the call of farm work and it took two seasons to follow the promising vein back into the cliff before it widened out and they found mica crystals large enough to sell.

Typically, mica flakes had to be four to six inches long to be worth extracting. Each spring the buyer from Dominion Mica set up shop in the Hotel les Draveurs, and for several years, the McCluskys filled one or two cartloads with fine crystals and hauled them down the twisted track which led from the hills to Crewe.

Argile knew that, by the early 1930s, mining in the region had mostly ceased. In most cases, the last years of these mica mines saw an unproductive scramble to find new quality veins, but work at the McClusky Mine ended for sadder reasons. Old Man McClusky lost both sons in the spring log drive, as they tried to break up a jam on the Akonaga. He could no longer work the farm and sold. Over the following years, the new owner farmed the bottom lands near Crewe and never reopened the mine. The mine entrance and surrounding heaps of discarded spoil were overgrown and obscured by vegetation when Argile found it the previous fall.

Argile reached the end of the main adit. Here the tunnel twisted to the left and ran for several metres before ending in a blank rock face. Argile knew that he must be close to one of the large geological faults that defined the edge of the Wilsonian

Escarpment. An age ago, the earth's crust had ruptured under immense tension, the movement bringing two very different rock types into abrupt contact. The mica-rich granite which formed the floor, walls and roof of the mine cast a pale reflection from Argile's flashlight. But facing him was a dull, dark rock. A fault contact, wet and glistening, separated the two rock types.

To the McCluskys this would have meant the end of the vein they were following, and possibly the end of the mine, if drowning had not ended operations. Argile thought there was still good potential; he had found a crystal of phlogopite mica eight inches across. It was like a dark brown mirror. He put it aside to collect when he had finished in the mine. Molly, at the rock shop, would love it.

Argile pulled a tangle of electric cable from his rucksack. The main purpose of his visit to the mine was to attach monitoring equipment rather than collect minerals. Argile ripped the backing from two adhesive metal plates and pressed them against the rock wall. After connecting the plates to his laptop with the cables, he put on headphones and plugged them into the computer. Argile hit the rock with his hammer. It rang like a bell. He called it "clinkstone'".

Through these home-made geophones, Argile hoped to hear cracking sounds, signs that the rock mass in the bedrock below Crewe was straining under pressure. He thought the resulting micro-quakes might speed the creeping movement of the shallower clays and soils. He hoped to hear the amplified sucks and groans of the overlying softer rocks, much as a conch transmits and modulates the sounds of the sea.

Argile listened intently to absolute silence.

Disappointed, he was on the point of removing his headphones when he heard a series of faint pops. He waited for another fifteen minutes but they were not repeated. It occurred to

Argile that the pops might be the sounds of fracking. He had read in *The Courier* that the company TiteGas was drilling a well, but that was kilometers away across the river. Argile attached a recorder to the geophones. The batteries would last a week; enough time, he thought, to see if any pattern emerged.

Argile repacked, but before feeling his way back towards the entrance, he used the curved pick of his geological hammer to ease out a slab of mica. It broke way with careful levering; no hammering, boring or blasting required. Perhaps the McCluskys had had an easier time of it than Argile had thought. Retracing his steps, he pushed through the arch of ferns at the mine entrance, blinded by the filtered light after an hour underground.

✧   ✧   ✧

MARSHA WATCHED ARGILE emerge from the mine entrance and scramble down the path towards the main trail. After he was safely past, she stepped from behind a tree. Waiting for Argile she had got very hot, bitten by bugs and was fast losing patience. She would return later with Priebus to investigate the mine.

Chapter 14

ARGILE WAS LEANING back in the kayak to ease a cramp in the small of his back. He had paddled down the Akonaga from the Crewe municipal boat launch, keeping a close eye on the near bank. He knew his destination but was always on the lookout for places where the current had collapsed the banks of Leda Clay leaving a fresh exposure. As he followed the river, he was getting deeper into the Leda: lower stratigraphically. Here the clay was older, deposited soon after the Champlain Sea had filled.

It was a glorious summer day. There was not a breath of wind and the water was limpid. The slight current carried Argile with the flow towards his destination, a narrow beach downstream from a sharp bend in the river. As he glided into the shallows to beach his kayak, he could see grey cobbles studding the bed of the stream. These were concretions, hard nodules eroded from the low cliff of Leda Clay he had just passed. The flow had carried them these few metres, washing them clean of the softer clay in which they were embedded.

The keel of the kayak grated on the sandy bottom and Argile let the bow of his craft nose up onto the sandy beach. He extracted his collecting kit from the storage space behind the seat of his kayak, slung the sturdy canvas bag over his shoulder, pulled on a pair of rubber surf shoes and walked into the warm, shallow water. Argile reached down, picked up a cobble and placed it in the bag. He waded further, stooping to collect additional specimens until he had about ten kilos of rock. Quite enough, he thought, and went back to the beach. He found a patch of shade near the bank and sat, arranging his collection on the sand beside him.

His kit was very simple; an angle of wood attached to a short board, similar in design to a tool for shucking oysters. It was large enough to wedge a rounded cobble firmly into place so he could attack it with hammer and chisel.

Argile had an eye for picking concretions which contained fossils. It was an unconscious talent. Most of the cobbles he selected contained something interesting. More often than not this turned out to be fragments of shell hash, or a battered fish scale. Sometimes, to his great satisfaction, he would discover an entire fish skeleton.

Sitting quietly on the beach, Argile worked methodically through his pile of concretions. He placed each in the vise formed by his angle of wood, looked for the best spot around the widest perimeter to insert the chisel, and tapped. He then carefully separated the two halves and laid them side by side in the sand. After thirty minutes, he had founded several with partial fish skeletons, one with an entire skeleton, and one with a group of three tiny fish.

Argile wrapped and bagged the split pairs of concretions which he felt were collectible. He left half un-split. He packed all the rocks into the sling bag and lugged them over to the kayak. He stowed the cargo between his knees to keep the additional weight near the centre of gravity. He pushed off the beach and turned into the current.

Slowly paddling upstream, Argile was pleased. It had been a good haul and Molly would welcome both split and unsplit concretions. He knew she had sold the fish fossils on Etsy, the internet shopping site.

✧   ✧   ✧

IT HAD BEEN a week since Marsha and Priebus had explored the McClusky Mine and Priebus was still barely talking to Marsha. He had hit his head several times on the roof of the mine, panicked in the dark, and lost his favourite hunting knife. It had been an unpleasant expedition, and entirely unprofitable: they had discovered nothing resembling a deposit of Crewe Stones.

Now, Marsha hoped they were on the right track. They were parked on Chemin de la Rivière two hundred metres back from the river, having followed Argile's trip down river with a surveillance drone. Priebus was having difficulty controlling the machine. It was at the limit of its range and a group of straggly bushes blocked his line of sight. He finally had it hovering and was getting a reasonable view of Argile's kayak.

After a few minutes, Argile appeared with what looked to Priebus like a heavy bag, climbed into the kayak and paddled back up river. The drone followed him upstream for a few minutes before Priebus recalled the machine to land on the roadside verge beside the camper.

"Good!" exclaimed Marsha Teg, after reviewing the video. "Get your boots on, Priebus. We are going fossicking. Bring those folding boxes."

They left the vehicle and pushed through tall weeds to the river. Scrambling down the steep clay bank to the beach, Marsha quickly found the heap of discarded rocks where Argile had been splitting concretions a few minutes before.

Half an hour later they had filled two boxes with rocks scooped from the river bed. The return trip to the camper carrying the heavy boxes was sweaty work. Marsha was confident that they had collected enough rocks, and was sure that some would contain the skeletons of fish, similar to the specimen she had first seen on the internet.

Initially, Harris had directed Marsha to send anything found back to Schenedy Falls. He envisaged a ceremony before a congregation when he would ritually split the concretions to reveal the fossilized witnesses to Noah's Flood. When Marsha said that she could not guarantee a fish in every concretion, he eventually agreed that Marsha should do the splitting in the field. There was a risk of embarrassment should the concretions prove devoid of any fossil.

Marsha and Priebus parked the camper in their usual spot in the RV parking lot at the Allways. Priebus went to buy a vise, a heavy hammer, and a chisel from the hardware department. Marsha judged that in the hour or so of daylight remaining they should be able to split most of their collection. She set out two folding chairs on the asphalt beside the camper. It was mellow evening and the residents of the other RVs in the lot had started their portable barbecues. She was in good humour, feeling that their mission was almost accomplished.

She pulled the tab on a Bud Lite and passed a Doctor Pepper to Priebus.

"Let's get cracking," she said.

PART II
AMBITION

Chapter 15

THE TELEPHONE WOKE Argile from a light sleep. He rather hoped that Ems would pick up one of the wireless extensions. The bedside phone was the only one in the house still attached to a cord. They had decided to keep the ancient technology after the ice storm of two winters past when the first service to go out was wireless communications. Cell towers had collapsed under the ice load. But picking up this phone meant being tethered to the bed.

"Hello, *Bonjour.* Dr. Argile? This is Mayor Hilary Beaubien calling. I hope to find you well. Is this a convenient time?"

Argile, who had half expected 'phishing', and was ready to slam down the phone, was silent for a few seconds before muttering a 'Good Morning'.

"*Bon.* Dr. Argile, I found your comments at our last Council meeting most interesting. I very much appreciate citizens sharing their expertise with us."

"Oh yes? Well, thank you, Madame Mayor." Argile made a shushing gesture to Ems who had just come into the room asking who was on the phone.

"Please call me Hilary. It is great that we have an expert resource in our community."

"I have a favour to ask," continued the Mayor. "Would you agree to advise the municipality on geological matters? If it is convenient, it would most helpful if you would come with me to a meeting in Margs Bay, over in Ontario, this Thursday evening.

There is a presentation by the company drilling for gas there and I would appreciate your advice. As you know, there are plenty of voices opposed to fracking coming to Crewe."

Argile put his hand over the microphone. "She wants me to advise her. She calls me an expert."

Ems raised an eyebrow and went into the bathroom.

"Well, yes. Thursday evening is fine for me," said Argile, returning to the telephone conversation.

"*Parfait*," said the Mayor. "Does six-thirty work for you? I will pick you up and we can drive down together. Thank you so much, Dr. Argile."

Argile replaced the phone on its stand and sat on the side of the bed for a minute. He decided that he felt slightly flattered. He would be doing his civic duty. He went downstairs to find Ems who was sitting at the table, nursing a coffee and looking out of the window. He relayed the conversation.

Ems snorted. "It just saves them the money of hiring a consultant," she said. "Now they get one for free."

✧   ✧   ✧

THE MEETING BEGAN with introductions by the Chairperson, a councillor from Margs Bay. TiteGas would be represented by the company's senior ecologist, a young woman introduced as Dr. Brakes.

"Please, it's Mandy," said the young woman. She looked down to her left. "And this is Brandon, from our engineering department."

Brandon, in his late twenties and bearded, ducked his head nervously.

"And beside Brandon is Leanne Turnbull, from drilling operations." Leanne stared impassively across the heads of the audience.

"And to my right," continued Mandy, "is Mr. Charles Bludston, to handle questions on company policy. Argile had already guessed that this must be the corporate lawyer, to judge by the expensive shoe projecting towards the audience from under the folding table.

Argile sat beside Mayor Beaubien at the end of a row, in a room slowly filling with people. They had a fair view of the stage and a large display screen. Argile had agreed to come as a 'citizen consultant to the mayor'. It was, as Ems had predicted, an honorary title with no per diem.

They were to hear a presentation about the TiteGas's deep-drilling and fracking program. TiteGas had, over several years, amassed a large block of land as 'expro' leases, which gave the company exploration and production rights. The target was the deep Windigo, a black shale formation underlying much of the region. TiteGas had drilled the southern end of their leases and was already producing gas from several pads around Margs Bay. The company now planned to expand their operations north towards Crewe.

Mandy dimmed the lights.

"Let me explain how TiteGas operates," she began. "We are a triple rated green company. Many of you here in Margs Bay will have worked with us over the last year and know that we 'walk the talk'."

The holo-cube projected by the Ayetech showed three bullet points. TiteGas promised to minimize surface disturbance, not to interfere with farming, and to have zero impact on quality of life for residents."

Argile sighed. He tried to concentrate on what Mandy was saying.

"We use 'cutting-edge' technologies, such as ultra-long-distance, horizontal drilling." Mandy emphasized the point by slashing her hand through the air.

"And we hide our surface operations behind camouflage screens. You would hardly know we were there at all."

The holo-screen showed a diorama of the area around Margs Bay. Cows ambled through meadows, geese angled across the sky and Argile swore he could hear robins singing.

"We concentrate drilling activity at a handful of pads; here, here and here," said Mandy, pointing with her laser pen. "We drill straight down to a depth of two kilometers to hit the top of the Windigo and then sideways for up to ten kilometers. We use a smart drill that steers itself to keep within the shale. That's where the gas is. The drill is like a mole under your grass, but there is nothing to see on the surface at all; no disturbance, no noise."

"I hate bloody moles," came a voice from the audience.

Mandy hurriedly pressed for the next projection, a view of the subsurface Windigo. It hovered above the stage in hues of purple and green.

"The dark green is the Windigo shale; the grey represents the overlying clays and limestones, and the wiggly blue tubes are the actual wells," she said.

"TiteGas has completed a network of boreholes which reaches and drains gas from almost every part of the shale reservoir around Margs Bay. There are over one thousand kilometers of well bore draining gas from the Windigo!"

Mandy paused for the audience to appreciate the model of the subsurface world beneath Margs Bay which shimmered above the stage. This had been Brandon's contribution to the presentation and what it lacked in zing, it made up for in detail. Argile heard the people in the row behind fidgeting in their chairs. There were several coughs.

"What about the burning water?" The shouted question came from the rear of the hall. Argile saw Mandy wince. In the audience several heads turned. They saw a man wearing a green rain jacket and a toque.

Mandy knew that, whenever there was talk of fracking, someone in the audience would remember the YouTube videos of tap water being lit with a match, of methane bubbling from glasses of drinking water. Yes, it was largely faked, concocted by an expert director who had since moved on to better paid gigs in advertising. But once seen, it was hard to forget: contamination of potable water by gas leaking from poorly completed boreholes was something that caught people's attention.

She tried her best. She explained that impermeable strata up to a mile thick separated the Windigo from the deepest water wells in the region. This made upward migration of gas and frack water unlikely. In her experience, she said, such contamination was rare, although she couldn't deny it happened occasionally. Operating procedures had improved enormously over the last decade, she added, and close monitoring of the water table would ensure that, should problems arise, they could be quickly localized and addressed.

The man who had shouted the question now grabbed the wireless microphone which the audience had passed backwards.

"Michel Monchagrin, EcoClub Canada. Madame Brakes, for each degree you add to global warming, ten million people die. How can you live with yourself for making this holocaust? When will TiteGas stop killing our future generations?"

"How can you guarantee at one hundred percent that you won't poison the water?"

"When will you stop polluting the groundwater?"

"Stop the drilling. Save the planet!"

Michel Monchagrin left no room for Mandy to attempt a reply. Montchagrin ignored a Margs Bay resident who rose to ask a question, and refused to relinquish the mike. The murmurs of support which had greeted the first question died away.

The Chairperson looked at her watch. The minute hand was crawling towards nine pm, and she wanted to get home to Skype with her daughter before the grandchildren went to bed. Several persons at the back of the hall were sidling out. Perhaps saving the planet could wait for another day. She pressed the button to turn off the floor mike.

"Well, if there are no further questions." It was more a statement than a question. "I would like to thank Dr. Brakes and TiteGas for such an interesting presentation. If anyone wants to speak with our TiteGas friends, I gather they are willing to stay for a few more minutes. Goodnight and drive safe everyone."

✧ ✧ ✧

ARGILE LEANED OVER to Mayor Beaubien.

"I would like to talk to Brandon."

"But of course, Dr. Argile. Now, excuse me, I have to network". The Mayor slipped between the chairs with practised ease and joined the group in front of the stage.

Argile followed. The Mayor was already shaking hands with Mandy and exchanging business cards. He saw Brandon and the Leanne hovering on the fringe of the group.

"Hi, excuse me. Brandon? Leanne? My name is Argile. Brandon, you must have put in a lot of work preparing the data for such a stunning visualization. I was really interested by your geological model."

The engineer gave Argile a wary glance. Leanne looked past Argile towards the side door to the hall.

"Going for a smoke," she said.

"Pleased to meet you, er, Mr. Argile," said Brandon. They shook hands. "Don't mind Leanne. I'm pretty used to these public meetings; experienced, you know. But it's a first for Leanne. Did you have a question on the geology or engineering? The finite element model doesn't fully capture the flow dynamics."

Argile listened as Brandon explained his model with increasing enthusiasm. After five minutes, Hilary Beaubien returned, and he introduced her.

"Brandon, this is Hilary Beaubien, Mayor of Crewe."

"*Bonjour, Brandon*," said Hilary. Your project has created lots of jobs here in Margs Bay, I hear."

"Hi," said Brandon. "Er, good to meet you. I can speak to the engineering detail but Mr. Bludston here can explain the economic benefits if you are interested." He pointed to the legal type behind him. But Bludston was talking fishing with a councillor from Margs Bay. He seemed to be arranging a trip for the near future.

"I was about to ask Brandon about the disposal of frack water," said Argile to Hilary. "That's the water that comes back up the hole with the gas. It is usually contaminated with the salt dissolved from the rocks, in this case the Windigo Shale." He turned back to the engineer.

"Brandon. I was wondering where you dump the excess frack water. Not in the river, I hope?"

"Oh sure, great question!" said Brandon, more at ease. He pulled out a roll screen from his jacket pocket and looked around for a flat surface. "Huh, this'll do." He flattened the screen on the seat of a folding chair and tried to hold down the four corners.

"Let me help," said Hilary, lending a finger.

Brandon bent to speak into the roll screen. "Windy, show injectors!"

"Windy is my name for the model," Brandon explained. "It's short for Windigo." He paused to see whether his audience was following this reasoning and then continued.

"You see those five wells in dark blue? Those are the injector wells and we dispose of over half of the frack water by pumping it down these holes. The rest is decontaminated at our surface plant and recycled for more fracking. Absolutely none goes into the river."

"Are you pumping into some deep rock formation?" asked Argile.

"Okay sure," replied Brandon. "We drill down to a deep aquifer with great permeability three kilometers down. It is two hundred metres deeper than the Windigo, and separated from it by impermeable limestone, hard as concrete."

"Ah, *imperméable*," said Hilary. "Dr. Argile, I think perhaps we should get back..."

"And we will soon be drilling another injector well!" continued Brandon, warming to his theme. "Then all the frack water can be pumped back downhole. That's a hundred metre cubes per minute at full capacity. Nearly five Olympic-sized swimming pools..."

"Call me Chuck, Madame Mayor." Charles Bludston had ended his fishing conversation and turned to introduce himself to Mayor Beaubien. He reached between Argile and Brandon to shake hands with Hilary. Bludston turned his broad back to Brandon, who was about to enlarge on the hydraulic behaviour of the Windigo reservoir. A curtain had been drawn and Brandon's final comment on hydrostatic pressure went unheard.

✧ ✧ ✧

"*TRÈS CHARMANT*, THAT Monsieur Bludston," said Hilary Beaubien, unlocking the car and sliding into the driving seat. They had finally quit the hall after Hilary had said goodbye to several of her fellow mayors. Argile got in beside her.

"So, Mr. Expert, what did you think? They seem a competent team."

She slipped her Ayetech from her purse and put it on the dash, where it unfolded and adhered.

Driving through Margs Bay to turn on route 132 towards Crewe, they passed an EcoClub vehicle recharging at a roadside Quickies. The power was priced reasonably at the franchise, but the snacks consumed while you waited were not. Argile wondered vaguely whether EcoClub gave a decent mileage allowance.

After fifteen minutes, they crossed the Akonaga River.

Hilary was listening to the news on her Ayetech, her hands on the wheel but with an earbud in. It was legal but distracting all the same, thought Argile. Traffic was light, but in the dusk there was a risk of deer crossing. He kept scanning ahead and wished it was dark enough for high beam. At this time of night, the deer were active. Slow down, Hilary, thought Argile. He felt the toes of his right foot curl.

"So, what was all that about injector wells?" said Hilary.

"Yes, I was curious," said Argile. "TiteGas have found a rock formation below the Windigo which is naturally fractured. That means they can pump—inject—the waste frack water into this zone. And problem solved: no need for surface disposal, and no water quality issues."

"Whoa!" Hilary steered abruptly to the left to avoid a small shape bounding across the road. Argile had a glimpse of white stripes. Argile looked in the side mirror but could see nothing on the road. The skunk had probably made it.

"So, is a fracture zone significant?" asked Hilary.

"The injection wells line up above a fault deep in the subsurface. The same fault marks the edge of the escarpment near Crewe but then it dives deep beneath the village and I'm guessing that it continues southwest towards Margs Bay. It is curious that they can inject into that rock; it is so tight and impermeable here."

"I am not sure I understand," said Hilary. "In your opinion, is TiteGas' pumping a risk?'"

"No," Argile replied. "It is highly unlikely that the pumping would affect such an enormous mass of rock. It would be like trying to lift a mountain with a hand grenade."

Argile watched Hilary nod her head slowly. He had kept it simple but, on reflection, he thought he should qualify his previous statement—the pumping might cause a minor tremor—but Hilary was already pulling into her spot behind the municipal building.

"A small probability. Only a hand grenade," said Hilary, quick to summarize the conversation.

"Dr. Argile, you have been a great help. Thank you. It has been an interesting evening."

Argile got out and walked over to his car, then looked across to the lights in front of the Drafters. He thought about a quick half pint of beer. He was thirsty after an evening of fracking, but Ems was expecting him back.

Chapter 16

BRYCE DESJARDINS HAD told Rob Freeman, the driver of the municipal excavator, to meet him at nine sharp. He had waited beside the gate into the woods for a full fifteen minutes, engine running. The sign on the gate clearly said 1025. *Chaulice!* Freeman had got it wrong, as usual, thought Bryce. He must have gone to the dump.

Bryce turned his SUV and drove up Chemin de la Rivière past the sign at the entrance to the village. *'Au revoir et à bientôt'*, it said. Just past the sign was the entrance to the dump, at number 1075. He turned in, drove around the mountain of road grit readied for next winter and into a rutted clearing where the garbage trucks turned and backed to the edge of the disposal pit. Crows clattered from the trees.

Sure enough, he saw Rob leaning against the bucket of the yellow Kobatsu, smoking a cigarette. He was chatting with the young Box kid, who he recognized. Bryce had nailed Sean Box for graffiti on municipal property a few years ago. The cops had let Box off with a warning, much to Bryce's disgust.

Bryce pulled up beside the big excavator and got out. He saw a dust-covered truck parked behind the Kobatsu. He supposed it belonged to the kid. On loan from his Dad, no doubt. Smelling the garbage did little to improve Bryce's mood.

"You can clear yourself off, Flatpack," he growled at Sean. "Freeman, you were to meet me at nine at number 1025! *Tabernac.*" The word came like a short burst from an automatic rifle. *Tab-ber-nac.*

Mind you, for all his effort to instill discipline, he knew that it was water off a duck's back to Rob. There was bad attitude among the *cols bleus*, the labourers, who were mostly locals and mostly Anglos whose family fortunes had declined as their farms failed. *Maudit* Irish, he thought. Typical.

Rob clambered up into the cab of the Kobatsu and held down the ignition for a count of five. The engine caught with a roar, backfired and blew out a cloud of diesel smoke which swirled around Bryce and his SUV. Rob gestured to Bryce that he would follow him down the road to the job.

Once back in his vehicle, Bryce called ahead to make sure that the realtor would arrive at nine-thirty. His morning was *chargé* enough at the municipal offices without the likes of Freeman screwing up his personal agenda. He listened to the phone ring and then switch to the recorded message. *Merde.* But he was confident that Alcee Dupree would be there because he wouldn't have much business at present. Bryce knew that the market had been slow. A hungry realtor is what Bryce needed right now; hungry but not too smart.

Bryce drove back down the road towards Crewe. He glanced behind to see the big yellow excavator looming in the rear-view mirror, its twin exhausts snorting grey diesel smoke into the air. After a few hundred metres he slowed and turned off at number 1025. This was the entrance to the undeveloped land that Bryce had bought at an estate sale the previous year for a ridiculously low price. The gate was wide open and he followed a dirt track through the trees for a short distance.

✧   ✧   ✧

ALCIBIADE DUPREE WAS named after his great-grandfather on his mother's side: a dubious blessing. It was one of the Old Testament names which the church had encouraged over a few experimental decades in the early twentieth century, to help distinguish between the multitude of Josephs, Pierres, Jeans and Matthieus that crowded the baptismal rolls of Quebec. At school he had always been 'Alcee'.

Sporting a bow tie, a younger Alcee was pictured on roadside signs around Crewe. When he sold, Alcee would attach a separate board announcing "*Vendu!*". Recently, it had seen little use.

Alcee had arrived right on time. He had suffered a streak of bad luck—sales scooped by Multimeuble, a rival outfit—and the call from Bryce sounded promising. Have I got a deal for you, Bryce had said. It would be the answer to Alcee's prayers.

"*Salut, Bryce,*" said Alcee, getting out of a mid-range Buick, an electric blue but now somewhat muddied. It was this year's model. Like several of the local realtors, Alcee had a leasing arrangement with a dealership.

"*Salut, Alcee, ça va?*" The two men greeted each other familiarly. They had attended the same high school in Constance, and had both enjoyed the favours of one Marie-Lyse Coude, now Dupree. Alcee thought Bryce didn't know he knew. But Alcee knew.

"'Ow's the wife?" Bryce asked. After a little further chat in which neither was really interested, Bryce said, "Okay—let's get this show on the road."

The two left their cars and walked across the clearing to where Rob Freeman had just arrived. They passed a stack of concrete paving slabs, timbers and other construction materials.

"Municipal stockpile," muttered Desjardins, in response to Alcee's raised eyebrow.

They reached the excavator and looked up at Rob, who was listening to music on his Ayetech. Alcee knew Rob Freeman: Rob had done jobs for him repairing driveways on some of Alcee's more remote properties.

"*Bonjour*, Rob," he said.

Rob Freeman pulled of his earphones and jumped down from the excavator.

"Hi, Mr. Dupree."

Both looked at Bryce expectantly. "So what is the plan, Bryce?" said Alcee. "What is this great deal you mentioned?"

"*Attend.* Wait a second Alcee, while I sort out this no-brain." He turned back to Rob.

"Your job is to cut a new access road through the forest for about five hundred metres. Think you can handle that? I marked the route with red flagging tape. It runs just above the base of the slope to keep the road clear of that there cedar swamp."

"And you had better get going," said Bryce. "I'm not paying you to smoke cigarettes. Don't forget to dig a deep trench beside the road. The base of the slope there is wet and needs draining."

It looked straightforward on the map. The new cut through the neck of forest from Chemin de la Rivière would connect Bryce's land to River View, creating a secondary entrance to the development. Currently, the existing single access limited the number of proposed holiday condos planned by Jack Shawcross. It was a matter of fire safety.

Bryce was not one to miss an opportunity created by municipal regulation. Double the building density meant twice the revenue and Bryce planned to benefit. It was trickle-down economics, *pur et simple*.

In the hierarchy of municipal staff, one manager with whom Bryce had never been able to see eye to eye was the Fire Chief, whose dictate on matters of fire and flood was absolute. Hoity-toity Madame Beaubien believed him implicitly. For once, Bryce was happy with the Chief's interference.

Merci le chef, he thought.

But Bryce had a small problem. He didn't own all the land between his lots and the River View lands. A thin strip intervened. He knew from the municipal tax role that the estate of a certain James Garrity held the title. The land had not been built on—it remained forested—and had not changed hands in years. The Garritys were almost extinct around Crewe anyway. This is where he hoped Alcee would work some magic.

Bryce and Alcee watched Rob climb into the cab of the Kobatsu. The machine juddered into motion and clattered towards the trees.

"*Écoute*, Alcee. You know Saint Ebenista's nursing home in Constance, eh?" said Bryce, once the excavator had moved away. Alcee nodded.

"They have a Madame Garrity there. That land that Freeman is cutting belonged to her uncle."

"I need that land transferred. You think you can make her an offer she can't refuse?"

"Sure: that's no problem. What's the deal?"

"With a new access road, Shawcross can expand his project and it will open up land for about thirty new units. If you can get this Madame Garrity to sign the land over, you can have the listings. But since I have already lined up one buyer, how's about five percent for your commission? List and sell, Alcee. You win coming and going. *Voyons!*"

The two men stood side by side gazing wistfully at the snorting excavator push down a row of trees. Both envied Rob Freeman; a man and his machine.

"Ten percent," replied Alcee.

✧   ✧   ✧

SEAN HAD NOT driven far. After waving to Rob he had gotten in his truck, retreated up the road past the municipal boundary and pulled over. He wondered what that bastard Desjardins was up to. He rolled a joint and smoked for a few minutes. Then he remembered a job he had to do for his Dad. It would take most of the afternoon. Sean turned around and drove back past the town sign. From this side, it read '*Bienvenue à Crewe welcomes you*'.

That same evening, Sean pulled into the parking lot behind the Drafters. There was a line of motorbikes taking up most of the space, and he had to squeeze into the last available slot. A bunch of riders up from Montreal, he thought, hoping they wouldn't be out for trouble. He walked through the door and glanced in the main bar, crowded with blue denim and black leather. Yep, the bikers were in town. Rob wouldn't have gone in there. He guessed he hadn't yet arrived or perhaps was sitting outside for a smoke.

Sean walked down the corridor leading to the back patio. It overlooked the river, and was a favourite spot for a quick drag. In the five weeks since the river had become ice free and the armchair consigned to the deep, the region had seen double the normal rainfall. The big reservoirs upriver were brim-full after ending the previous summer at abnormally low levels.

Sean leaned over the railing at the edge of the patio. Brown river water washed over the pile footings. The levels had risen about a foot overnight and Chemin de la Rivière was already partially flooded. A crew from the municipality had been putting up temporary closure signs. Soon there will be some flooded basements, Sean thought happily. There was good money to be made working for the companies specializing in *sinistres*, emergency stripping of sodden gyprock and insulation. Some of those companies weren't too fussy about credentials.

There was no sign of Rob, so Sean returned to the snug bar and looked more carefully into the nooks. Finally he found him sitting in the corner stall with a dark-haired girl Sean vaguely recognized.

"Hi Flatpack," said Rob. "Get a couple of beers and come on over. Meet Dara. She works at *The Courier*."

Sean went to the bar just as Argile, who had decided that Ems would not expect him back at the cabin for at least half an hour, was ordering his half pint of draft.

"Whatsup Professor?" said Sean. "I didn't know you drank here. Why don't you join us? Hey, three more drafts. *La table là-bas*," called Sean to the server behind the bar. The barkeep nodded to Sean. Sean nodded towards Argile, who sighed.

Argile said "Hi" and slid in along the seat beside Dara. Rob was describing a discovery he had made that afternoon.

"I backed right out of that trench," said Rob. "I thought it was a skull but I wasn't about to dig it out of the bank to make sure. I guess I should have called the police but, well, it was past six o'clock, so I shut down the machine and walked back to my truck. All I wanted was a beer."

The server came with a tray of beers. He dealt three beer mats onto the table and placed the dripping glasses on the mats. Argile noticed the image on the beer mats. It was a large motorbike, a Harley probably. The word 'Les Bleus' was stamped across the mat. The server noticed his interest.

"New management," he said, giving the edge of the table a half-hearted wipe.

By now, Rob was four or five pints in, and Argile's arrival encouraged him to retell his story. He had been digging on the Desjardins land when he had noticed a pale object embedded in the sandy clay beside the bucket.

"I got down from the cab and poked with a stick," said Rob. "Jeez, and there was this eye socket, just staring at me. Just like last Halloween when we went trick and treating. When that skeleton tumbled over and the skull rolled along the ground. How you jumped."

"I never jumped," said Sean.

Rob now felt he was really warming up his audience. When sober, Rob was pleasant and easy company. But after a few beers he started to talk too much, and then became surly. Rob leant over to Argile and in a loud whisper started to recount the many injustices visited on the Freeman family.

"When great-great-granda Freeman came over after the famine, they gave us that shit land up on the ridge. And then that tightarse Scot at Constance cheated Da on the trees. I'll tell you something—he pulled Argile even closer—they're worse than those Frenchie lawyers and their hypotecks." Which reminded him of Desjardins and he gave vent to his feelings about his employer.

Sean winked at Argile and Dara. "Rob, your round. Go get some beers." Freeman stood, and lurched against the edge of the booth.

"Have to go fur a piss" he mumbled. "Where's the bog, now?" He wandered off leaving the other looking at each other.

"He does seem to have discovered a skeleton," said Argile. "I didn't know they were excavating that land." Argile was keen to see any new excavation into the Leda Clay. He knew the slopes above Chemin de la Rivière well, knew their potential mobility. Wet weather triggered two small landslides along a nearby section of road only last year; a pair of beautiful rotational slumps had moved two slugs of soil half way across the road, where they had congealed like cold porridge.

"It could be an old grave," said Dara. "Maybe even a tribal grave." That would make a good story, she thought to herself. She could write the story from the inside, from the perspective of the local band.

"It could be a murder," said Sean, cheerfully. "Maybe Bryce did it."

✧　✧　✧

ARGILE WAS MAKING his excuses to leave after his single drink when Dara insisted that he join them in the morning to look at Rob's find.

"You know lots about science, Dr. Argile," Dara said. "You can tell us how old the bones are."

Sean agreed. "For sure, Professor. You must come!"

Argile was pleased to be asked. He suggested that they meet at nine-thirty. Ems would be in town staying at their condo, so he was pretty sure he had no other commitments.

Rob returned from the toilets.

"I think I had enough," he said, slumping on the bench.

"Hey Rob," said Sean. "We all want to go see your skull to-morrow. Nine-thirty? You reckon if you can make it?"

"Whadya mean 'if'? Sure I can," said Rob.

Rob pulled out his Ayetech to show them how to get to the work site. After a minute of fruitless search for the right app, he gave up.

"Here," he said. Rob dipped his index finger in a puddle of spilled beer and sketched a crude map on the table top.

"It's right here," he said, stabbing his finger down. "Off Chemin de la Rivière just before the town limits. On bloody Desjardin's land."

Chapter 17

AFTER DAYS OF cramped observation of the Argile driveway from the camper van, Marsha had worked out weekly and daily routines for Argile and Ems. Argile took the dog for an evening walk shortly after five and seldom returned within the hour. His wife seemed to spend Monday to Friday away.

So it was now five-thirty on a Thursday evening in mid-June, and Priebus was backing the camper up into the side road which climbed to the fire tower. Marsha, in the passenger seat, was pulling on hiking boots. They were about half a kilometer from the Argile property.

The younger trees now crowded the single-track road, having put on two to three feet of new growth in the heat of early summer. With the forest canopy filled in and the spring flowers of the forest floor a memory, ferns had taken over. It was damp and gloomy. Mosquitoes hummed in the dim light which filtered through the leaves. The rear-view cameras on the tailgate of the camper were out again and Priebus, leaning out of the side window to reverse, was bitten several times.

"That's far enough," said Marsha. "I am going to have a closer look at the cabin. Back in an hour."

After Marsha left, Priebus took ten minutes to find the faulty connection in the camskin controller. The camskin would shroud the camper, make it invisible. Finally successful, he switched it on and the white van became a mottle of dark greens, indistinguishable from the enveloping woods.

After ten minutes of scrambling uphill, Marsha pushed through the scrub oak to emerge from the trees near the highest point of the ridge. The clouds had broken up to the northwest, and shafts from the setting sun were casting long shadows across the farmlands three hundred feet below.

"God, what a view. I could live here for ever," whispered Marsha to herself.

The cabin was now below her and along the ridge to her left. Marsha squatted on an outcrop of granite. She could see the driveway which led from the road to the cabin and ended in a wide turning space. She hurried across the rough grass to the front veranda. Argile and Ems never locked the cabin, so she could push open the screen door and walk in. The door slammed shut behind her.

"Shit," said Marsha, angry with herself for such a basic error in field craft. "No hurry. No hurry. Breathe. Breathe."

There seemed to be rocks everywhere—on shelves, around the fireplace and on windowsills. She picked up a fist-sized, triangular rock from one end of the mantel above the fireplace. A label informed her that this was a rock impacted by an ancient meteorite, collected from a stream bed in the Canadian Arctic. Beside this specimen was a large crystal with a purple tint. She read 'Rock salt. Attention—mildly radioactive'. Marsha quickly replaced the rock on the shelf.

Moving across the room Marsha saw a shelf of smaller specimens. They look like fossils but there was nothing from the Leda, with or without fish. She looked around what seemed to be Argile's office space in the corner of the large room. There were no obvious maps on the wall. She had half hoped to find one marked with a large 'X'. Well, that would have been too simple, she thought.

Marsha was disappointed not to find any Crewe stones but

she had only intended the briefest reconnoitre. To be honest, she just needed some distance from the van and Priebus. She checked her watch. Argile would be back soon: it was time to go.

She let herself out of the cabin—silently this time—and retreated under the eaves of the woods into the deepening dusk. Marsha threaded silently through the trees, slanting down the hill to intersect the road and the parked camper. It felt good to follow her instinctive sense of direction, feel the high of emerging from the trees onto the track just where she expected. Like Afghanistan with trees. Except: there was no sign of the camper. Suppressing her irritation, she realized that Priebus must have finally got the camskin working. She sighed and checked her Ayetech. Sure enough, the device assured her that the vehicle was only metres away.

Chapter 18

CANDICE FROM THE Café Pontiac had tipped Sean off that the motel in Constance was hiring for the summer. It had sounded like a sweet gig; better than mooching around the garage doing odd jobs for his dad. He had called the manager and—much to his surprise—had been invited for interview the following day. He had rejigged his resume, ignoring the advice of his mother to emphasize his skill with small motors. Without bothering to ask, he had put down Professor Argile as a reference.

Two days later, Sean was behind the front desk. He was wearing a uniform and a lapel badge which said 'Reception'. The manager had assured him he would have plenty of opportunity to try different jobs in the motel and learn new skills. He was pleased that he had passed the interview so easily, not knowing how difficult it was for businesses to hire staff through the summer season. Sean supposed that the clincher had been his claim to being perfectly bilingual.

"Anyway," thought Sean. "It is what it is".

He was staring below the desk at the Ayetech which managed the booking and billing. The device communicated with the larger network of Ramble Inns, updating customer profiles and preferences. Sean was glad the machine seemed preoccupied and hoped it wasn't monitoring his performance. True, his job was not complicated; he was there to greet, carry bags and ensure that the guests understood how to use the key codes.

It was a miserably wet morning and Sean had seen little action at the front desk. At ten o'clock a car turn in to the motel parking lot. Sean glimpsed the plate on the front, 'Empire State'. Up from New York then. He pulled his attention away from the vehicle—it was a smart, black sedan—and focussed on the driver, a large man dressed in somber clothes and struggling to pull a raincoat over his shoulders. As he turned, Sean caught sight of a dog collar; a referend gentleman, then. Sean guessed that he might be here to play the slots at the Akasino on the reservation up the road. It was one of the more successful businesses in the region.

✧　✧　✧

PASTOR BOB HARRIS retrieved his briefcase and grip from the trunk. He usually tried to stay at this chain. Ramble Inns had spread north across the border and were now on the outskirts of many Canadian towns. He was gratified to see that they were moving east into Quebec: *Le Ramble Inn.*

After locking the vehicle, Harris stepped back onto the strip of sodden turf which bordered the parking lot. His shoe sunk into mud. Muttering, he ran to get under the cover of the awning which only partially sheltered the entrance to the Inn. He went through the automatic doors into the lobby, shaking the raindrops from his coat, and marched up to reception.

The cheery greeting from the young man standing behind the desk did not improve his mood. "*Bonjour, 'Allo, Monsieur. Vous avez une reservation?*" The pastor grunted and held his Ayetech under Sean's nose. The device gave Harris's name, quoted the reservation number, and gave the plate number of his car. It spoke in French with a Parisien accent.

Harris watched the receptionist glance at the screen below the counter. He was assured that his room, number 234, was ready and accepted the young man's offer to carry his bag. Harris followed up a single flight of stairs and down a long corridor, barely listening to a recitation of the Inn's amenities. Reaching the door of Harris' room, the young man waved the Inn's Ayetech towards the lock sensor, heard the click and pushed open the door. He stood aside for the pastor to enter. Harris did so quickly and, shutting the door firmly behind him, cut short the description of the self-service breakfast arrangements.

With a grunt of relief, Harris turned the lock on the room door. Here was familiar comfort. Every Ramble Inn had the same furnishings: a teak desk and a swivel chair in dark faux-leather, an 'L'-shaped settee long enough for Harris to stretch out, a heavy glass-topped coffee table to rest his feet, and a large screen television. An excess of pillows and bolsters graced the 'emperor' bed. On one wall there was a framed print of dried grass, number 52 of 200. He recognized an old acquaintance from other Ramble Inns.

Harris walked over to glance out of the window. Through the rain he saw several vehicles parked in the lot facing a clay bank which rose behind the Inn. Muddy water ran down the slope in runnels into a growing puddle the colour of chocolate milk which was slowly spreading across the asphalt. The day was satisfactorily grey.

Harris lay on the bed, pulled open the bedside drawer and smiled with approval; all Ramble Inns now had copies of the Mission Guidebook. He always liked to read the preface, text to which he himself had contributed.

Harris had arranged to meet with Marsha Teg and Priebus that evening. He knew that they were camped in the long-stay lot at the Allways Supermarket, which he had noticed driving in to town. However, it was fitting that they should come here. He had booked the conference room off the lobby for six p.m. Before that, he wanted to contact the developer Shawcross. It might be useful to remind him of the clause in the contract which specified penalties for delays in construction.

✧ ✧ ✧

MARSHA WAS THINKING about her report as she and Priebus drove to the Ramble Inn. A warm rain was slashing across the windshield. She had put together a short presentation for Pastor Bob's benefit which summarized their findings, but she knew that Harris would be angry with the little progress to date. She had been so confident that some concretions would split to reveal perfect fish, as the pastor had ordered, but they had failed to find any. Sitting in the Allways parking lot, she and Priebus had worked methodically through the two boxes of concretions which they had recovered from the river. After some false starts, they had found the best way to crack the nodules was to apply pressure across the widest circumference and tap along the seam. Priebus had shown himself quite adept but every split concretion proved disappointingly barren. At the end of two hours, they were sitting beside a pile of broken rock and no fish.

On their arrival, Marsha passed the car which she recognized as belonging to Pastor Bob and backed the camper into the slot beside it. They hurried into the lobby. After enquiring at reception, Sean led them to the Business Centre, a cramped boardroom with an overlarge table, surrounded by eight high-backed orthopaedic chairs. In front of each chair were small reading lamps with attached microphones. The blinds were drawn. The hum of the motel air-conditioning unit could be heard just outside, competing with the drumbeat of the rain.

"I will page Monsieur Harris for you. Please help yourselves to refreshments over there on the side counter," said Sean.

Left alone, Marsha and Priebus sat and gazed at a picture of

Lake Louise on the wall opposite. Although possibly the most reproduced picture in Canada, neither of them recognized it.

"That's nice," said Marsha.

Harris gave them five minutes before coming down to the meeting room, Ayetech in hand.

"Good evening! And God bless!" Harris surged into the room. "I just had to finish a call," he said, waving the device by way of explanation for keeping them waiting. "Have you helped yourself to sodas? I'll have an iced tea, thank you, Marsha."

Marsha had struggled from her chair which she had failed to get out of 'auto-posture', and went to the beverage counter. Meanwhile, Priebus had leapt up and moved to shake Pastor Bob's hand. She had noticed but failed to mention to Priebus the rim of dirt under his fingernails from scratching grey mud from his black pants, the dried residue from his rock splitting.

"Okay, Marsha," said Harris. "Please tell me your team has made progress. I can tell you I am disappointed about the fish."

Marsha put her Ayetech in the middle of the boardroom table and touched the screen. She intended that her device lead Pastor Bob through the presentation. Her hologram manifested at the far end of the boardroom and she watched herself mouth the opening words of her speech. There was no sound. Pastor Bob stared pensively at Lake Louise until Priebus, diving beneath the table, discovered how to connect the speaker system. He plugged in the audio jack, and Harris' geniality returned. Ramble Inns south of the border had gone completely wireless, in his experience.

Marsha's began her presentation by describing the geography of Crewe and region. She explained the extent of the Leda Clay formation, of particular interest to Mission as the source of the fossil-rich concretions they were seeking. She acknowledged again their failure in locating a supply, despite their successful tracking down of Argile, the local enthusiast who provided the fish specimens to Molly's Rocks. Changing theme, she noted the two cultures of west Quebec, the French and the English, and touched on the low attendance at church where the three main denominations combined could only muster a few percent of the overall population on any given Sunday. She finished with a slide showing land prices gleaned from the websites of local realtors.

"You asked me to check these property prices, Pastor Bob," she said. "As you know, I am not an expert so I hope this is what you want."

"Very good," said Harris after the images had faded into rest mode at the end of the presentation. "But I wonder if perhaps you made an error on that table showing property values?"

Marsha flushed. She was regularly caught out by arithmetic. She referred to the slide in question and stared at it blankly and with rising panic for a full fifteen seconds before she finally saw the problem.

"Oh! It's in Canadian dollars! Thank you, Pastor Bob, for catching that. The average lot price is one hundred and twenty-five thousand Canadian, not US."

"That's much better," said Harris, who had already concluded that Crewe fitted well with Mission's strategic goals. He pulled from his briefcase a sheet of paper with Mission letterhead.

"This," he said, "is a directive from The Reverend Dean Polkhammer, Mission's Senior Executive for Marketing. He is much taken with your fossil fish, Marsha. He grasps the merchandizing potential. Dean agrees with me that this local connection to the biblical flood is essential to the success of a new Mission here in Crewe."

"So, it seems," continued Harris, "that this Argile who supplies Molly's Rocks with Crewe Stones is key. We need him to find a regular supply. Although I suppose plastic replicas would do at a pinch."

Harris stood and walked round the table to look more closely at Lake Louise. Then he turned and placed his hands on the shoulders of Marsha and Priebus.

"It is because of Dean's enthusiasm for your concretions, Marsha, that Mission has decided that Quebec is a strategic opportunity. We are coming here to Crewe to launch our good work. My team—that is you and Priebus—will lead the charge. We are negotiating with a local developer, Jack Shawcross, to adjust his plans for a major development on a site called River View, here on the outskirts of Crewe. Mission wants a physical presence in the community, and this new development is an opportunity not to be missed. You two are my eyes and ears. Now, any questions?"

Priebus coughed. He was still brooding on his frustration with the nodules.

"Sir? Why can't we just grab this Argile and ask him where he finds these fish?"

Marsha rolled her eyes. Her preferences were surveillance and stalking, skills perfected in Afghanistan. She had enjoyed her recce around the Argile cabin, even if the results were disappointing, and she still believed that stealthy observation of Argile's movements was the best approach. She was just about to ask about the plans for River View and the implications when Harris interrupted.

"You may be right, young Priebus," replied Harris. "Direct methods can be effective."

Priebus caught Marsha's eye and smirked.

"And since you will now be in Crewe for some time," continued Harris, "you should start the usual missionary activities. Going door to door is a useful way to judge the mood of the population."

Marsha's heart sank. Door to door was a depressing exercise in rejection, but she understood that talking on the doorstep was a favoured way of gathering intelligence for Mission.

Harris rose to signal the end of the meeting. Nodding to Marsha he reached across the table to shake his nephew's hand.

Retaining his grasp for some seconds he said, "It's God's work, Priebus. Just follow the guidebook."

✧ ✧ ✧

THROUGH THE WINDOW from his perch behind reception, Sean watched the young kid and the guests of Monsieur Harris climb into the large camper in the parking. He had recognized them as the pair he saw beside the road near the Professor's place a few weeks back.

After a few minutes, Harris emerged from the Business Centre and came to the front desk. He pushed his Ayetech in front of Sean who waited while the device asked him in French for directions to the Akasino.

"Just turn right out of the parking lot, Sir, and follow route 148 north for twenty kilometers," said Sean. "You won't miss the big sign on the right."

"Oh, huh, right. Thank you then," said Harris, who turned and went out to his Lincoln. Sitting behind the wheel, he took an antacid tablet from the glove compartment, put it in his mouth and crunched down. He remembered that it had been Dean Polkhammer who had suggested the Akasino as a good place to relax. The Lord knows what Polkhammer was doing this far north. Mission executives moved in mysterious ways. Still, he was grateful to escape the Inn for the evening. It had been a tough week and the dish of fries, gravy and cheese curds he had eaten in the Ramble Inn's restaurant had disagreed with him. At the casino he would down a couple of Caesars to settle his stomach.

Chapter 19

IT WAS FRIDAY and Ems was leaving the city to drive back up to the cabin. Forty-five minutes ago she had finished the first draft of her report and pressed 'Send'. She worked for an architectural firm with a flexible work policy that minimized office space at headquarters. Hot-desking was the norm, but Ems was senior enough to work mostly from her 'home office' which occupied a corner in the Argile's city apartment. If and when Chester came into town, she would tidy up.

It took her only five minutes to quit the building, struggling down the stairs with arms full and kneeing closed the front door. She threw a bag containing a week's worth of dirty clothes onto the back seat of her car, beside a large cardboard box containing seventeen pounds of grumbling cat. The cat's name was Lalique, after the green jade of his eyes: 'Lally' for short.

After driving quickly through the back streets, Ems joined the traffic on the parkway. With some rapid lane-changing on the approaches to the bridge, she managed to surf the wave of the five o'clock drive for the hills.

Ems pulled into the driveway at the cabin to find Argile weeding one of the front flower beds. Jet rushed to greet her, turning in circles of delight. Argile stopped struggling with the couch grass and came to open the back door of the car, allowing Lally to jump out from his box onto the warm gravel. Ignoring the dog, the cat lay down and rolled onto his back, purring satisfaction. It was clear: he was finished after another hard week confined in the city apartment. Lally was not one to take work home.

"Look at that lazy cat," exclaimed Ems, giving Argile a per-functory *bec* before bending to rub Jet's chest. "I beat the traffic for once, but I am nearly finished. All those last-minute changes. *C'est trop.* That client has a *tête de cochon.* Stubborn like you wouldn't believe!"

"Well, you're back now. You can relax. And it will please you to learn that young Sean helped me take two boxes of rocks down to Molly's while you were away. The garage is much less cluttered now."

"*Bon.* I'll believe that when I see it. Did you get everything for this evening?"

Argile nodded. He had just put the wine and beer in the fridge to chill. He had remembered to replenish their stock of alcohol at the SAQ in Crewe that morning after picking up the groceries. Their 'cave' now boasted five bottles, none of which would remain unopened for more than a couple of weeks.

✧   ✧   ✧

THE GOUGHS ARRIVED twenty minutes early. An urge for company had come over Argile earlier in the week and Ems had agreed to a Friday evening barbecue. Provided the weather held, he would cook outside: pork tenderloin with chopped aubergine and red peppers, and those tiny multi-coloured potatoes. Local strawberries were still in season and would do for dessert. Ems had texted Jilly Gough to see if she would make meringues.

Jet had a special relationship with the Goughs, developed over several years of outrageous spoiling by Jilly, whose pockets always held fragments of dog biscuits. His happy barking alerted Argile to their car pulling up in the driveway. Mildly annoyed at the futility of his efforts to inculcate some dignified reserve into his dog on these occasions, Argile stopped scraping the grill and walked around the house to greet the guests. Ems had beaten him to it and was bringing Peter and Jilly through to the back veranda.

"God, I hope you didn't invite the Marshalls," called Jilly as Argile emerged onto the veranda. Jilly was nothing if not forthright. It was true that their last party had been uncomfortable. Cade Marshall was not one to pull punches and had spent much of the evening bemoaning the latest idiocy coming out of the federal government in Ottawa. Cade had been manoeuvred into retirement by an unsympathetic manager and had since emerged as a libertarian, fiercely so by Canadian standards.

Argile steered Peter back into the kitchen and rummaged in a kitchen drawer for a corkscrew to open the bottle of wine which Peter had brought.

"Have you got them?" he asked when they were out of earshot of the veranda.

Peter late in his career as an electronic engineer had developed a passion for micro-drones, tiny aircraft fitted with custom sensors. His pet project was a swarm of micro-drones which he had originally intended to use to pollinate the Gough's vineyard. When the results of this proved disappointing, Peter looked for another project, and when Argile mentioned his survey work on the slopes above Crewe, Peter volunteered his drones. The price of this help was for Argile to enthuse about Peter's wines. This vintage was year two. It was, to be fair, an improvement on year one. It was a varietal genetically modified to discourage the pests of a Canadian June. By some reports, the new grape had proven successful on the harsh soils of western Quebec. Wines from grapes grown on the rude terroirs of the north had attained a certain cachet among younger oenophiles.

The prognosis of a warming climate had encouraged many hobby farmers to try growing vines. But not all parts of the globe were warming evenly. Since planting his vines, Peter had endured a succession of cooler and wetter summers. He knew that greater variability in the weather matched with climate models, but he felt it would be fairer if the temperature varied back to above average for a season. Let somewhere else be cooler and wetter for once.

"It's not really a red," Peter was saying. "It's more of a rosé, really. Slightly crackling. The girls should like it."

Argile poured a couple of glasses of wine, then opened the fridge and took out the six-pack he had bought at the dep the previous day.

"Here," he said, passing a beer to Peter.

"Mm, that's good," said Peter, taking a long pull on the bottle. "Yes, don't worry, I remembered. The mini-drones are in a cardboard box in the back of the car. We can launch them later when it gets dark. You will like the LEDs I glued to their backs. It took me all yesterday afternoon."

Argile and Peter went to join the women on the veranda, stepping carefully over Lally who was lying across the doormat. Argile carried the drinks. Their brief absence did not appear to have registered. The two women were still engrossed in conversation.

Jet rose from under the table and stared at the plate of tortilla chips which Argile had carried outside from the kitchen. Jilly fed him a chip when she thought Argile wasn't looking.

Peter sat down beside Ems and Jilly, sinking awkwardly into one of the Adirondack chairs on the veranda.

"You have the most magnificent view from here," said Jilly. "I am surprised you get anything done. I could sit here forever."

"Please excuse me while I turn the vegetables," said Argile and went down the veranda steps to a small paved area on which crouched the ancient gas barbecue. He had lit some coils earlier to deter mosquitoes but dusk was falling, the patrolling dragonflies had disappeared and the first bats had yet to appear. Taking advantage of this changing of the guard, the blood-seeking insects rose from the long grass en masse. Argile thought his guests would be lucky to tough it out for another ten minutes before being driven inside. Argile flipped over the meat and shovelled the roasting vegetables into a pile in the corner of the grilling mat to remain moist.

Argile returned to the group on the veranda. Peter was explaining his work on drone bees. Both women were silent.

They went inside and sat around the dining table. Argile brought in the food, slipping through the screen door with practiced deception to leave behind his train of pursuing mosquitoes. In the middle of the table Ems had placed her Ayetech which was now unfolding into a rosette of fern-like fronds.

"That is so pretty, Ems," exclaimed Jilly.

The two couples knew each other well and enjoyed each other's company, provided—in Argile's view—that their mutual invitations came at decent intervals. Early in the evening, their conversation had focussed on upcoming holidays or absence thereof. Later, alcohol had helped the talk to diversify. As was usual there was frequent recourse to their Ayetechs or factual corrections on conversational matters such as ancient British monarchy, the name of that town in Provence, or the next opportunity to view the aurora borealis.

It was Peter who brought up his concerns about fracking. The Goughs were on a deep well and, like many of their neighbours, worried about their water supply. They feared potential contamination of groundwater. Sensational reports on social media stoked these fears: stories of fracking breaking the cap rock which pressed the salt brines deep underground, allowing noxious fluids to wend towards the surface; of cracks in rotting cement around the well bores prized open to release methane gas; and of cups of tea igniting spontaneously.

"What I can't believe," complained Peter, "is that damned Hilary Beaubien saying that we had nothing to worry about. That's typical. The government does nothing when some big oil company moves in. Now here we are with fracking on our doorstep. We have electric vehicles, we live in a green home, we are insulated to our eyeballs and they say we need the gas? It's all about profits and backhanders, I say".

The last time Argile and Peter had talked, back in March, Peter's rant had focussed on spring potholes—their depth, number and persistence. This, granted, was because his mechanic had told him that the ball joints on his car needed replacing.

"They should have lasted for years if we had decent asphalt around here," Peter had said. "They go for the cheapest. It's dubious contracting. That's why Beaubien can't repair the roads effectively."

"You have a bee in your bonnet about the Mayor," said Argile. "As for the fracking, well, I changed the propane on the barbecue yesterday, so if you want some supper, you had better support gas development." The mood lightened.

That there was local opposition to the prospect of fracking near Crewe hardly surprised Argile. Opponents of fracking used emotive words—explosion, fracture, contamination. People sought answers from the internet but had no means by which to sift fact from exaggerations and untruths. Argile got a couple more beers and poured more wine. The conversation drifted to more neutral subjects.

After dinner, Peter arranged his swarm on the table in front of the window. By now it was dark outside, and the air had cooled. The party put on jackets and sat on the veranda steps to watch. Peter switched on the green LED lights on the backs of the micro-drones settled on the charging ramp.

"*Bees*—that's what I call them, but don't worry, they won't sting. Now sit back and watch."

Peter bent over a small console and gave a terse command. The swarm rose from the table in a glowing cloud and then moved out from the house towards open space.

"I don't have to do a thing," said Peter proudly. "I programmed the general flight pattern but the detailed navigation depends on the bees learning their new environment. The swarm can even invent new patterns by itself. They will all come back to the ramp when their power levels drop below ten percent."

The swarm was now about twenty-five metres in front of the veranda and was swaying left and right.

"They're mapping the landscape," said Peter. "They do it in infra-red, if you were wondering. It usually takes about a minute, after which the program will start."

Suddenly the swarm organized into several smaller groups and the individual bees spaced themselves evenly. The cloud expanded to occupy much of the sky in front of them. As wide, Argile thought, as the big screen viewed from the fifth row at the one independent movie theatre that still survived in Crewe. He had to credit Peter with an impressive achievement.

"Now watch," commanded Peter, as the swarm organized itself into letters. The words "Gough Prod*ctions" danced before their eyes for a few seconds, before being swept away as the swarm rose in the sky.

"Damn," said Peter. "One of the LEDs isn't working."

A descending spiral of letters froze to hover in the air before them.

"*No to fracking, Hilary,*" they read.

"Hah. You see, I read in *The Courier* that la Beaubien is in bed with TiteGas. Typical politician, don't you think?" asked Peter.

Argile felt guilty: the Mayor had announced a measured and balanced approach to future applications to drill beneath Crewe. She had listened to Argile's opinion after the Margs Bay meeting. He had said that fracking shouldn't be a concern, either for causing earthquakes or for contaminating groundwater.

For *The Courier*, the Mayor's comments had been a gift, meriting the front page of its latest edition. The paper painted the Mayor as recklessly pro-development.

Talk died. Returning inside and lighting the lamps, Ems suggested that it might be amusing to ask her Ayetech to start a new topic of conversation.

"What about that weather, eh?" ventured the Ayetech, after a moment's pause.

Chapter 20

HILARY BEAUBIEN SKIMMED through the brief for her ten am with the River View team. Her Ayetech had extended into a screen sized for optimal reading with a font customized to correct for the Mayor's myopia.

Municipal staff had presented several options for Council to consider, but for various reasons had winnowed these down to one recommendation: that the development be given the green light. The proposal now ticked all the boxes. It included a review of accessibility (appended at tab A); environmental screening (tab B); and results of a community survey (tab C). The report covered the economic benefits at length and these appeared to be several, including a projected rise in property tax revenue of twelve percent.

By the time Hilary had reached tab D (infrastructure) it was five minutes before ten. She flipped back to the staff recommendation. In Hilary's view, there were two issues with the development. One was the lack of secondary access for the large number of new condos planned for the development. A provision to require secondary access to the development—at least for emergency vehicles—was proposed as an important condition for approval. She recognized the Fire Chief's input.

The second issue which nagged at her was the geotechnical report (tab F). Test drilling had identified Leda Clay beneath most of the site, which could be a problem. But the proponents advised that injecting a stabilizing brine would strengthen the sensitive clay. They called this technique 'chemical piling' and cited several successful examples from Europe where the resistance of clays dramatically increased with this treatment. Building on these treated clays proceeded with no problems. After thumbing through the glossary at the back of the report, Hilary discovered that the 'stabilizing brine' was just salt water.

The Mayor flagged this for the meeting. Otherwise, it seemed to be a thorough report from municipal staff. The recommendation to allow the project to go ahead was clear, with the reasonable but important caveat about secondary access.

The Mayor had invited Argile to the meeting. He had already arrived—she had seen his bicycle in the rack in front of the building—and the receptionist had shown him to the conference room. She closed the file on her desk but waited before leaving her office. She made it a rule to be the last to enter any meeting. Bryce Desjardins could entertain Argile and the party from River View until her arrival. She told her Ayetech to open Facebook.

✧   ✧   ✧

FROM HIS OFFICE window, Bryce Desjardins saw the River View SUV pull into the municipal parking lot. He went to the reception area, welcomed Jack Shawcross and his assistant, and escorted them towards the conference room.

"*Faites attention*," he said in a confidential tone. "There will be a tax payer-observer attending the meeting. You know how the Mayor insists that meetings are all open to the public. It's stupid, I know, but don't worry. Dr. Argile is a bit of a crazy: no one takes him seriously around here."

Bryce showed the visitors into the conference room where Argile was waiting. Argile turned from gazing out of the large window which looked out, rather unfortunately, on the municipality's composting test area.

Jack Shawcross nodded to Argile. "Ah yes. Dr. Argile. You were at the last council meeting."

Denisse Lafriche sat beside her boss on one side of the table and Argile took a seat opposite them. Jack Shawcross pulled out his Ayetech and laid it on the table.

"It's good to have your own record of these meetings, don't you agree?" he said to Argile.

The Mayor entered with an older woman, followed by Bryce.

"*Bonjour*," said the Mayor, shaking hands with Jack and Denisse across the table. "Please call me Hilary. And welcome, Dr. Argile. I am glad you all could make it. I believe you have already met our Director of Public Works," she said, nodding towards Bryce. "And this is Madame Bellesrides, municipal secretary."

The Mayor and Madame Bellesrides took the chairs at the end of the table. Meanwhile, Bryce moved to the side table where a coffee machine stood beside a collection of mugs.

"I have invited Dr. Argile as an observer," said the Mayor. "As you know, he raised a concern about potential landslides and has some expertise in those matters. We can offer coffee or tea."

Jack accepted coffee but with no milk while Denisse demurred. Bryce pressed the button for a long black and made a latte for himself. He placed a small bottle of mineral water on a small napkin in front of the Mayor.

"All the coffee materials are supposed to be compostable. We are testing some of those new coffee pods made entirely of organic materials." Hilary gestured to the collection of composters outside the window. "Unfortunately, we just don't drink enough coffee for a rigorous experiment, so your contribution is very welcome!"

"Ah yes, coffee grounds; important for Crewe as a fair-trade town, I suppose." Jack paused. "To business, then?" He was looking directly at the Mayor. "It is good of you to take this meeting at short notice. You have our application, which I hope you agree is comprehensive, but I wanted an opportunity to answer your questions in person."

Jack hadn't become successful without self-awareness. He had managed after long practice to score highly on the emotional intelligence tests on the Ayetech application. Peripherally, he felt the cold regard of Madame Bellesrides but kept focussed on the Mayor.

"And I wanted to make you aware of a slight re-purposing of the project," continued Jack. "Nothing substantial has changed in the plans, but we have been fortunate to find a new investor who has put the project on a firmer financial footing."

"I thought your project was a sound investment. Are you saying that isn't the case?" asked the Mayor.

"Yes, of course it is," said Jack. "But the economics of the project were marginal, which is why I asked you for relief on property taxes. With the new investor the finances are rock solid. It's an educational group from the States called Mission who believes Crewe is perfect for a campus. Their focus is adult education, and they plan to adapt the buildings for student accommodation. You may have seen their advertisements on television."

Madame Bellesrides paused writing on her steno pad. She had read the file on River View and prepared the briefing note for Madame Mayor. She did not have a favourable opinion of Jack Shawcross. Although this was the first time she had met him in person, she knew of his reputation around Crewe. She was friendly with Denisse's mother from the 'bring and buy' sales at the community hall. It would surprise Jack to know how thoroughly his morals had been dissected by the village women of a certain age.

At the mention of Mission, Madame Bellerides' ears pricked

up. Denisse's mother had confided that her daughter said that some religious organization was invading the village, an American sect. The Lord knew what the Father would have to say about that, although the new man might not be reliable in such matters. Perhaps she should write to her cousin the Bishop to warn him. A short letter, or perhaps a text. Bishop Jean-Baptiste had finally learned how to use his Ayetech.

Madame Bellerides heard Madame Mayor cough beside her.

"Well, I think your investors are your business, Jack," said the Mayor. "Although you may expect some blowback on social media. However, I believe you had a provision for some assisted living for elderly people in the original plan?" She glanced sideways at Madame Bellesrides, who gave a curt nod.

"Yes," replied Jack. "The residence is still in the plan but we have moved it to a much better waterfront location."

Jack unrolled a map and pointed to the Akonaga River.

"It will be here on the river bank, with easy access to the village and great views across the water."

"*Bien.* Okay," said the Mayor. "Now what about the soil stability issue? You must recognize the problems we have here in Crewe building on Leda Clay. With a large project like yours, please remind me of the special measures you propose?"

"No problem," replied Jack. "My consultants have paid particular attention to drainage. Our plans emphasize control of run-off which, as you know, is key to avoiding stability problems."

"*Merci*, Jack. I understand the drains, but what confused me was the piles, the chemical piles which you mention in the report. Perhaps you would explain...?"

"Tab F in the report, isn't it, Denisse?" said Jack. He flipped to the place in the ring binder.

"Yes, our consultants recommend the use of chemical piles to stabilize the Leda Clay below parts of the River View site.

Chemical piles are just boreholes drilled into the clay and pumped full of stabilizing brine. The brine changes the chemistry of the clay—actually glues the clay particles together—and dramatically increases its strength."

"Ah, where does this brine come from?" asked the Mayor.

"Well, it's just salt water really, Hilary," said Jack. "This is where my project benefits from collaboration with TiteGas. That's the company drilling for gas over on the other side of the river. TiteGas has agreed to include the twenty water wells we have just drilled on the River View property in their groundwater monitoring program. They have inserted state-of-the-art meters to record pressure variations in the Leda Clay. Monitoring around the clock will give us early warning of any pressure increases in the clay while we are building. But our consultants assure us that this is adding precaution on top of precaution."

Jack glanced around the table to see that his audience was following him. Satisfied, he continued.

"TiteGas also offered to provide me with saltwater from their fracking operations. They propose to tanker the brine onto the River View site and to inject it into the Leda Clay."

"But surely that is experimental?" interjected the Mayor. "I mean, it hasn't been tested here in Crewe?"

"Well, think of it this way. I am sure it will be successful and Crewe can use this technique more widely in the future. That means, Madame Mayor, that you will be able to green light development on the unproductive farmland around Crewe where there were concerns about Leda Clay. Municipal tax revenues will soar."

Jack paused briefly to allow time for the Mayor to reflect. He imagined that over her term, she had been obliged to shelve several vanity projects for lack of funds.

"Now let me conclude with my personal assurance that public

safety is my number one consideration," said Jack. "River View builds in a large margin of safety for all our projects, especially when it comes to the Leda Clay."

He sat back in his chair, smiled at the Mayor and looked across the table at Argile.

Argile, who was doodling a series of stick men on bicycles on the pad in front of him, tried to concentrate. Shawcross had been saying something about TiteGas. Had they extended their fracking patterns towards Crewe? Their nearest drilling pad was a good fifteen kilometers from the far bank of the Akonaga. From there, it was another two kilometers to the centre of Crewe. That seemed a long way for horizontal drilling.

"Perhaps I could ask Dr. Argile if he has any comment," said the Mayor, breaking the sudden silence.

Argile pulled himself together.

"I agree the monitoring of groundwater is welcome," he said. "But the Leda Clay is tricky, and any excavated soil piled near the river bank could trigger a landslide. And the brine might contaminate drinking water. Have you thought of that?"

"Our engineering consultants are extremely experienced," replied Jack. "We have included all their recommendations for setbacks and drainage in our plans. They are confident that all issues are entirely manageable. And the brine is just like the salt water from domestic water softeners—people have never been concerned about that!"

"But chemical piles are not an instant remedy. They take a long time to become effective."

"A matter of weeks," said Jack.

"Years, more like," said Argile.

"Gentlemen, gentlemen," interrupted Hilary. "Perhaps Dr. Argile agrees that the precautions you are taking are appropriate. Even though we can acknowledge that he still has reservations, I am sure he appreciates that the municipality's land base is highly restricted and that we are forced to develop on ground which may not be ideal. River View does seem to be following the advice of their consultants."

Argile shrugged. The Leda seldom failed when and where he predicted. He looked at his notepad. His later stickmen appeared dismembered and smudged by little whirlpools of ink.

Chapter 21

FUCK MODERATION, THOUGHT Dave McClintock as he stared glumly at the screen. Ever since Elsie Truelove had added 'moderator' to his job description he had grown more depressed. Yes, his title now included Chief of Social Media. It looked good on his *c.v.* but made no impression on his pay. Instead, he found himself more and more frustrated, trying to apply the code of ethics that *The Courier* had developed through focus group sessions earlier in the year.

He was watching a rapid rise in the volume of posts to *The Courier Online*. He sighed. There were rumours of earthquakes, magic crystals and secret deals between Mayor Beaubien and energy companies. Lucky Crewe, he thought.

Take earthquakes. Usually, *The Courier*—Dave, that is—would try to pair the out-and-out crazy with something saner, but so far no purported expert or authority had weighed in with a rational view. After the tremor during the council meeting, some were convinced that TiteGas was destabilizing the bedrock. Others had a more mystical take—that some mysterious force was to blame. Several posts verged on the hysterical.

What are 'aural convulsions' anyway, wondered Dave as he read the most recent to pop up in the in-box. Wikipedia wasn't a great help. He gathered an aura could be a premonition of an epileptic event, or a psychic phenomenon for which there was dubious evidence. Perhaps 'aural convulsions' could predict earthquakes? He re-read the post and failed to decide which definition made more sense from the context. Dave was skeptical. He pressed 'delete'.

The Courier had recently bought an artificial intelligence program to help scan and sort through electronic mail. Among other functions, it checked for trolling, cyber-attack and abuse. Dave ran the program to check whether people posting to the site were bona fide individuals or advertising robots, and whether they were potential subscribers. The program also scanned for text with any taboo words or phrases—anything touching on ethnicity was out. Dave relied on the AI to flag hints of sarcasm or irony or innuendo to help him decide whether to accept or edit a post. Straightforward Anglo-Saxon obscenity was easier for Dave to catch than unacceptable words in the French feed. He would ask Lise whether *un maudit grand pot-de-vin* was acceptable or not. He was pretty sure it had nothing to do with drink.

Dave knew he was fighting a losing battle. Dave knew the program needed upgrading: its capacity and judgement were being overwhelmed by the deluge of messages from media engines trying to push products or influence opinion. He thought he was looking at a media push now with the earthquake thing—some kind of campaign, but to what end?

He looked over to Lise. She was laying out the next edition on the big table. Now that was a fun job; one that Dave had had to relinquish. There was a game he used to play: matching stories to advertisements in ways which appealed to his sense of humour. It required careful judgement so not to be caught by Elsie in her final read-through. Dave tried to think of some inappropriate advertisement to run with the earthquake story; something about milk shakes perhaps? Or a two for one special offered by Foundation Services, specialist in drains and retaining walls. Which reminded him he hadn't seen Dara for hours. Where the hell was she? She had gone to find some local geology expert to interview about the earthquake. But coming into the office no longer seemed a high priority for Dara. The editor seemed to be pretty lax with her, Dave thought. Bloody old dyke.

✧ ✧ ✧

EMS WAS SCROLLING through her daily news feed. In *La Presse* it was the usual stuff; another shooting in Montreal, the latest in a war between rival gangs. Ems guessed that it would be tit for tat: someone else would be for the chop. The economy was not doing well, and a Quebec Minister was launching a blitz on English signs. *Rien de neuf*—nothing new.

She switched to the local news. Ems had finally weakened and paid the subscription for *The Courier Online*. One item caught her attention. She too had felt the earth tremor which had disturbed the council meeting a few weeks past, and there was a quote from a Dr. Roch Legalet, a geophysicist friend who Ems knew from her university days. Roch predated Chester Argile in Ems' affections. There was a picture of the scientist looking earnest and Ems guessed the photo must date from at least ten years earlier.

The Courier had finally found its expert on the subject of earthquakes. Ems read that, in Roch's informed opinion, the low level of seismic activity was perfectly normal and nothing to concern the populace. He carried the authority of the Geological Institute which constantly monitored seismic activity in the region. A magnitude 3.5 was a minor shake and caused no significant damage.

A pity, thought Ems, that Chester could not state matters as clearly.

Ems skipped to the foot of the article and started to read the online comments from readers. It surprised her how upset people were about that little earthquake. Mind you, she supposed that she was a little de-sensitized to geological events from living with Chester. But no one was injured, and the only casualty *chez eux* was cracked glass in one picture frame. She had been happy to have an excuse to put the frame back in storage. It contained Chester's certificate of retirement, an occasion for congratulations after thirty years of loyal service, signed by the mechanical arm of the Prime Minister, no less. It was *dommage* that they had misspelled Chester's name.

As Ems followed the thread, she read that *Chapterandverse101* viewed earthquakes and floods to be sent by God to correct errant humanity. Very Old Testament: Chester would be amused. *Dare2luvJesus* held that such disasters were the works of the devil. Others blamed the fracking by TiteGas, or terrorists.

Unknown to Ems, Dave at *The Courier* had finally decided to close the thread but before he did so, one final post slipped through. Ems read that ungodly geo-terrorists were hiding in plain sight in the community. 'DON'T BELIEVE THE SO-CALLED EXPERTS', it cried. 'Trust your own judgement. All you need is a guiding hand!' The poster, signing itself *activeMission*, warned that the citizens of Crewe would pay a high price if they were not vigilant.

A large advertisement appeared beside this last post. It urged readers to contribute to Mission, shortly to open a study centre in Quebec. Ems was curious. She google 'Mission' and found the website. It was an organization headquartered in the States. A smiling family welcomed visitors to the home page. Promoting progressive evangelism, she read, lending a guiding hand to followers everywhere. Ems was lapsed catholic and pro-choice; proudly Quebecoise.

Sapristi!! Here in Crewe? *C'est pas vrai!*

✧　✧　✧

WHEN ARGILE RETURNED from the evening walk with the dog, he seemed on autopilot. Ems recognized the signs; Chester was still thinking geology—lost at some horizon in the Quaternary Period, as he had once told her. *Bon*: a drink would return him to the present fast enough.

"Have you seen this in *The Courier Online*?" she asked.

Argile moved over to sit beside her on the couch and she began scrolling through the thread.

"I see they got hold of Roch for an interview. He's not shy to oblige the media, you know," said Argile.

"You know that's not fair," replied Ems. "No, look further down in the comments."

"The Mayor keeps calling me her expert," said Argile after reading the post. "'Geo-terrorists'—that's a good one."

✧　✧　✧

MAYOR HILARY BEAUBIEN always checked the news feeds before breakfast and at intervals throughout the day. The postings about the Crewe earthquake made her sit up. By the time she had drained her first coffee of the morning, she had decided to downplay her reliance on Dr. Argile. She wrote 'less of the geo-babble' on a sticky note to remind herself. She liked Argile but he did come across as aloof, too academic. It was a pity he wasn't more down to earth, like that fellow Legalet.

In these times of public mistrust of experts, Hilary wondered whether it would have been wiser to take a stand against TiteGas, rather than her favoured middle of the road approach. People had perfectly valid common sense concerns, and she took pride in listening to the people. Take that burning water, for instance, which that EcoClub agitator had raised at the meeting in Margs Bay. She had looked up the video on YouTube. Oil companies had mixed gas into people's drinking water. Or perhaps it was a conspiracy of geo-terrorists: the posts seemed a little confused on this point. The charming Mr. Bludston's mellow assurances did not seem as convincing now.

Chapter 22

WITH SOME TREPIDATION, Dr. Mandy Brakes steered the company pick-up along the narrow dirt track which ran beside the river towards River View. It was raining, and the surface was slippery. Even with the four-wheel drive engaged, she felt the tires skidding sideways. She was driving directly on clay, which was swelling under the rain. The ruts were pooling with grey water. Finally she gave up and steered onto the coarsely vegetated verge.

Not the best environmental practice, but to hell with it, she thought.

Mandy was proud to work for TiteGas. It was a new kind of gas company, one committed to winning 'social licence'—a measure of trust—from all who came in contact with it. Unlike conventional companies that focussed on either exploration or distribution, TiteGas explored for, produced and distributed its own natural gas. This had become possible with new fracking technologies that could extract gas from almost any rock rich in mature organic matter. TiteGas produced gas only for local consumption, so there was no need for controversial long-distance pipelines. This successful strategy was reflected in rising profits for the company's private owners.

The company boasted that its operations put the environment first. TiteGas planted dense buffers of fast-growing trees around its drill sites to offset carbon emissions, trees which also shielded the company's operations from public view. Corporate advertisements explained how consumers could lower their use of fossil fuels and save money; a message that perversely had the opposite effect.

TiteGas saw high potential in a geological trend extending north from Margs Bay towards Crewe. The company had drilled successful wells a few kilometers south of the Akonaga River, and the next wells planned would be close to the southern bank, almost within sight of the town of Crewe.

Mandy's responsibilities included monitoring groundwater in areas where TiteGas planned to explore and develop gas. Acquiring baseline data for water quality was high among the company's social licence commitments and the data was potentially useful for deterring lawsuits of parties who imagined that fracking might affect their water supply.

TiteGas had drilled several holes in the bottom lands bordering the Akonaga to install piezometers, devices that measured the groundwater level and pore pressure. The Municipality of Crewe had agreed to the drilling, and she knew that Jack Shawcross, the developer of River View, allowed TiteGas access to his lands. The holes ran in a rough line beside the route Mandy was following. The remote-monitoring system had failed on several of them, and Mandy felt the need to check the installation despite the rain. She was conscientious and hated to have gaps in her records.

Peering through the windscreen Mandy spotted the florescent tape flagging piezometer number sixty-six. She saw immediately that a falling branch had knocked sideways the solar panel powering the data transmitter. She hoped the problem would be as obvious on all of them.

Putting on her gumboots and pulling the hood of her rain jacket to shield her head, Mandy plodded over to the piezometer, found the manual data port and connected her Ayetech. She repositioned the solar panel and checked that the transmitter was charging. Everything seemed copasetic.

She walked carefully back in the truck to avoid slipping but could not avoid accumulating sticky clay balls under the arch of each foot. Climbing in, she slipped out of her boots and settled in the driver's seat to review the last twenty-four hours of data which the monitor had recorded but failed to transmit. Her Ayetech screen showed a graph of groundwater pressure.

To Mandy's surprise, the record showed a marked hike in pressure. Over a period of several minutes overnight, the pressure had risen, in a series of steps, to almost a third higher than the baseline which it had followed closely for the previous six months. It was almost as though a pump had driven the pressure higher. This was an anomaly. Perhaps there was an issue with the sensor.

Anyway, she thought, preparing to drive on, piezo sixty-seven and sixty-eight will either confirm the error or not.

A few hundred yards down the dirt road from her last stop, Mandy turned towards the gate leading to the River View lands. The remaining piezos on her check-list were on the far side of the fence, but she saw that she might not get to them. A white truck with 'ECOCLUB' stencilled on its side in large green letters blocked the entrance. On seeing Mandy's approach, a handful of protesters waved banners. One read 'No to oil pollution' and another 'Save our water'. She wished she was not driving the company truck. The TiteGas logo on the side would hardly escape notice.

✧   ✧   ✧

FOR MICHEL MONCHAGRIN it had been a long morning. First, he had to round up his group of activists—not known as early-risers—and then drive from Montreal. They needed breakfast, so they stopped at a *casse-croute* on the way. Several in the group insisted on espresso, so it took longer than Michel anticipated. On their arrival in Crewe, they erected their protest banners across what he assumed was the main entrance to River View. It was actually the back entrance.

After an hour, it was becoming hard to keep the group energized. Michel began to feel that he had made a mistake in choosing the new development in Crewe to protest. Yet, since the meeting in St. Margs, he had researched TiteGas. Although the company downplayed the subject, he was convinced that this would be the first fracking in Quebec and it would be right under this development. He had even heard that the company planned to pour frack water into wells on the River View project. They were going to poison the drinking water. It all stank of collusion between capitalist developers and corrupt government officials.

Seeing her through the approaching vehicle's windscreen, Michel thought the driver looked familiar. As it slowed, he glimpsed the TiteGas logo and recognized the woman Mandy Brakes from the meeting at St Margs.

The early morning espresso had given Michel acid reflux, but he forgot his discomfort in a rush of angry revulsion. Here was a turncoat, a betrayer of the cause; one of those *soi-disant* 'ecolos' who worked for an oil company.

"*Bonjour*, Madame Brakes," he called, stepping firmly into the path of Mandy's SUV. One of the EcoClub protesters clustered around the vehicle. They shouted "*Non á TiteGas, non á TiteGas*".

Someone began banging a pan.

Mandy pushed the button to crack open her window.

"Bonjour, Monsieur. I really need to get through to do some safety testing. It is very important."

Michel shrugged as if to say she would be going nowhere. He knew the testing she meant. The unregulated production of gas was always just 'testing'. He leaned towards the window.

"I am Michel Montchagrin, committee chair for EcoClub, Laval local. I was at the Margs Bay meeting where your stupid company tried to sell its lies. I asked you a question and you couldn't answer."

"Well, I'm sorry if we didn't answer your questions at the meeting but you don't understand. It is vital that I get through. I..."

Michel's derisive snort interrupted Mandy. "You company slaves are all alike!" he shouted. "Call yourself an ecologist. How can you live with yourself? There is no way we are letting you through. You can—*mais c'est quoi le mot en Anglais? Ben oui*, you can 'frack off'."

Mandy was not usually at a loss, but Michel's furious regard six inches from her face stunned her. A mollifying response froze in her throat. She flushed, feeling a real anger which she couldn't articulate. She closed the window and reversed to turn the vehicle around. As she did so, she heard jeers from the protesters. She retreated back the way she came until the gate was out of sight and stopped, her heart pounding.

After waiting a few minutes to calm down, she drove on. Passing piezo sixty-six, she decided that the anomalous reading was just that; an anomaly. She would log it as instrument error on her return to base. As for Michel Montchagrin and his idiot friends, they could go to hell. She didn't earn enough to put up with that crap. Let the president of TiteGas deal with EcoClub.

Chapter 23

S EAN'S DAD, THOMAS-JOHN Box, was Crewe's go-to guy. His towing and wrecking business at the edge of the village had grown over the years to include repair and servicing for a wide variety of motors from snowmobiles to all-terrain vehicles. Cars and trucks of various vintages now beyond further salvage littered the back of his three-acre lot. The original red tow truck of T-J Box *et fils*, now retired, was displayed with pride beside the avenue of white-and-red-painted tractor tires which guided hesitant customers towards the entrance to the wrecking yard. There was a large garage for repairs, where locals trusted that the excellent Monsieur Box would charge less than the dealerships in town. *Mille mercis*, he would say to his customers with smiling Irish eyes. Everyone knew they could trust T-J, even if he was an Anglo.

Sean reserved a corner of his dad's workshop cum garage. His snowmobile was there under a plastic sheet. For summer wheels, he had built a four-by-four all-terrain vehicle by scavenging various parts from the lot. His VTT, *véhicule tout-terrain*, was not street-legal but, by keeping to the road verges and side streets, Sean had successfully evaded the attention of Officer Manon Patinaude. Compared to the Ford, the VTT was cheap on gas and a cooler ride altogether.

Sean knew his dad wanted him to work on rebuilding an engine that morning but he had begged off an hour to meet with Rob who had promised to show his drinking buddies of the previous evening what Rob called 'his bones'. Twenty minutes later, Sean pulled up behind the big yellow Kobatsu. Dara was already there, her parked Civic looking small and fragile beside the squat bulk of the excavator.

"Hi," said Sean, "What's up?"

Rob offered cigarettes to Dara and Sean. Only Sean accepted, ignoring Dara's disapproving glance, and was lighting up when he saw Argile and his dog emerge from the forested hillside above.

"Morning Professor!" called Sean. Argile waved, and changed direction to walk towards the group by the excavator.

"Good morning, Sean. Hi Dara, Rob," said Argile. "Thanks for the invite, Rob. Now, where is your find?"

"Over there, below those trees," replied Rob, pointing behind him. He turned and started to walk up the cutline. The others followed, stepping carefully to avoid the rocks displaced by the blade of Rob's machine. Argile put Jet on an extensible leash.

Rob had been digging a trench parallel to the cutline when he had quit the previous day. The ditch was about four feet deep and a stream of water trickled along the bottom. The smell of leaf mould mingled with the tang of ozone, and something sulphurous.

"There it is," said Rob, pointing to the far side of the trench where torn roots dangled in the air. Below a thin layer of dark forest soil, the walls of the trench were cut into a stiff yellow sand. From near the top of the sand stared the empty eye socket of a skull.

Dara took her camera out as Argile jumped into the ditch for a closer look. He poked gently at the skull.

"Most of it is stuck in the sand. I would have to dig it out to be sure it's human," said Argile. "I don't think I should do that. Oh, and there's the end of another bone." Argile pointed to a pale knob to the right of the skull. The end of a humerus, I would guess. That's an arm bone, Sean."

"How old is the skull?" asked Dara.

Argile didn't reply immediately. He was familiar with these sands—deposited by rivers flowing from melting glaciers as they retreated to the northeast. Their age might be anything from nine thousand years before present to yesterday.

He took out his penknife and carefully scratched at the sand just below the skull. He held up a small angular object.

"Pottery," he said. "This is definitely an archaeological site. This shard looks pre-contact. See these wavy scratch lines on the surface?" He passed the fragment up to Dara, who held it out for Rob and Sean to see.

"I think this decoration is probably diagnostic. It could be at least several hundred years, maybe older. It needs a proper archaeological dig and radiocarbon dating to know for sure. Ah, there are some wood fragments."

Argile worked with his knife at the sand and flicked some dark fragments into a ziploc bag he pulled from his pocket.

"This charcoal should give us a date," he said.

Sean scrambled down beside Argile.

"What's 'pre-contact' Professor?" he asked. Argile started to say that the term referred to indigenous culture before the French landed, but Sean was no longer listening. He was poking with a stick at the wall of the trench about five feet from Argile.

"Hey, what's this?" Sean said suddenly. "There is something shiny there." Before Argile could stop him, Sean tugged the object loose and held it up. It was a man's shoe, pointed at the toe with a raised heel.

"This doesn't look Indian. More like Italian. Fuck, there's a foot still in it."

He flung the shoe aside with a snort of disgust.

"Hold on, I have a poop bag here," said Argile. He pulled out one of the green plastic bags he always carried when walking with

Jet. Gingerly he picked up the shoe from the bottom of the trench and dropped it into the bag.

Dara was looking pale. Argile tried to reassure her.

"Don't worry, Dara," he said. "The other bones are definitely old. The foot is from a recent burial. The skull is embedded in the sand below the soil layer where Sean found the shoe. It is almost certainly older. Mind you, we have to call the police now."

"I'm fine," said Dara. "This is great. Let me just get another picture. How about a selfie with all of us?"

Argile motioned to Sean. They started to clamber out of the ditch when they saw a vehicle pull up at the beginning of the cutline.

"That's Desjardins," said Sean. "There's going to be trouble. I'm out of here." Sean slithered over the lip of the trench and, crouching low, ran into the trees and out of sight.

✦ ✦ ✦

BRYCE DESJARDINS PARKED beside the excavator. He could see Rob Freeman standing fifty yards away, smoking a cigarette and looking down at something. Some woman was beside him holding a dog. Bryce pulled on his rubber boots and stomped up the cut line.

"What am I paying you for, Freeman?" he called angrily. "Why aren't you digging? This job needs to be finished. Christ!"

When Bryce reached Rob, he saw a third person on his knees in the trench. It was that meddling Dr. Argile. He also recognized Dara Odek, who had interviewed him a few weeks ago about potholes on municipal roads. There had been a new provincial rule which had delayed repairs, he had explained. They could have pushed ahead but, *ma chère*, at additional cost to taxpayers.

"Why, *Bonjour*, Mademoiselle Odek. What is going on, Rob?

And the doctor there, what is he doing, eh?"

Dara finished speaking into her Ayetech, turned and to Bryce.

"Monsieur Desjardins, it is nice to see you again," she said. "We were passing the end of the road when Mr. Freeman here waved us down."

Argile had stood and reached up to offer his hand to Desjardins, but Bryce ignored it. Jet, never very discriminating with humans, was circling the new arrival, tail wagging.

"This is very exciting, Monsieur Desjardins," said Argile. "I am sorry if we came on your land without permission, but you don't seem to have the land fenced or signs posted. I thought this was a municipal lot."

"Anyway," said Argile, pointing to the skull in the trench, "it looks as though you have an archeological site on your property. There's the skull, some other bones, and this." He held up the green poop bag.

"*Bien que non!* I don't want your dog shit, Monsieur," replied Desjardins, ignoring the bag.

Desjardins foresaw delays and extra cost. He glanced down into the trench.

"Those are deer bones," he said firmly. "It is sad 'ow many hunters trespass on my property. I will ask you to please leave now. Freeman has work to do."

Bryce turned to speak directly to Dara.

"And be careful where you put your feet, *ma chère*. This is a work site, and these trenches can be dangerous."

Bryce knew that an hour's work with the excavator and all this nonsense would disappear. Rob, however, made no sign of starting up.

"The hydraulics have blown a gasket, Monsieur Desjardins. I will have to get a part tomorrow before this baby moves any more earth."

Rob looked past Desjardins and winked at Dara.

"Oh, I almost forgot, Monsieur Desjardins," said Dara, taking the green bag from Argile. "We also found this on your land. And I have already called the police." She opened the bag for Bryce's inspection.

'*Ta-ber-nac*', swore Bryce, bending over to retch.

✧   ✧   ✧

THAT EVENING BACK at the cabin with Ems, Argile recounted the day's events, focusing on the archeological aspects, and leaving out the gruesome discovery of the foot.

"But call Roch at the Geological Institute!" she said. "He can have your sample dated at the labo."

Argile was none too happy at the prospect of seeking Roch's help. Roch Legalet irritated him. Although by profession a geophysicist, over the years, Roch had brown-nosed effectively—in Argile's opinion—to acquire various managerial responsibilities as colleagues retired. Responsibility for the geochronology lab had come under his wing. He knew for a fact that Legalet had zero expertise in that domain. In an unkind moment Argile had mentioned to Ems that they probably kept Roch on because of his name, which translates as 'cobblestone'. Ems had not found this particularly amusing. She had known Roch since their university, when she had been impressed by his intensity.

Next morning, Argile telephoned Legalet at the Institute about the discovery on the Desjardins land. Roch agreed to have the wood fragments he had found in the trench analysed using carbon[14] dating.

"*Alors*, we could meet tomorrow. I will up in Crewe with the cycling club. How about I find you at the Café Pontiac around lunch time? You can give me the sample."

"And how is dear Marie?" he added.

Chapter 24

THE LEDA CLAY is sixty feet thick under the ninth hole of the Crewe Golf Course. Bordering the rough beside the fairway is a steep-sided valley, a notorious trap for sliced drives. The valley cuts deeply into the Leda. In the stream-bed, the clay looks blue beneath the water.

Although Laurentian Miniput occupied only a small corner of the full-size course belonging to the Crewe Golf Club, it generated a large proportion of the club's annual income. Families swarmed the Miniput on weekends, and during the week it was often used by companies from the city for out-of-office away days. Colleagues could network while having fun. Morale would be boosted.

For Alcee Dupree, his summer mini-golf tournament was his most important business event of the year. In support of local charities, the realtors of the region set aside their professional rivalries at this annual event and took up clubs instead. Alcee had launched the tournament three years ago and with the help of cooperative weather plus a handsome discount on fees, it had become a regular fixture in the real estate calendar. It was cheaper than a real golf tournament and more acceptable to the ladies.

Alcee had lucked out on the weather this year. The sky was a hazy blue on the afternoon booked for the tournament. It was the last Sunday in July; hot, yes, but there were plenty of cold beer in the refreshment tent. He had sold a lot of drinks tickets.

The tournament was an opportunity to invite prospective

clients. Not the retirees downsizing from their country homes to condos in the city—the last of the baby boomers seemed remarkably resistant to perfectly justifiable fees. No, the right clients, in Alcee's view, were the developers with projects which could see hundreds of new homes. Crewe was now within one easy charge for an electric car in and out of the city. And there was plenty of abandoned agricultural land, crying out for subdivision.

Alcee had taken particular care to match certain individuals with inappropriate partners. It was an opportunity to even accounts, after a rough year. Alcee had partnered 'Flipper' Sheen from Multimeuble with Bryce Desjardins. It was revenge for a dubious move that Flipper had made on one of Alcee's listings. Flipper would get an earful of Bryce's complaints about the Mayor and get no leads: Alcee already had the deal with Bryce sewn up.

The seventeenth hole was called 'the Crest'. Making par here was hard: in some ways it was more difficult than on its full-scale equivalent a hundred yards away behind a screen of shrubs. The hole included a flowing water feature where the water was blue like mouthwash, its colour a brand signature for Laurentian Miniput.

There was a trick to this hole known to regulars. Alcee could consistently score one under par four. His partner today, Jack Shawcross, was already at six strokes and looking none too happy.

"Damn it!" said Jack, as his ball rolled into the gutter for the second time. "You know what, Dupree. Some people in this town just don't appreciate what it takes to build a new development."

Shawcross retrieved his ball and replaced it on the mat.

"Last week, I had to listen to a tame idiot of the mayor telling me about Leda Clay. As if I hadn't paid enough to my consultants. He was a real pain in the butt. Do you know someone called Argile?"

"No, I mean, yes, Jack. That would be the Dr. Argile who writes letters to *The Courier*," replied Alcee.

"That's right; one of that crowd. I suppose I should feel sorry for those types; lonely at their keyboards. Not! Hah ha!"

Jack's ball finally wobbled its way past the fountain and dropped into the hole.

Perhaps thought Alcee, as he entered the score on his Ayetech, he should confide the secret of the next and final hole to Shawcross. One had to drive the ball firmly through the curving tunnel when the rotating arms of the clown pointed to three o'clock; otherwise, the ball would hit the far lip at the wrong angle and fall into the water. No, he decided: he would not.

"Looks like you could do with another beer, Jack," called Bryce Desjardins from the neighbouring fairway.

Alcee saw Shawcross grunt in acknowledgement and grit his teeth as he teed up for the last hole. Players had to drive the ball a full fifteen feet between the waving legs of a clown.

There was a special prize if you got a hole-in-one on the eighteenth. There was also some side betting on it, and Alcee had persuaded his partner to wager fifty dollars. Alcee himself had taken the safer route, betting against a hole-in-one. Shawcross was almost sure to fail, and the fifty dollars would pay for drinks later. It was all for charity of course but there were expenses to take care of. Alcee stood to one side as Shawcross squared his shoulders and set to strike his ball.

Meanwhile, Jack had concluded that the best strategy was to appear indifferent. He did not care about the bet. He thought the attention he was given by the assembled realtors was amusing. He enjoyed their attempts to woo him and liked to despise people like this Dupree for sucking up to him. Jack did not bother to analyze the angles. He tapped the ball gently along the contour of the fairway. It looked as though it had just enough pace, passing between the legs of the clown towards the hole. But then, on the very lip of the hole, it hesitated.

✧   ✧   ✧

ON THE FAR side of the Akonaga River from the golf course and set back from the water by the regulatory distance of one hundred metres, TiteGas had built a gravel drilling pad. Over the previous week, the company had drilled a well to a depth of two kilometers and had run steel tubing to the bottom of the hole. This was now cemented into place and firmly bonded to the surrounding limestone. Testing confirmed the presence of a highly permeable zone near the bottom of the borehole, immediately above the Precambrian basement rock. This zone had been encountered in other wells across the field, and the company had used these wells to inject waste fluids from the fracking operations.

As play proceeded at Laurentian Miniput, TiteGas' engineers were pumping waste water—a salty brine—into its most northerly disposal well. Powerful pumps forced the fluid through perforations in the steel tubing into the surrounding rock, to be swallowed in a vast underground labyrinth of natural fractures. This was just as modelling predicted.

Unknown to TiteGas, their geophysics had failed to reveal a fault in the deep basement rocks. The tectonic forces which caused the original displacement had dissipated long ago and the fault, welded into rigidity by the precipitation of mineral cements, had seen no movement for at least three hundred million years.

In recent geological time, freed from the weight of glaciers, the land under Crewe rose, gently bending and deforming the underlying bedrock. This new stress reactivated the fault, its binding cement already weakened by meltwater percolating through the rock. The fault was now on a hair trigger.

When TiteGas began pumping waste fluids into the zone targeted for injection, the heightened pressure reduced the friction across the fault. The fault slipped briefly, then locked once again. Yet the movement was minor—a mere blip on surface gauges at the drill site—and pumping continued uninterrupted.

The brief shudder sent a compression wave radiating outwards and towards the surface. The wave undulated rapidly to the northwest at speeds close to that of sound. The players at Laurentian Miniput felt a slight vibration, as if a small truck had driven past on the nearby road. Although the wave was barely noticeable, its motion aligned with Jack Shawcross' ball teetering on the edge of the eighteenth hole. In a game like mini-golf the tiniest of nudges often works wonders: the ball tipped slightly and fell in.

"Yesssir!" cried Jack. Other players scattered around the course clapped as he retrieved and held the ball aloft.

Maddie Latique, also from Multimeuble—'we have agents everywhere'—had the nerve to jump across the water feature to embrace the man.

"*Chaulice*," swore Alcee, sickened by the sight.

As four o'clock approached, most of the party were standing around in the shade of the marquee, waiting for the stragglers to complete their round. Alcee had stocked a cooler with beer bought from a discount store and six bottles of wine from the Société des Alcools; white, labelled as *fruité et généreux*. His fellow agents were not discriminating when it came to drink. The barbeque was going strong under the management of Flipper Sheen, who was living up to his name working the burgers.

Most of the players were relieved to escape the hot sun. The back nine—all tortuous fifty yards of them—had been brutal. Their thirst quenched with two or three beers, the golfers had revived from their exhaustion to a general feeling of good will.

Not for nothing were most of the group realtors, garrulous as a species. Their professional small talk was less guarded than might normally be the case. Inevitably, Jack Shawcross, as the main act in town from a development viewpoint, was the centre of a hopeful group.

Bryce had cornered Alcee, who was balancing a hot dog—all dressed—on a paper plate while drinking a light beer. He was looking mournful.

"Alcee, *est-tu malade*?"

Bryce was standing squarely in front of Alcee, so there was little hope of escape.

"*Non, mais...*" he replied, "I just dropped fifty to that bastard on the hole-in-one." He nodded over towards Shawcross.

"That's tough," commiserated Bryce. "He's a lucky *mec*. Anyway, *écoute*, Alcee. Did you do that little job I asked? Madame Garrity?"

Alcee had indeed been over to the old folks' residence in Constance and spoken with Madame Garrity. It had not gone well. Even at eighty-five, the woman had a fierce head for figures and surprising strength in the claws with which she had clutched his forearm. He had spoken about the land she owned. It was a small sliver—an accident, really, left over from the subdivision of the Garrity family farm. He had explained that her land blocked access to another property and how the owner of that property had asked Alcee to see if Madame Garrity would consider selling. The owner didn't really need it—his own lot was big enough, since he was a widower whose wife had recently passed—but thought that by adding the sliver of land he could better protect the wildlife corridor which ran along the back of his property. Alcee said the owner was, of course, willing to offer a fair price.

Alcee happened to be experienced in valuing country property. He could show Madame Garrity several recent examples from the region where similar sizes of lot had sold for tens of thousands. However, most had some interesting feature, such as deeded access to water or a view. Really, and he was sad to say this, her land had no selling features. It really was a leftover, a tag end. Surely she would be happy to be relieved of the responsibility? The municipality had been making noises about undeveloped property. Taxes were likely to go up.

"Forty thousand and not a cent less," Madame Garrity had interrupted him.

For a moment, Alcee lost the thread of his pitch; his famous smile briefly slipped to the left, a mannerism which he had worked hard in front of a mirror to correct. Recovering quickly, he took Madame into his confidence. He agreed that there may be some value after all. She had seen through his initial pitch, and he respected that. Madame clearly was familiar with the market, and she must realize he was merely testing the ground. As a matter of professional ethics it was his responsibility—nay, duty—to work for both buyer and seller. He would be completely frank.

Madame Garrity called for tea, and Alcee endured a further half hour listening to the recent adventures of her innumerable relatives. At the end of the interview, he made his excuses and walked pensively back to his car. Twenty-five thousand was the lowest the old lady had been prepared to go and, for that, Alcee found he had agreed to work on another project for her, at a cut-rate commission. Who knew that she and her *maudit* family owned a string of rental properties on the mountain at St Marie? And now he had to contact her financial advisor, a Monsieur Latâche in Laval. Alcee guessed this was an aging relative who did the family's tax returns.

Bryce was less than pleased when Alcee told him Madame Garrity's price. He grudgingly agreed that it might be closer to a fair value than the ten thousand he had been expecting to pay. But he felt that perhaps Alcee had not put in a hundred-percent effort. Still, Bryce wasn't about to jeopardize the deal. It was timely, and he would now have some good news for Jack Shawcross.

Bryce left Alcee to finish his burger and went to rejoin the group around the developer. Maddie Latique was helping Shawcross into a green jacket as winner of the hole in one. Multimeuble Group's golden insignia graced the breast pocket.

Chapter 25

THE PHONE RANG at the cabin late that same afternoon. Usually, on the old land line, it was calls from marketers or persons purporting to represent the Canada Revenue Agency. Ems picked up.

"*Mais oui*, he is just here, Madame Mayor."

"Chester, it's your friend Hilary," she said, and passed Argile the phone.

"Dr. Argile, I hope I don't disturb," said the Mayor. "I find that I am in need of your advice, again. Did you feel the earth tremor this afternoon?"

Argile had felt nothing because he was napping in his hammock at the time. It had already been swaying gently.

"Well, no," he replied.

"I'm worried, Dr. Argile. I felt it at the municipal building, just like the one at the last council meeting. I have had several calls from concerned residents. Surely this is unusual?'

"Not unusual, just chance," said Argile. "Tremors strong enough to be noticed recur every two to three years around here. But the interval between quakes varies. Having two close together could be just a matter of chance."

"Could be?" said Hilary. "Some people are saying that it could be the fracking. You said that wasn't possible when we were in Margs Bay."

"Yes," replied Argile. "I thought it unlikely at the time, and still do."

"Perhaps you could recommend someone with expertise in earthquake science?" said Hilary. "*Bien sûr*, I rely on you when it comes to issues with the Leda Clay, but for these earth tremors I think I need a real earthquake expert. I was thinking you might have a contact at the university."

"I gave her Roch's coordinates," Argile said to Ems, after putting down the phone. "Hilary seems to think he will know more about earthquakes than I do."

"'Hilary' now, is it?" said Ems.

Argile thought about his data recorders in the McClusky mine. He was curious to know whether the trace would show the latest tremor. Roch might know the maths but Argile would have real data.

"Going out," he called to Ems who had gone back into the kitchen. "Down to the old mine."

"Chester, take the Ayetech," she replied. "And supper is at six."

Argile went out to the back veranda, pulled on his boots and called Jet. He sprayed his ankles and elbows with mosquito repellent and rubbed the remaining liquid behind his ears and over the back of his neck. The bugs would be brutal in the deep woods. He jammed his bush hat well down on his forehead.

Argile marched down the path leading to the main trail, the quicker to get into the shade and out of the late afternoon sun. In the heat, Jet trailed behind. In about fifteen minutes, Argile reached the signal rock and turned up the winding path between the boulders. Here the air was still and oppressive. On reaching the mine, Jet walked straight into the pool guarding the entrance, scattering frogs.

Argile tied the dog to an old wooden prop in the shade of the ferns overhanging the mine mouth.

"Stay here, Jet," said Argile sternly. Jet flopped onto the

ground beside the pool and closed his eyes.

Argile entered the mine slowly to allow his eyes to adjust to the gloom. It took him ten minutes to negotiate the puddles and minor rock falls to reach the end of the adit, stooping to dodge projections from the uneven roof. He retrieved the data card from the recorder and inserted a new one. He checked that the geophones were still firmly stuck to the rock wall, and retraced his steps to the mouth of the mine.

When Argile emerged into the sunlight, he found Jet standing alert, staring fixedly across the small clearing towards the trees beyond. A squirrel, probably, thought Argile. But the dog was making a subdued growling noise very different from the hopeful whine with which he normally addressed squirrels. Perhaps a bear? Argile looked more closely at the trees but saw nothing but green.

Argile checked that the data card he had just retrieved was secure in the pocket of his bush jacket, and then headed down the path. He glimpsed movement in the trees to the left of the trail, but kept Jet close and concentrated on navigating the stony path. Porcupines were the most feared animals in this part of the forest, feared for the vet bills should a dog get a face full of quills.

Chapter 26

H E HAD ALREADY lied to the young woman facing him across the desk. Father Lawrence Bonenfant shifted in his seat, sat back and looked at the old black and white photograph on the wall behind her. Father Pelletier, an early priest of the parish, returned his gaze with his eternal air of reproof. Long dead, he was supposedly buried beneath a concrete slab in the sub-basement where they stored the folding chairs.

They were sitting in the office on the ground floor of the red brick presbytery that squatted beside his Church. Bonenfant had been here for six months now and was still adjusting to his transfer from Africa. He had been prepared for the cold and snow, but the summer heat surprised him. It was positively tropical.

He remembered the Bishop's words when he first arrived. "There is a need, my boy, for a dynamic priest to bring back the lost sheep of Crewe. They drift into sin."

Bonenfant was still struggling to find his flock.

At first sight, he thought the church admirable. It was simple but elegant, with a tower and steeple sheathed in tin which gleamed like a silver beacon in the snowy landscape. Painted wood carvings of the Apostles attested to the devotion of past parishion-ers. But now, in the sultry dog days of summer, the church looked shabby; the peeling white paint had a greenish tint and much of the exterior wood was rotten and needed replacement. Although he was comfortable with the heat and humidity outside where it belonged, Bonenfant missed the air conditioning in the fine megachurch in Gabon where he had spent the last five years.

✧   ✧   ✧

DENISSE LAFRICHE HAD been worrying about the Shawcross development for several weeks. Should she tell somebody about what she had discovered? Finally, her Mother had lost patience with her.

"*Bien.* If you won't talk to me, go see that new Father Lawrence."

So here she was, sitting before the priest, explaining that she would surely come to mass next Sunday, but what she needed to talk about wasn't really confession. And yes, she would definitely think about baptism, but that was a way off yet. No, her brother Pierre-Louis wasn't married, but he was living with a good friend down in Montreal. It occurred to Denisse that perhaps the Father didn't quite understand her French.

Her concern was not the backdoor dealings she had witnessed with the municipal director; that was standard operating procedure in Quebec, according to Jack Shawcross. What troubled her was discovering that the Shawcross development, far from being a residential condo complex as originally described, was to become the home of an American religious group, something called Mission. Catholic, even if *non-practiquante*, she nonetheless respected the Church. Her *arrière arrière grand-père* and *grand-mère* were buried in the churchyard, plus eight of their children. Later generations of Lafriches had followed them.

The thought of a plantation of religious conservatives on this soil, from *les États*—and Protestants, *bien sûr*, offended Denisse's sense of what was right. It upset her sense of place, what fitted here in St.Pet.

Bonenfant had already met with the Reverend Robert Harris

of Mission, a fact that he omitted to mention to Denisse. It had been at Harris' invitation and the two had discovered that they had much in common. Bonenfant had been glad to discover that Mission's stand on moral issues regarding family and sexual orientation aligned closely with those of the Church. He considered that the new Pope's pronouncements on such matters were flagrantly Eurocentric and could hardly be expected to apply outside that continent. Bob—he had insisted on the familiar— had told him about the plans to launch a Mission here in Crewe.

Bonenfant was reassured that Mission was not—as he had first feared—anti-Catholic. Clearly Pastor Bob and he had common cause in encouraging Christian devotion and St. Petraphile could benefit from some of the techniques that Mission had perfected. Pastor Bob had generously lent him a copy of *The Guiding Hand*. The chapter on how to use social media fascinated him. Such techniques had hardly seemed necessary in Africa. But here? Mass had been a lot livelier in Gabon.

"Well, my child," said Bonenfant. "I am so pleased that you have come to see me, I think for the first time? I understand these concerns of yours, but surely we should welcome others in our Christian communion."

"*Bien*, it's just I wanted you to know about these people coming in. Oh, I guess I am just worried these people will take over the village."

"I see you are anxious," replied Bonenfant. "Perhaps—and I myself have found this technique very useful—if you have specific questions about these people from Mission, you should try writing them down."

Committing thoughts to paper had served Bonenfant well for managing anxiety, and he never missed an opportunity to suggest this technique to his flock. As a product of a high school in West Africa where he had learned an exquisite Parisian French, he was convinced that Quebecois could alleviate many of their problems by paying more attention to correct grammar.

Bonenfant looked at the clock on the wall beside Father Pelletier's photograph. "*Écoutez, ma chère*," he said. "Leave this with me and, when you your questions written down, please come back and we can work through them one by one. *Précision et clarté*; it is essential to be clear and precise. Now, I am needed at a meeting of the churchwardens. Please say '*Bonjour*' to Madame Lafriche."

"*Eh, merci mon Père, je suppose. Au revoir*," said Denisse. She would never, she swore in her head, take her Mother's advice again.

After showing Denisse out of the office, Bonenfant went outside and sat on the steps in front of the Church. He had a fine view across the valley: the church stood on a knoll at the east end of town, and on either side the land fell away to terraces formed by the sands and clays on which most of the town stood. The foundation of the building itself was the solid bedrock of the Canadian Shield.

Behind the church a path wound up through the trees to the foot of a small cliff, where a vein of pure white marble was exposed. Here there was a hollow informally called *la Grotte*, where loose blocks had been gathered by past parishioners and roughly cemented into a conical cairn. The flat summit of the cairn was graced by a plaster statue of St. Petraphile herself, who was protected from rain and snow by a pink half-dome. Her skirts had weathered to the palest of blues. Her head was crowned by a circlet of Christmas lights which came on at night. When Bonenfant had first been shown the Lady of Crewe, he asked that the faded plastic flowers at her feet be removed.

Harris' words had appealed to Bonenfant's own sense of mission. He would consider Pastor Bob's proposal. In return for

Bonenfant's support in Crewe, Mission would help finance the installation of air conditioning and wireless hubs throughout both the church and presbytery. It was a generous offer and Bonenfant was gratified that his influence in the community was so valued. He and Bob had in common the furtherance of Christian morality, after all. And wasn't this the mid-21st century? The warming climate made air conditioning vital to Church attendance.

With the upgrade, the Church could charge more for the rooms on the second floor of the presbytery. Bonenfant knew this would meet with the approval of his churchwardens. The refugee family who rented the rooms for a nominal amount—an unfortunate arrangement agreed to by Bonenfant's predecessor—would have to find cheaper accommodation elsewhere.

Chapter 27

AFTER BEING CHASED off by Bryce Desjardins, Dara parked on the verge close to the turnoff to the Desjardins land, and waited. Before long, a police cruiser pulled up beside her. The local officer had set an ambush for speeders, just behind the town welcome sign, and responded quickly to Dara's call. Dara knew Officer Manon Patinaude.

"*Bonjour*, Dara. *Comment ça va?* Not so great I suppose. Where's this foot you called about, then?"

"Hi, Manon," said Dara. "That was quick. Just follow me. It's just a short distance up that track."

When they arrived and parked beside the excavator, Bryce Desjardins was still giving Rob Freeman a piece of his mind. Argile had found a stump to sit on some distance away and Jet was investigating ground hog burrows in a nearby bank.

"*Bonjour*, Messieurs," said Officer Patinaude, interrupting Bryce. "We have received a call from Madame Odek here about human remains found on this land. Which one of you found the bones?"

Rob Freeman raised his hand.

"And your name is?"

Rob muttered his name, watching as Officer Patinaude wrote in her notebook.

"*Alors*, Monsieur Freeman. Show me," she said.

Rob led the way up the cutline. A Dara and Argile got up from the stump and followed them. Rob showed the officer the skull exposed in the side of the trench.

"And this guy found a foot," he added. Argile stepped forward and held out the green bag for the officer to inspect.

"*Merde*," muttered Patinaude, peering into the bag. Breathing heavily, she ordered Rob and Argile to go back to join the others. She placed a large rock to hold down the end of a roll of police tape, then clambered across the trench to tie the tape to a tree. Once she had cordoned off the site to her satisfaction, she went back down the cut line to rejoin the group.

"*Alors*, I will need a brief statement from all of you," she said, taking out a notebook. Rob described how he found the skull. Dara and Argile explained how they came to be present that morning. By the time she got to Bryce Desjardins, the latter's impatience finally boiled over.

"*Ecoutez*, Officer. These persons are trespassers on my property. So, they have found some old bones. These delays are costing me money, *calice*! And why is this reporter here? You need to get these people to leave straight away. I can tell you that..."

"*Ça suffit*, Monsieur Desjardins. *Il n'y a rien à faire.* No one must touch the site before the Inspector arrives."

After learning from Manon that a forensic team was coming up from Montreal in the morning, Dara returned to the office. She already had a story, but she had an idea and wanted a green light from Elsie. There was an Aboriginal slant she wanted to pursue, and Elsie, when she hired her, had encouraged her to explore her roots. Stories in *The Courier* seldom mentioned the views of the Ako Band.

✧   ✧   ✧

TEN MINUTES LATER, Dara walked into the newspaper office. It was an older building and as poorly insulated against summer heat as winter cold. An oscillating fan was going full blast on the big desk in the centre of the room, but it was still stiflingly hot. Lise was in a tank top and Dave in shorts.

A live screen above Dave's head showed the daily click count. It was down this week and Dave was looking pensive. He needed a killer post.

"She's out of office," called Lise across the room in response to Dara's questioning look.

"Yeah," added Dave. "An important meeting." Dara shrugged. Everyone knew their editor had a pool at home.

Dara sat down at her desk and scrolled through her contact list to check the number she wanted for the Ako Band. It was a revolving door at the Band Office—Dara never knew who she would get when she rang. It was Kitsi who answered the call. They had been to primary school together but Dara knew that whoever was working the phone was told to take a message and put people off. Kitsi told her that the Chief was down at the new filtration plant, testing the water, and wouldn't be back soon. He couldn't be contacted.

"Hey, Da, why don't you drive out, have a coffee? You city folks don't get up here often enough."

Dara agreed that was true. She probably had just enough volts in her car to drive the fifty kilometres up to the Rez. She liked the idea of just dropping in. She would leave a note for Elsie.

Dara waved at Dave to catch his attention.

"I am off out again, Dave. Tell Elsie I have gone up to the Rez following a story. Back later this afternoon!" Dave mumbled a reply, by which time she was already out of the door.

Half an hour later, Dara passed the new casino. It was an imposing building in the architectural style known as 'native revival'. A long, curving berm enclosed a shallow lake, now full of water lily flowers in this early summer. Partly surrounded by this lake was the Main Lodge, which housed both the casino and a hotel. To reach Reception, visitors passed beneath an impressive cedar gateway surmounted by a carved beaver, and the words 'Welcome to the Akasino'.

A short distance after the entrance to the casino, Dara turned onto the dirt road leading into the Rez. She pulled up beside the coffee shop, confident that Kitsi would already be there. Nodding to the old timers sitting on the steps, Dara went inside. Sure enough, Kitsi was sitting at a Formica table nursing a large mug.

"Hey," said Dara.

'Whoa, here's city girl!" replied Kitsi. She got up from the table and went into the kitchen to grab a mug from the sink for Dara.

"Still cream and full of sugar, Da?" Dara nodded. Back at *The Courier*, espressos were the order of the day.

"So, Dads is gone fishing again?" said Dara, after a few minutes chat learning about the recent doings of Kitsi's family. Everyone called Chief Odek 'Dads'. She knew he hated being called by his first name Clive.

"Yeah, fishing. But Harvey is in the office," replied Kitsi.

Dara groaned. Harvey was a white guy and the assistant administrator. The Band had hired him over two years ago on a three-month contract, but he had ingratiated himself with counsellors and the contract had been extended first to a year; now it seemed indefinitely. Dara supposed Harvey felt himself indispensable and she knew he held the Band's Ayetech. Dara had no intention of discussing matters with him. His body odour repelled her. The man was a creep.

Dara sat with Kitsi, telling her about working at the paper and the room she rented above Molly's Rocks. After refilling their coffees, Dara finally explained her reason for coming up.

"You really need to speak to an elder, Da," said Kitsi, after

Dara described the discovery of what she was ready to call a grave. "I could make some calls, but Jo is just outside."

Gravel crunched on the road outside the café and Dara looked out to see Dads' battered truck slide to a halt. Chief Odek got out, and lifted his rod case and a sack from the back of his truck. He stopped to talk to the small group sitting on the steps. He pulled out a pack of cigarettes and offered them around.

"Dara," said Chief Odek, as she and Kitsi emerged from the café. "Your cousin here was wondering why you didn't say 'Hi'".

Dara and Kitsi joined the group sitting on the steps, Dara rapidly running through clan genealogy in her head until she located the right cousin.

"Hi Joseph. Didn't see you there."

Dara's views on tobacco were general knowledge, so no one offered her a cigarette.

"So Dara, what brings you up here? It's been a while." Dads coughed and looked past Dara's shoulders to the trees which screened the river. He was still thinking about the large trout he had hooked an hour earlier but which had managed to escape.

Dara recounted the story of the discovery of the bones in the woods near Crewe, and the opinion of Dr. Argile that the bones might be old.

"Dr. Argile found a piece of pottery. He said it was 'Indian'."

"So this Dr. Argile is some kind of expert, you say?" said the Chief, forcing himself to concentrate on what Dara was saying.

"Well. He is a geologist, so he knows about dates and stuff." Dara replied.

"Hum," said Chief Odek. "A grave you think? Yeah, that's possible. One clan moved down there before grandfather's time."

Joseph, who had remained silent during this exchange, cleared his throat and said quietly "You say there is a development going in just east of Crewe, near where the creek joins the Ako? That land is unceded—they have no right."

The assembled group looked grim. This was another development on Tribal lands without consultation, let alone compensation.

Chief Odek scratched the eczema on the back of his neck. He knew what was coming. It was unavoidable and meant an early start to the protest season. Which was a pity, because the river was unusually high for this time of year, and the fishing was still good. He had even booked a fishing excursion for some moneyed lawyer up from the city, keen to try for muskie. It had been a while since Odek had fished the Akonaga near Crewe: it was a long way downriver from his usual haunts. In his mind's eye he saw the broad reed beds bordering the deep channel: perfect for pike and, he hoped, for muskie. With an effort, he refocussed on the matter at hand.

"Okay," he said. "We can get things organized. We go down and meet with this developer, make our point, and at the same time have a look at this grave of yours, Dara. Joseph, you can drop by Tackle's and tell him to get all the kit loaded for a barricade."

By the time Dara had consumed her fourth cup of coffee, the arrangements had been agreed. A small convoy of trucks would drive down to Crewe led by Chief Odek. She and her photographer would meet them at the gate to River View. Dara was excited by the thought of a scoop: land rights, ancestral burial and a white, Anglo developer in the frame. It was an embarrassment of riches.

Chapter 28

THIRTY KILOMETERS DOWNSTREAM from the Ako Band reservation, the Akonaga River leaves the forested hills of the Canadian Shield and meanders across a broad floodplain. It passes beside the town of Constance, gathering breadth and volume from several tributaries, before entering a long reach near the village of Crewe. Along this stretch of the river are holiday cabins, mostly dilapidated wooden structures, which have—despite their temporary appearance—weathered several floods. On their private docks are piled a variety of canoes, pedalos, and an occasional laser sailboat.

The Crewe Canada Day raft was a less conventional craft. There had been a tradition of raft building in the Akonaga valley since the days of the *drave*, when the loggers up-river hauled their winter's cut to the edge of the ice waiting for the spring thaw. They would lash together pine logs to build a raft and, with such a quantity of building material at hand, they often erected a log bunkhouse on top. The main logging runs were during the flush of spring high water and, only after the river had grown tranquil, were the rafts drifted downstream and beached along the river bank between Constance and Crewe. Here the men dismantled the bunkhouses, and carted the wood away for new barns and extensions to cabins. The loggers, now turned farmers, focussed on their homesteads until the snow flew the following winter.

The foreman at Crewe usually turned a blind eye to this re-purposing of the timber, although the mill owner, Hardy

McClintock, frowned on the practice. The men stole the wood, in his opinion. Still, it was a small amount, and he knew he would need the same labour back the following winter.

The first colonists to penetrate the Akonaga Valley had followed the Ottawa River up from the Saint Lawrence, leapfrogging ever westwards, looking for land to settle and exploit. In the early eighteen hundreds, they reached a river flowing from the north and followed it upstream between banks rich in tall timber. Now they were a thousand kilometers from the Atlantic Ocean.

After fifty years, logging had stripped the white pine from the sides of the valley, and settlers had tamed the flatter ground for a patchwork of small holdings. Half the land was for corn, potatoes and beans; half for cattle. The forest on the hill provided fuel, maple syrup and the occasional deer.

The farms just about managed for three generations and then faded; the livestock sold off. Landowners subdivided the dying farms for residential development, or sold to enthusiasts keen to grow the latest in organic vegetables, by hopeful bee keepers, and by retirees keen to try viniculture. Most of the local youth, once destined to be farmers, had drifted into town, where they worked multiple jobs to afford city rents. Those who returned relied on their creative talents, supported by stints on construction sites, or up north planting trees.

Perhaps inherited wood skills, dormant for most of the year, stir in spring. Or perhaps the joy of getting outdoors in a T-shirt after a cold winter ignites an urge to build. For whichever reason, the youth of the Akonaga Valley have their own traditions around wood and water. Every year, on a meadow upriver, the Connor twins, with the help of assorted friends, gathered to build the annual Canada Day Raft.

Over the years, the rafts had become ever more elaborate, incorporating old settees and La-Z-Boys, a hot tub, a bar/disco and even a pool table. The authorities, after some grumbling, initially judged this year's raft mostly safe, but required it to tow an inflatable Zodiac large enough to carry six. If it sunk, any additional passengers would have to swim for it, but that was the general idea anyway.

The twins had floated this year's edition downriver the previous week. This was not without some excitement as it swayed through the rapids upriver from the village, its first and only test of seaworthiness. It was shepherded by a snub-nosed timber boat, built to work with floating logs and which had found a new vocation in nudging the raft to a safe harbour along the river bank by the Drafters. The boat was only ten feet long but deep-keeled, with the screw protected by a heavy cage. Redundant after the last of the logging runs on the Akonaga, it had been rescued from its ignominious resting place in a local playground and fully restored.

The twins had run a power cable from the raft to the shore, and had regaled passersby on Rue Principale with the sounds of partying pretty much non-stop throughout the Canada Day weekend. As in previous years, the Counsellor for the River Ward received complaints. This year, on Councillor Black's insistence, a snap inspection by the provincial river keeper generated a list of environmental infractions which the Council could hardly ignore. It was with regret, and to the angry muttering of Crewe youth, that the Mayor ordered the raft removed until the issues could be addressed.

It did not have to float far. The twins found a quiet spot downriver beside a high bank of grey clay, out of sight of the village, and close to a straggling lodge built by river beavers. A gang plank reached from the raft to shore whence a path followed the river bank, winding through the stumps of shrubs coppiced by beavers to join a dirt road. A short distance down the road was a gate, padlocked to discourage access, but it was easy to slip past the mesh fencing.

This was the route followed by Sean Box and Candice from the Café Pontiac, after he had asked her out to thank her for the tip on the motel job. They had walked from the raft and were standing in front of the gate looking back at a sign which announced the coming development at River View.

"They are already building on the other side of that patch of bush," said Sean. "The plan said three hundred condos, but they changed their mind. Now the rumour is that it will be a private foundation, like a college, with some condo development on the side. *Attention!*—that's poison ivy!"

Sean and Candice had spent a relaxing afternoon on the 'penthouse' of the raft, helping the Connor twins drink a case of beer and playing beer pong. Misdirected balls which fell overboard had to be retrieved, and the easiest way was to ride the raft's slide into the river. The slide was the emergency escape route. The slide mirrored the beavers' chute further along the bank, although the latter was slick with grey mud. Climbing back to the penthouse up a knotted rope was more of an effort, and the game, after its initial frenzy, became more leisurely as the afternoon progressed.

Now Candice had to get back to town for a shift at the café. Having cleared the wire, they turned around to look at the signs by the gate: 'River View Development—*Terrain privé*—no trespassing; no hunting; no motorized vehicles; no dogs'. It said nothing about mooring rafts.

Chapter 29

I T WAS A fine Saturday morning, and Sean had given the Professor and his friend a ride in the back of his Ford truck. By nine-thirty, the day was already stoking up and the humidity rising. It looked like it would be a similar pattern to the last week: hot, hitting thirty degrees in the late morning, followed by heavy downpours from pop-up thunderheads in the afternoon. There was plenty of water ponded in ruts on the track and that made Sean cautious. His summer tires were slick, and he had no wish to get stuck again on a mission with the Professor. Sean had tried the old quarter-in-the-treads test and they had failed miserably.

"I'll drop you off here," said Sean. He had driven along the track to the edge of woods above Crewe, but had no wish to chance his luck further. The track had more or less petered out anyway.

Sean helped them unload their equipment, reversed the truck, and disappeared with a roar and a spatter of gravel.

Two hours later, Peter Gough and Argile were wading through shoulder-deep golden rod. They had been gradually working their way downslope from fairly open maple-oak and pine forest towards the outskirts of Crewe. The ground was much damper here. The wet spring had ensured the explosive growth of ranker weeds and the thick vegetation made it hard to see Argile's blaze marks from earlier in the year. Cascades of pollen tumbling from the sprays of yellow flowers had already triggered a fit of sneezing in Peter. His nose was now streaming.

"Is this the last one?" Peter called hopefully to Argile, who was struggling through a patch of the invasive dog-strangling vine which had run rampant around Crewe over the last few years. Over the last couple of hours, Argile and Peter had walked back and forth across the slopes above the town, attaching small, metal disks to various trees and rocks designated by Argile. They had hoped to attach fifty that morning but Peter had lost count.

"Yes," replied Argile. "Let's go down via the Church to fix one last reference point. And then I fancy something cold at the Café Pontiac. We should be in plenty of time to meet Roch there."

They angled across the slope to reach the path leading to the shrine of St. Pet. Argile attached the last disk to the cairn supporting the statue.

"That will do," he said. "I hope they work as well as you say."

Before setting out that morning, Peter had been entirely confident that the disks, each with a tiny, embedded emitter, would be perfect targets for his swarm of mini-drones. Now, dripping with sweat and suffering from innumerable mosquito bites, he realized that conditions in the field were less than optimal. The distraction of various insects, the deeply overhanging foliage along the eves of the wood, the wretched clouds of pollen which might scatter his signals, the sheer tangle of the unkempt forest—all these could confuse the drones' navigation. The size of the dragonflies he had just seen worried him that they might actually attack his drones. Peter didn't bother to reply to Argile.

Ten minutes later saw them both sitting in the shade on the patio beside the Café. Argile had just emerged after ordering two beers from Candice. The two men leaned back to relax and cool off, watching the languid stream of cars heading up to cottage country for the weekend. After a few minutes, a group of cyclists pulled up in front of the Café. Among them was Dara Odek, wearing hip-hugging cycling pants—*cuissards*—and a tall man, probably in his thirties, whom Argile vaguely recognized as also being from *The Courier*. It surprised him to see Molly Laberge locking a smart-looking road bike to the rack in front of the Café. Until then he had not thought of Molly wearing anything other than long, flowing cotton prints.

Roch Legalet brought up the rear of the group. He was sporting a bright red spandex suit with reflective silver stripes. With drivers like Sean Box on the roads around Crewe—types who had little compunction about roaring past groups of recreational cyclists at high speed—it was a prudent precaution, if a little over the top.

Roch spotted the two men on the patio and waved. He leaned his bike against the fence and came over. In contrast to Argile who was tall and deliberate in his movements, Roch was short and sported a bushy beard; the squat and bustling type of geoscientist. His rolling gait hinted at years spent aboard seismic survey vessels, suggesting a life of past adventure which he hoped impressed junior research assistants.

"Peter Gough! Long time!" exclaimed Roch. "*Salut Argile. Ça va bien?*"

He grabbed a menu and sat down across the table. Argile offered to order an extra beer.

"*Non, merci,*" said Roch. "I will have one of their specials." He turned to Candice, who had just arrived with two beers. "*Eh oui, Le Veggie-Vélo, s'il vous plait.*"

The three men sat around the table in the shade: two rather grubby in stained khaki pants and shirts after their morning in the bush; the latest arrival bulging and perspiring in his colourful cycling gear.

"Whew," said Roch, and sat down. "You have something needing my expertise, Argile?" The veggie-vélo arrived, and Roch began sucking noisily on the voluptuous green smoothie.

"Yes, Ems suggested I call you." Argile described the discovery on the Desjardins lands. "Would your lab run radio-carbon on some wood fragments? I'd like to pin down a date."

Roch sucked his smoothie and set it aside. "Archaeology is not really my thing, as you know Argile, but since you already have samples, I suppose I could ask the lab to run the tests. Do you think you could get an official request?"

"If that's what you need." Argile knew Roch would be keen to display his influence.

"*Bien*," said Roch. Get me the samples and I will see if the lab can fit them in. They are busy these days, but I will try."

"Now, I have a question," he continued. "Did you feel an earth tremor up here last Monday? I had a call at the Institute from a charming woman, a Madame Beaubien, asking for my help, so I am interested to know if you had heard reports of any damage here in Crewe."

Argile had expected Roch to mention the recent seismic activity. He had not noticed the tremor, and he was reluctant to describe his acoustic monitoring of the clinkstone. He knew that Legalet would scoff at his makeshift geophones in the mica mine.

"Many in the village felt the tremor, but I heard no report of any damage," said Argile.

"*Bien*, at the Institute's observatory we have noted several events over the last six months," continued Roch. "This is above the historical trend. The highest magnitude was a four-point-two but most registered at about magnitude three, probably too slight for you to feel. The epicentres align along a trend which runs beneath us here in Crewe."

"So why is this happening here?" asked Peter. "Is it something to do with the fracking over towards St. Margs?"

Roch raised an eyebrow.

"*Mais non*, Peter! The tiny amount of energy released by the fracking process could not possibly cause an earthquake. The forces needed to overcome the inertia of the rock mass would have to be several orders of magnitude greater. You should not have any concern there. No, what we are seeing may be unusual over the short time we have records, but if we could go back far enough, it would become clear that these minor tremors merely represent a long term pattern of minor crustal readjustments."

"Well, that's a relief," said Argile.

Roch changed the subject. "Peter, what are you doing with your micro-drones? I hear you have become quite the expert."

Given this invitation, Peter could hardly resist explaining how he was planning to deploy the whole swarm later that day.

"Argile and I have been placing markers all over the hillside above the village. The plan is for the swarm to fly to the markers and develop a detailed map. It will be down to millimeter scales, far better than the resolution we get from satellites. It's about Argile's obsession with the Leda Clay. Have you seen much creep lately, Roch?"

Roch stroked his beard. He didn't realize the question was in jest. It touched on his professional expertise, and he framed a serious reply.

"No, Peter. But it is true you have some issues with the Leda Clay around here. We call creep 'solifluction', by the way." Roch was nearing the bottom of the vegi-vélo and blew ruminatively down the straw: "blug, blug", like farts in the bath.

"It is easy to avoid these problems with good management practices," he continued. "My colleagues and I at the Institute refined the geohazard maps for the region only a few years ago. The earlier versions were, in my opinion, alarmist. No real understanding of risk. Frankly, the local authorities were happy with our new map. We changed the red, so-called 'high-risk' zone on the map to yellow. There is no problem, provided developers follow the recommended set-backs. Just don't build too near the edge of slopes—that is my advice. Argile?"

Argile had only been half listening. A whiff of rotten eggs had stirred a memory of mud eruptions he had seen in Yellow Stone. In a flash he imagined Roch Legalet on his knees blowing through a straw into the Leda Clay, the clay turning to liquid and rising to the surface in seething boils.

"Yes," said Argile, banishing the image. "The array of ground markers allows me to monitor movement across the entire slope behind the village. I have been doing it with hand-held GPS, which was laborious to say the least. The hillside swells and shrinks with the seasons and now I can measure that change precisely."

"Better watch out, Roch. Next he'll tell you that the clay sings to him".

Argile frowned at Peter. He wasn't about to reveal to Roch his more fanciful ideas about the Leda.

"Hah ha. Yes, Peter. The harmonics of geophysics," said Roch. "It's a pity Argile can't do the math. Isn't that so Argile?"

"Mathematics is not up to the job of describing the moods of soft rocks, Roch."

"Huh, *belle excuse*, Argile. Anyway, you know Marie invited me up to the cabin this evening?"

"Yes," Argile replied. "But be aware that Peter and I will be training a swarm of bees on the veranda."

A vehicle pulled up beside the Café Pontiac. Draining his glass, Argile added, "Time to get going. That's the car from 'UCall'. It must be for us."

Argile left a twenty on the table. "That should cover it," he said.

Argile and Peter got up and walked over to their ride. To his surprise, Argile saw it was a familiar, battered truck, with the

'UCall' logo on the windshield. Sean Box was driving. He was in animated conversation with Dara Odek, who stood at the curbside with her bicycle. Argile and Peter climbed into the cab, catching the end of the conversation.

"And if you cut me close again, Sean, I'll be on your case like you wouldn't believe!" shouted Dara.

"Hey, Professor," said Sean, turning to his passengers. "I don't suppose you expected to see me again so soon. How do you like my new job? Dad arranged it with 'UCall'. We are the first in Crewe. I have an Ayetech now," he added, pointing to the device clinging to the front dash. He started the engine, then nodded towards Dara now sitting with her friends on the steps of the café.

"I don't think she likes me," confided Sean.

✧   ✧   ✧

ROCH LEGALET WATCHED the truck drive away. He didn't think much of Argile, or his soft sediments. Marie could have done better. Clarice came by the table and left the bill. Forty dollars with tip. The veggie-vélo had been outrageously expensive.

Chapter 30

THE AIR WAS usually clear for late summer, with no mists or residual smoke from distant forest fires. A thunderstorm overnight had cleared the humidity, and the view across the valley went to the far horizon.

Argile sat in a deck chair on his veranda, Jet at his feet. Argile was examining the traces from the geophone records. The most recent tremor—that which had alarmed Hilary Beaubien—was marked by a sharp deflection, followed by a train of lesser waves gradually diminishing in amplitude over twenty seconds.

Argile played the recording back in audio, listening on headphones. The background noise was a faint, crackling sound with random louder pops: the geophone had recorded the sound of strain in the surrounding rock amplified by the clinkstone. He sped up the playback and the background crackle rose in pitch to a shriek. He reduced the speed again until the sound in the headphones was a faint murmur. Then, with no warning, he heard a loud bang in the earphones, like the back flap of a dump truck clanging home, followed by trailing reverberations. He checked the time on the recording: it was three-thirty one in the afternoon on the preceding Sunday. Unknown to Argile, this was exactly the date and time of the Jack Shawcross hole-in-one at the golf tournament.

✧   ✧   ✧

AT FIVE O'CLOCK Peter drove up with a cardboard box full of mini-drones.

"We won't fly the swarm until dusk," he said. "The sensors work better in the evening."

Peter placed three charging plates on the grassy slope in front of the veranda, and, with Argile's help, they placed the mini-drones on the plates. They had just about finished when they heard a vehicle draw up in front of the cabin. A car door slammed, and Roch sauntered around the side of the house. He had changed into slick jeans and a purple T-shirt in pure merino.

"*Salut*, guys!" called Roch. "Argile, is there somewhere I can plug in the beast?"

"Oh, *Bonjour*, Roch!" called Ems emerging from the cabin. "I didn't hear you drive up. *Bec?*"

Ems leant over to offer her cheek to Roch.

"I love the new car," she said.

Roch was driving a new electric sports cabriolet. He liked the fact that it drove in complete silence but still had pangs of range anxiety. He suspected that driving on these winding, back-country roads cut the range considerably. Roch pulled a charging cord from a special compartment in the front of the vehicle, and handed the end to Argile.

After plugging the charging cord into an outlet, Argile turned to the assembled group.

"So, this is the schedule for this evening. Peter says that his swarm is ready to launch if you want to watch from the veranda. Supper is ready to go on the barbecue for later, and I have put Peter's wine to cool."

Roch looked dubious at this last remark, and decided not to mention the bottle he had brought and left in his car cooler. It was from the higher-priced '*cellier*' side of the provincial wine shop, the SAQ. The assistant with whom he had discussed options had assured him that his selection was *bon pour le barbecue*. They had enjoyed a little laugh about it.

The party went around to the veranda, settled into Argile and Ems' eclectic collection of 'outdoor' chairs, and looked out across the valley. Peter picked up his computer tablet to confirm that the drones were fully charged. He sat back in his chair and pressed the launch button.

"That is all there is to it," he said. "They are on their own now. It will take a few minutes for them to agree on a launch sequence and then away they'll go."

By now it was dusk and Argile saw a bat flutter along the overhang of the veranda hunting for moths. He wondered if the rising swarm would disrupt its echolocation.

At six precisely, the first of the mini-drones rose from its charging pad and hovered some thirty feet out from the veranda. Its colleagues followed in rapid succession, each seeking a pre-defined position in the array. They gathered like a threatening regiment, a dark spatter against the afterglow in the western sky.

Peter looked smug, like a proud father of disciplined off-spring.

"Now they will disperse to seek the ground markers we placed across the hillside this morning. By the time we finish eating, I expect to see them all returned to base and we shall be able to download the data."

✧　✧　✧

THE NEXT MORNING, Argile woke with aching head and dry mouth. Ems was snoring softly beside him. He might have known this would happen with Peter's homemade wine, especially when washed down with whiskey. He now regretted his idea of the previous evening to toast the safe return of the drones.

He gargled with mouthwash, and spat out wine-flecked phlegm. He swallowed two painkillers and started his computer. Peter had promised the results as soon as possible, and had already sent a text with a link to the data cloud.

Argile opened his mapping program and downloaded the drone data as a new layer. The newly registered survey points sparkled on the screen, a fresh new stratum on his growing stack of data. The new data appeared to match with his surveys of earlier in the year, data collected—Argile thought ruefully—with great labour using his makeshift methods. He allowed the program to best fit the new data to the older surveys and then map the 'deltas'—the discrepancies between the old and new surveys.

A red bloom appeared in one area of the map, highlighting an anomaly beside Crewe Creek. The red showed the greatest differences with earlier surveys, suggesting a bulge in the Leda, promising a landslide. Crewe Creek, having meandered languidly across a ridge of resistant granite, fell onto the softer Leda, its churning momentum carving a deep ravine. There had been repeated slope failures in this sector as the twisting stream plunged down the gorge, undermining the clay slopes on either side as the creek tumbled towards the Akonaga River.

❖   ❖   ❖

LATER THAT MORNING, with his hangover from the previous evening slowly dissipating, Argile was walking the path by the ravine. The bulge in the slope had looked impressive on the survey data, but finding signs of imminent slope failure on the ground was a different matter.

Beech leaves, early sacrifices to the advancing season, lay in yellow-brown drifts across his route, the leaves curled and crisp like breakfast cereal. The drifts obscured the path and made footing less certain. Argile began to question his choice of route before he recognized his blaze marks high on the tree trunks. He had been on snowshoes at the time he made the cuts, and they were three feet above summer eye level.

On reaching the ravine, Argile found a white pine had slid down the slope, tearing a long grey scar in the clay. Its root mass had heeled into the creek bed and the trunk now leaned back against the slope. By his calculation, and confirmed by his GPS, Argile should be standing directly on the bulge. He walked back from the lip of the ravine, looking for signs of tension cracks. These would confirm the extra strain he had observed in the data. Nothing was obvious, only the single pine that had slid downslope. It was, he thought, a question of not being able to see the wood for the trees.

It was frustrating. Argile had hoped for a landslide in the Leda, perhaps a slope failure triggering a retrogressive slide, one where each failure triggered another, causing the landslide to bite back into the slope, gnawing backwards in a surfeit of chaos. He had seen videos of such events—some within this region of Quebec, others in Scandinavia, where similar clays existed and were just as hazardous. The rhythm of the successive failures as the slide retrogressed was beautiful, leaving perfect, vase-like scars, and the transition to fluid flow was something he would dearly like to see in person. Willing the Leda to get on with it and fail, he retraced his steps. Waiting on geological process demanded patience.

On the way back, Argile detoured to take the trail sloping uphill towards the McClusky mine. He would check on the geophones and recover the latest recording.

PART III
REVELATION

Chapter 31

AT TEN DOLLARS a day, daycare was a *maudit bon* deal, thought Réjean Latâche. He had dropped off *la petite* Véronique and had returned to his house in Laval, a town just north of Montreal. It was a detached bungalow built in the nineteen-sixties, surrounded by thick, straggly hedges and quite private. He had quiet neighbours which he hardly saw because they avoided meeting him. This was unsurprising since Réjean was a disconcertingly large man, bearded and extensively tattooed. He rode with the Blue Beards—les Bleus, the senior biker fraternity in greater Laval.

Réjean pulled the cover from the heavy Harley e-motorcycle in the driveway and stowed supplies for his morning ride. On top, so they wouldn't be crushed, he placed a bouquet of chrysanthemums.

The day promised to be fine but not warm enough to do without his heavy, studded leathers. He walked the bike back off its stand and realized that he was looking forward to the hundred-kilometer run up to Constance. Today, though, was not solely a joy ride; there was business to conduct. He would meet the outriders from les Bleus at the discount gas station on his way out of Laval before hitting the AutoRoute.

Fall was approaching fast and an early frost had heightened the colours in the woods; the maples would be flaming in October. This was the best time of year for a road trip, thought Réjean, as he settled in the saddle, put his boots up on the pegs and open the throttle to exactly ninety kilometers per hour, the outriders closing behind in formation. He flicked the switch the Ayetech to autopilot and settled back, his wrists draped over the extended handlebars, more for show than guidance. The Ayetech would ensure that the pack kept formation. Today it was a twelve-pack of Blue; an old joke. The cool morning air had a bite to it—a relief after the heat of summer.

Their route took them along the broad valley of the Ottawa River paralleling the range of low hills to the east. The road ran straight through brown and yellow farmlands with few hedgerows to interrupt the views of the river, light glinting from stretches of still water between the reed beds. They rolled past farmhouses with front porches covered by the ski-jump overhang of the roof style favoured in Quebec. The older buildings in stone dated back to the nineteenth century. Often beside the original structure was a new and larger house built to accommodate a smaller but richer family with expanding aspirations: signs at the entrances along the road announced Plouffe, Ménard, Patry. Facades clad in artificial stone and an excess of windows attested to the profitable subsidies accorded to dairy farming. Cattle stood in narrow fields which ran back from the road, the land rising gently towards the forested hills.

Réjean glimpsed the orange of ripening pumpkins in fields. They were choose your own. He had promised Véronique the biggest *citrouille* this year. Maybe he would stop on the ride back. The side paniers on the bike could carry a large pumpkin or, better, two for balance. The countdown to Halloween had begun: shops in the small villages along their route were festooned with spider webs, plastic gravestones sprouted like toadstools on front yards, and skeletons were lashed to the hydro poles with duct tape.

With Réjean's big, electric motorbike in the lead, the *motards* swept sedately through the villages, careful to observe the speed limits. The electric motors of the bikes were virtually silent. In appreciation, a *vieux monsieur* on his lawn tractor smiled and waved. A first. *Tabernouche.*

The riders stopped for breakfast at the *le Roi des Oeufs*, a favourite of les Bleus. The proprietor, after some initial hesitation, had agreed to accept their protection and over time had encouraged the rest of the village to do the same. It felt like home and the annual country and western festival in June featured a ride through of the full clan, some three hundred machines. It was a considerable honour. It had been a long time since the Patricians over from Ontario, a gang of rival bikers, had caused any trouble.

After another hour's ride, les Bleus arrived in Constance, where Réjean needed to make a certain visit alone. He would meet up with the others in the parking lot at the Allways. He drove slowly down the street to the old peoples' residence, pulled into a slot marked '*Reservé pour visiteurs*' and switched off his motorcycle. Réjean retrieved the flowers from his saddlebag, climbed the steps to the wooden porch, pulled open the screen door and walked into a small hallway. The room to his right, originally a front parlour, had been converted into an office.

"*Bonjour, Monsieur Latâche. Elle est en bonne forme,*" called the receptionist. Réjean had been a regular visitor for several years, and she recognized him immediately. Most other visitors to elderly relatives sported fewer tattoos.

Réjean walked down the long corridor, descending ramps which connected the extensions made to the building over the years. He knocked on the last door and entered. The room overlooked the gardens with a pleasant view across the river to the west. The sunsets were often spectacular. An elderly woman sat in the rocker before the window, her back to the door.

"*Bonjour, Ma Tante,*" he said and leaned over to give Madame Garrity kisses on both cheeks.

✧ ✧ ✧

NÉE LATÂCHE, ODELINE Garrity was the fifth of thirteen children. This was unusually large even by the standards of the time and the family enjoyed some notoriety in the neighbourhood of Laval where she grew up. The family was large enough to field two hockey teams although lack of equipment led to some competition among Odeline's brothers for possession of shin pads and other essential equipment. As the older children hit their teens, they began to show a talent for minor crime, aptly fitting the description 'juvenile delinquents'. For other kids *du coin*, there was no question of crossing *les gars Latâche*. It would have meant suicide.

Odeline watched her two older sisters dutifully marry, the first to a local *garagiste*, and the second to an Italian-Canadian called Mario who had a small business renting out slot machines to the many taverns of north Montreal. Odeline haunted the public library, reading stories of travel to exotic places and adventurous young women whose lives bore little relation to the monotony of Laval. At sixteen, she determined to visit Europe and scrupulously saved what she could from the traditional jobs of baby-sitting and house-cleaning for neighbours. She thought she had won the lottery when she got a cashier job at the big Steinberg grocery store on Laval's *Boulevard de la Concorde*.

Odeline met James Garrity three days after landing in Paris. He was getting the treatment from a waiter in a café on the left bank and was struggling to explain in awful French about having misunderstood the price charged for a bottle of wine. Odeline leaned over and berated the waiter in Quebecois so astonishingly vulgar that the man paled to the colour of his long apron and hastily reached to pour the wine.

"*Espèce de con...*" she muttered, turning to Garrity, who by now was grinning broadly at the small, young woman.

They spent three weeks in France, renting a car and touring the Loire wine country to the Vendée coast and then north into Brittany. It had been a voyage of adventure. For both, it was their first time in Europe. James came from a town in west Quebec, not too far from Laval in distance, but a different world culturally. His was an Irish corner of the province, settled a hundred and fifty years ago by immigrant small-holders. Many of the older inhabitants were still stubbornly Anglophone.

James and Odeline married at the end of March the following year. Garrity was Irish and, since Odeline's parents had never met an Irish who was not Catholic, he met with their guarded approval. That there might be protestant Irish never occurred to them. They could even overlook James' difficulty with French: the Latâche family sometimes found it useful to exchange comments *non-entendu* by the anglophone. And anyway, it was appreciated that Odeline was extremely stubborn, having inherited a *tête de cochon* from her grandfather, so that was that.

Given that the maple sap was in full flow, James and Odeline had agreed to have the reception at the sugar shack of one of Odeline's cousins. James was an only child, his father had died a few years previously, and the only representative of the Garrity family was his mother, who was overwhelmed by the boisterous crowd of Odeline's well-wishers. She was taken in hand by Madame Latâche, and seated at a table beside a *'mon oncle'*, Raymond Poutre, who was known to speak some English between gin and tonics.

The meal had been lamb, cooked on a spit over an open fire. James was told that it was a real *meshwi*. With plates loaded with meat, scrambled eggs and a *salade de chou*, James and Odeline sat on a hard wooden bench, wedged between two of Odeline's larger female relatives, Marie-Claude and Pierette. After the meal, confused by drinking red wine from a variety of bottles, each appearing as if by magic on the plastic table cover; having shaken hands countless times and been kissed by a seemingly endless stream of *cousines*, James and Odeline were driven off in a limousine to the Queen Elizabeth, finest of Montreal hotels. The honeymoon had been arranged by Mario, using his connections.

Under James' quiet guidance, Odeline learned how to farm the Garrity property overlooking the Akonaga. She loved the work; in the black November mornings before the pale dawn crept slowly across the eastern horizon, and even when the coyotes killed the hens and carried off the cat. When, three years to the day after their marriage, James died of brain cancer, Odeline was numb for months, going through the rhythms of routine chores on automatic. Then she pulled herself together, put the farm for sale and, with the insurance money from James's policy, bought a practical house back in Laval.

At the farm, Odeline's head for figures had been sharpened calculating the futures in goat cheeses and organic vegetables, a viciously competitive business where she had learnt some hard lessons from the city buyers. Back in Laval, she realized that her relatives were treating her with deference, partly out of respect for her loss but also because they recognized her as someone who could actually do math. Taking over the books, Odeline soon realized that she was the only one in the family with oversight over all the various operations of the siblings, cousins and various hangers on. After several months, she slowly brought the brought the family business under her control. The Latâche family finally enjoyed effective management.

It wasn't overtly organized, nor was it exactly criminal; it was simply the Family. Ma Tante ensured that the numerous children of her siblings found work in suitable business and professions, preferably in modest occupations or small, marginal businesses which did not attract the attention of tax authorities but which together functioned as an ecosystem. It was a black economy comprising construction, trucking, roofing, some restaurants, some retail, all serviced by compliant professionals in insurance and accounting. To deal with the occasional legal woes, Odeline had recourse to her brother-in-law Mario's experienced team in Montreal. Ma Tante saw the organization as an iceberg, a pinnacle of gleaming purity above the water level with a much larger mass of shaded ice below.

✧   ✧   ✧

DANNY, THE SIXTH of the Latâche siblings, had a trucking business. In fact, he had owned a small share in a large truck, with the Family bank owning the rest. He had moved with his wife and young son Réjean to an isolated bungalow on a country road near St. Nicolet sur Lièvre. Homes were cheap, and he had paid cash. The house was built on flat land, but on the other side of the road, the Lièvre River flowed in a deep ravine. Sometimes Daniel and young Réjean would cross the road and scramble down the steep bank to fish.

Danny would park the sixteen-wheeler on the large gravel pad beside the bungalow where it would dominate the house. *Transport Latâche, Daniel Latâche Prop* was stencilled on the doors of the cab. Gazing up at the name, as he and his mother waved goodbye when Danny left on another long-distance haul, was one of Réjean's earliest memories.

One evening soon after Réjean's sixth birthday the truck, heavily laden with printed concrete forms destined for a building site in Toronto had been parked as usual beside the house. The family went to sleep as usual; the night was quiet, and even the faint murmur of the river was soothing.

Next morning, the driver of a school bus—the first on the road at seven thirty a.m.—had been slowing to pick up Réjean for school when she realized that the Latâche house was gone. She pulled to a halt inches before falling into the void left by the landslide which had swept away part of the road, the house and several hectares of land into the river. Getting down from the bus, she crept close to the edge of the large semi-circular bite out of the asphalt, to look down at the crushed roof of the house.

She called the police. When they arrived, they found themselves on the opposite side of the slide, a hundred yards across the gaping chasm from the school bus.

Réjean's parents died under the wall of the house, collapsed beneath the weight of moving earth, but rescuers found the young Réjean conscious and lying on his back on a bed of liquefied clay that had squirted from the base of the landslide. The mud had carried him from the ruin of the house, running several metres downslope before freezing into a tongue-shaped lobe. Shocked and stuck to the clinging clay like some spread-eagled insect, Réjean had spent hours gazing up at the semi-circular outline of the lip of the slide, outlined against the faint glow of the sky. It seemed as if the stars were watching him like the eyes of countless spiders, the black maw of the slide waiting for his slightest movement, its mud tongue preparing one last swallow to engulf him.

By nine o'clock, a volunteer fireman from St. Nicolet had shuffled across the hardening crust on planks and pulled Réjean to safety. By the time they regained solid ground, both were smeared with grey mud, last licks from the landslide that had opened in the night to eat Réjean's world and which had now settled back into gaping indifference. Réjean knew fear that night. Only when he was much older did he learn the name his fear, the name of the ravenous beast that destroyed his childhood: the Leda.

✧ ✧ ✧

ODELINE HAD TAKEN young Réjean into her household. She had had no children with James and she lavished her affection on the boy. He grew up in a world of *mes oncles, mes tantes* and numerous cousins who drifted in and out of his life at family gatherings. His size and strength began to show in his early teens, together with a willingness to take risks which made him a regular on local hockey teams. By the age of fifteen he had lost both front teeth.

Following his father's career path, Réjean worked in the transport side of the family business, although the packages he generally carried were light and could be easily stowed in the saddlebags of a motorbike. A stay in a *centre de jeunesse* had fostered his interest in art, and over the years he had used his skin as exhibition space, cramming more and more tattoo renderings of the paintings of Renaissance masters on his body. He was particularly fond of Leonardo.

While inside, Réjean discovered that working with his hands was most enjoyable; his strong, beringed knuckles proved highly successful in negotiating small business deals.

Later, when she decided to retire, Odeline was confident that her adopted son would be a suitable successor as leader of the Family. Les Bleus would keep her more uppity nephews in their place. Odeline chose to move back to Constance, where she could cherish her memories of her brief years with James, who lay in his grave cut deep in the clay in the cemetery nearby.

"*Ma Tante?*" Réjean said gently.

"*Bonjour, mon petit,*" replied Odeline. "Oh my, thank you for the flowers, Réjean. Yes, there is a little problem which you can help me with."

Odeline sketched out the story of her interview with the real estate agent Alcee Dupree. She had immediately suspected that there was much he had not told her and she was not one to ignore the whiff of opportunity. She knew a large development project was in the air for Crewe, and that it might be a fit for the Family.

"Talk with this Dupree. I expect he will be entirely reasonable." Both Aunt and Nephew smiled at the word. '*Soyez raisonable*' might as well have been their Family motto.

Réjean bid au revoir to his aunt, and climbed back onto his bike. He would rejoin les Bleus and drive up the valley to Crewe. He cracked his knuckles and grimaced, none too happy about venturing back onto the Leda.

Chapter 32

THE HOUSE WAS described as a 'mansion' in the real estate listing. Built five years previously, it stood on a circle at the end of a cul-de-sac close to the Crewe village limits. With its high, cathedral ceilings and steeply pitched roofs in Canadian gothic style, the building was extravagantly spacious even for a large family. Its excess was further proclaimed by the triple garage in front, but the garage doors were shut, blankly facing the cracked asphalt of a driveway empty of vehicles. The lots to either side remained undeveloped.

Now in late September, the rear of the house had a view through a screen of trees towards the forested hills, a blotchy plaid of browns and reds. The thinning foliage was golden in the morning sun, with a scatter of precocious maples already a flaming red. Surely the prospective buyers would love the setting? After all, they had specified an isolated property with a vista.

Alcee Dupree knew why the lots on either side were empty. The land here was close to a ravine cut deep into the Leda Clay. Almost every spring, a landslip would occur somewhere along the edge of the ravine, when the clay was heavy with water from the melting snows. The sides of the valley were scalloped by past landslides.

The zoning map published several years ago highlighted in red a broad margin along the edge of the ravine. The map was controversial, as was the accompanying provincial regulation which prohibited building in this zone. In the adjacent yellow zone, building was permitted, provided the plans allowed for adequate drainage to carry runoff well away from the building. The mansion's foundation straddled the boundary between yellow and red. Since the province later repealed this restrictive regulation, Alcee hardly felt compelled to advise prospective buyers of the fact.

Alcee was struggling with the lock box. It was attached to the iron railing beside the front door but it had been three weeks or so since the last showing and Alcee thought there must be a touch of rust in the mechanism. He punched the key code again: he was sure he had remembered it correctly. Fiddling with the lock box was always embarrassing with a client on the doorstep: Alcee tried to arrive a few minutes before the appointed time, just to make sure he could get into the house.

"*Maudit* fucking lock boxes," he muttered.

Alcee was still struggling when he felt a hand on his shoulder. He had heard nothing and turned with a start to see a large man before him, bearded and wearing a heavy, leather jacket. Behind him, neatly drawn up around the curb of the turning circle, was a row of whisper bikes, their riders sitting quietly, helmets on.

"*Monsieur Dupree?*" the man asked pleasantly. "*Je m'appelle Latâche.* I hope I have not mistaken the time of our appointment?"

An hour or so later, the business benefits of having an understanding with the Family Latâche and les Bleus were entirely obvious to Alcee. He had told all he knew about the development at River View, and hurriedly explained his arrangement with Bryce Desjardins for listing and selling the additional properties that would be approved, provided Madame Garrity—a charming lady—still agreed to sell the land for the new access. When speaking of his commission from Desjardins he mentioned a lower figure than the ten percent he had got Bryce Desjardins to agree to. Which was brave, since Réjean's grip on his shoulder was quite painful.

For Réjean, Alcee was just the type valued by the family as 'associates'. Réjean was able to assure Alcee about the Family's approach to rewards. Pay was related to performance but, and here the pressure on his shoulder increased to make the point, there would be unspecified sanctions for underperformance.

"*C'est compris?*" he had asked Alcee.

For his part, Alcee was able to update Monsieur Latâche on the latest intelligence: that a turf-cutting ceremony was to be held for River View next Saturday, and that a major American group was now funding the project as some kind of centre for religious education. This had piqued Réjean's curiosity. It had been a while since there had been significant interference from south of the border. He wondered if a turf war was in the offing. The religious centre sounded like a front to Réjean: when combined with real estate development he thought it might be for useful for money laundering and other profitable angles. He sighed: organized crime came in many different guises these days.

When Alcee had volunteered the arrangement he had with Bryce Desjardins and described in detail the work to build a secondary access to River View across Madame Garrity's land, Réjean's face had remained impassive. He visualized the geography: he knew that piece of forest; secluded and well back from the road to Constance. Les Bleus had occasion to use the land for burials. He had not mentioned this land use to Ma Tante for fear that she might not have approved. It had been a while since the last burial, but he thought that it might be an idea to drop by to see whether the grave had been discovered.

✧   ✧   ✧

THE FLEET OF whisper bikes slowed to take the sharp turn onto the Desjardins property. Réjean led the procession to the clearing where a large excavator was parked. The others stopped neatly beside him. He pulled a tall coffee cup from its holder and took a sip. Then, signalling the outriders to stay with the bikes, he stomped up the newly excavated cutline to a large, white pine with twisted branches which he recognized.

This looked like the place, but whereas it had once been a private spot deep in the trees, the excavator had cleared much of the bush and dug a deep trench which, in Réjean's recollection cut straight across shallow grave of one Henri Toulouse, known on the street as 'Murmurs', whom he had laid to rest in this very spot five years previously. At the time, he had explained at length to Murmurs the consequences of passing information to the cops on certain lucrative activities of les Bleus. Yellow and black police tape now cordoned off a section of the trench and it would not be wise to linger. *Tant pis pour Murmurs.* He walked back down the cut line to the waiting bikers, and tossed the dregs of this coffee onto the ground.

"Okay, let's go. *Allons-y!*" said Réjean, straddling his bike. The riders followed as he rode off to take the road back towards Constance and the route for Montreal. Plenty of time to stop and buy that pumpkin, he thought.

Chapter 33

IN HER WAKE, Counsellor Agnes Black had left a career path strewn with damaged people. Her toxicity as a manager was notorious to those staff whose misfortune it was to fall under her control. Senior management loved her for her ruthless pursuit of performance goals, until rumours of harassment began to mount. At that point, Agnes usually transferred, often with promotion. Only towards the end of her career had a perceptive superior encouraged her early retirement. Agnes had devoted her life to her job, ignoring gentler paths to personal fulfillment. She resented being manoeuvred into quitting, underappreciated and frankly owed.

To her surprise, Agnes found stimulation in local politics, something she had previously thought beneath her. She discovered, after winning election for village counsellor, that the community could benefit from her many years of experience. Admittedly, the monetary compensation was derisory, but the position allowed her to practice techniques well-honed in countless meetings to deliver verbal warnings and correction. These days, her favourite target was Hilary Beaubien, who was, in Agnes' view, a hapless do-gooder.

"*Bonjour*, Agnes. *Tu vas bien?*"

Entering the Café Pontiac, Hilary had found it hard to avoid greeting Agnes Black, who was sitting with a small group of her particular cronies. To Hilary's mild surprise, one of the party was Jack Shawcross, who rose and waved her over.

"Madame Beaubien, what beautiful weather!" called Jack across the room. "Do sit down. No? Can I buy you a coffee?"

Jack Shawcross' business had profited from recent improvements in the town, including extensions of sewer and water lines, which had improved the economic viability of River View. Various projects to beautify the town had resulted in it being perceived more as a destination rather than a place hurried through by cottagers on their way north. For once, Hilary thought that she and Agnes might agree about the proposed development at River View—it was frankly too big for Crewe and Hilary had a nagging concern about the Leda. So why, thought Hilary, the wheels spinning in her head, was Shawcross chatting up Agnes, whose favoured position on any development was usually a fervid "No".

"*Mais non*, Jack. Thank you all the same. I have to run to a meeting. But I look forward to the opening ceremony next weekend. As you say in English, knock on wood for the weather."

"About that," replied Jack. "I just invited Agnes here. It will be great to have such strong representation from the local council."

"*Merde de merde de merde de merde*," muttered Hillary as she returned to her car with a large takeout coffee.

✧ ✧ ✧

"WELL, THAT'S THAT. She's gone," said Jack when he returned to the group. Several around the table sniggered and Agnes smiled. Her vote would ensure that River View would get its needed re-zoning amendment and the Mayor would be unable to veto. That a green light for River View would kill any possibility of a natural area was a bonus. No 'Beaubien Natural Area'. No, not on her watch.

After the party dispersed, Agnes drove slowly home, turning right onto the road running beside Crewe Creek, left onto a side road, then left again on Vista Terrace, a cul-de-sac. The housing development dated from the nineteen-eighties and overlooked the town. Reaching number eight, Agnes drove across the small culvert which separated her newly asphalted driveway from the gravel road and pulled to a stop. That morning, her gardener had run the riding mower across her lawns, mainly to blow the fallen leaves onto the neighbour's untidy property, Agnes hoped for the last time this fall.

She liked her property to be neat; the grass cut short with trim borders. In the middle of the front lawn was a lonely ornamental tree, supported against the wind which whipped around the corner of the house by a stout iron post. Pruning this tree was for Agnes a form of relaxation and her only contribution to yard maintenance. When she trimmed the tree she talked about the trials of her day. The tree never answered back. As she drove up, she noticed one trailing twig. She would deal with that later.

Behind her house, a level, green sward ran back some distance before sweeping down to a winding stream at the bottom of a long slope. The stream separated her property from public lands which she was quite determined would remain undeveloped.

The stream joined Crewe Creek a few hundred metres down-hill. After the spring snowmelt, the flow reduced by late summer to a mere trickle. With the recent rains, however, it was flowing strongly, with muscular eddies working to exaggerate its meanders.

As a village councillor, Agnes dismissed complaints from residents about damage to their property from floods, erosion and other natural processes. *Caveat emptor* was her motto. As for landslides in the Leda Clay, she felt the risk overblown by an overcautious mayor. When it came to her own property, however,

Agnes was annoyed by the stream nibbling away the bottom of her garden. It was a kind of theft which she was loath to tolerate. But, frugal in matters of both public and private finance, she hesitated to pay for the work necessary to reinforce the stream banks and control the erosion.

Agnes' house itself was one of several built along the edge of the terrace. The view and proximity to the village made these prime sites, and the buyers had opted for extravagant models. During construction, the developer had excavated large volumes of soil and clay and redistributed them across the site to raise the surface above that of the original damp pasture.

Agnes believed that the municipality should dig a deep ditch at the base of the slope, but her discussions with Jack Shawcross had proved illuminating. He had dismissed the idea as inadequate. The real problem, he explained, was the danger of a landslide. What Agnes needed—he had sketched the solution on a napkin in the Café Pontiac—was to load the toe of the slope with heavy rock to prevent any such a possibility. A 'berm' and a retaining wall would, he assured Agnes, solve her problem for good.

Shawcross had offered her the loan of an excavator and his best operator for the job.

"Rob Freeman is a professional," he said. "He'll get the job done."

Jack would deliver the necessary loads of rock at no cost. Excavations at River View had unearthed a large number of boulders, and this would be a handy way of disposing of them.

"To tell you the truth, Agnes, you would be doing me a favour. And I absolutely refuse to accept any payment for Rob's time."

Agnes was well aware of Jack's motivation and was amused to see how he went about trying to woo her vote. But no money would change hands, and accepting a help from a friend for a little drainage work was merely efficient use of available resources. She was in control: men were so transparent. She agreed that the work could commence later that week. Agnes collected her secateurs and went to confide in her weeping mulberry.

✧   ✧   ✧

THE FOLLOWING THURSDAY, Rob Freeman was working at the bottom end of the Black property. The curve of the slope hid the body of the machine and its operator from the house. Jack Shawcross had told Rob that the work should only take two days. He was to excavate along the base of the slope to make a level berm, place a row of interlocking wire baskets—Shawcross called them "gambions"—along the berm, and then to fill the baskets with boulders. The gambions would form a heavy retaining wall, their weight preventing any future movement in the slope above.

Rob Freeman liked this kind of unsupervised work. He excavated the base of the slope to create the level berm, and a crew positioned the empty wire baskets. Two of the Shawcross trucks had unloaded a pile of boulders at one end of the site. Now Rob was slowly filling each basket with rock. Two buckets to a gambion and then a backfill. He might almost be finished by dusk. Not that he need hurry.

At six pm, Rob Freeman shut down the Kobatsu and drove off in his battered truck. Beneath the dead weight of rock loaded into the gambions, the pressure in the underlying Leda Clay increased. This pressure wouldn't dissipate for weeks.

The gambions might prevent a rupture above the berm, but they were ill placed to prevent a failure in the underlying Leda Clay where the heightened pressure weakened resistance to a landslide. That calculation had not figured in the drawings on the back of the Shawcross napkin.

Chapter 34

MOLLY CAME DOWN from the higher plane with a slight bump. With some reluctance, she put aside the white selenite crystal she was clutching. The crystal had really helped her meditation, and Molly had sensed stars from far above connecting to her scalp through a filigree of tenuous threads. She was methodically testing the rock and crystal specimens from the cardboard box that Argile had left with her. Conscious of the importance of the scientific method, she ticked off the boxes for 'astral projection' and 'aid to meditation' against the list entry for selenite. She was sitting on a prayer mat in the back room behind the shop. A joss burner was sending tendrils of smoke to the ceiling. Molly's headphones played a selection of sea sounds, and a semi-circle of scented candles cast light of sufficient intensity for her to jot down her observations.

The next specimen from the box proved to be a block of plated mica. Molly composed herself, holding the rock in her left hand, and attempted to become one with the crystal. After a few minutes, she sighed in frustration. What was it with phlogopite? No matter how hard she concentrated, she could not sense any transcendental property, and yet Argile had insisted that this was a most powerful mineral.

Molly often thought about Argile. She had met him quite accidently last year as she was gathering pods of milkweed for a weaving project. She had seen a man struggling up the side of Crewe Creek with a large block of clay, and guessed he meant to sculpt the clay, or even to turn it on a wheel. She knew local potters whose claim to authenticity lay in the use of local clays: some of their rough-glazed products were on consignment in the shop. She blushed to remember their first conversation.

"Hi. Are you going to make pots with that?" she had said when the man got closer.

"Not at all," the man had replied. "This is Leda Clay. I am going to test its strength. My name is Chester Argile. Call me Argile."

Molly hadn't known much about the Leda Clay. Half an hour later, she was slightly better informed. Sitting at one of the picnic tables, Argile had pulled a round object and a hammer from his knapsack.

"It's a concretion from the Leda," he had told her. "Watch." Wedging the concretion between two planks of the table, he had hit the edge sharply with the hammer.

The freshly broken surface appeared to be blank. "One can't be lucky all the time. Often I find bits of fish skeleton inside these concretions."

"Let me look." Molly had taken the rock from his hand and stared at the flat grey surface. "I suppose if there was a fish there, it must have dived."

"Yes, when you break these things open, you must believe you will find the perfect fossil in the very next one."

Molly had stood, smoothing her long skirt.

"You are pulling my leg but I don't mind."

Molly knew that Argile watched as she walked away. He was, she decided, grey but interesting, a bit like the Leda.

Chapter 35

E MS AND JILLY Gough had arranged to meet for coffee at the Café Pontiac at ten a.m. Although it was a weekday, Ems had decided to take the morning off and drive up to Crewe. The place wasn't crowded and they found a private table to chat.

Ems was explaining her concerns about Argile's growing obsession with geological catastrophe. Again this morning she had come downstairs to find him sitting with his laptop, scrolling through images of disaster. She had looked over his shoulder and felt him stiffen slightly, half closing the cover of the computer. He had then explained that he was looking at images of landslides; recent monsoon rains in Nepal had devastated the country's road system.

"Then he asked me to watch a video," Ems said. "Chester pressed 'Play' and I saw a still image of what looked like a dry riverbed. In the background I heard faint birdsong. Then I saw something dark far up the channel and heard a growing murmur. It looked like a dark line which gathered breadth and height as it rushed towards the camera. The murmur increased in volume and suddenly a wall of mud surged into focus. I had to hold tight to the back of Chester's chair."

"Well, that doesn't sound too bad. You know he has a professional interest in these things," said Jilly.

"No I suppose not. I could see that Chester was quite excited, watching the wall of mud rushing below the camera. There were boulders the size of cars shooting past. I don't mind that he has his enthusiasms. I know he needs something in his retirement. But he watches these videos all the time. Hundreds of people are dying because of these events. Don't you think it's macabre?"

"I suppose it is a kind of pornography really," said Jilly trying to be helpful. "Something you just have to ignore in men of his age".

Jilly was familiar with obsessions in husbands. She had felt for months that a swarm of electronic bees had come between her and Peter.

"Well, he is off for another of his solitary walks. He said he would meet me at Rosty's Scars Picnic Area in half an hour. Will you walk up there with me?"

✧   ✧   ✧

MEANWHILE, ARGILE, OBLIVIOUS to the speculation about his mental health, was halfway down Crewe Gorge. He had started at the bridge where the creek tumbled over a hard edge of Shield rocks and fell twenty feet into a deep pool. During spring floods, the water gushed at high velocity through the concrete box culvert supporting the bridge and crashed down the gorge. At this tired end of summer, the falls were reduced to a trickle.

Argile was thinking about the text from Roch that morning. The radio-carbon dates had come back from the lab; four hundred years old, plus or minus fifty, for the carbon fragments on the horizon where he had found the piece of pottery, and somewhat younger for the bone. So it might be an Indian grave, but the results were inconclusive.

Argile followed Jet down the steep banks to the base of the falls, holding onto saplings for support. He moved downstream, cautiously jumping from boulder to boulder, while the dog wandered along the sandy bed of the stream in the few inches of water. As the valley widened slightly, Argile could walk with relative ease along the trace of a path which followed the eastern bank. After a few hundred metres, the creek emerged from the gorge where the hard rock plunged beneath the cover of sands and clays deposited by the retreating glaciers. The gradient eased: Argile was standing on the highest terrace of the Leda Clay.

At these low water levels, Argile was hoping to explore the undercut outer bank at the creek's first meander. Here the stream doubled back on itself in a tight loop, eddies eroding and undermining a low cliff of Leda Clay.

Standing on the gravelly beach on the inside of the bend, Argile could see the clay exposed just beneath the water surface. He was wearing rubber boots and stepped into the water to get a closer look. Below the water surface the clay was blue and slick. Above, the clay had dried in the warm air to a light grey.

The clay was not uniform. Water oozed from certain layers which were slightly darker. He smeared some of this material onto his finger and tasted it gingerly. He felt the grittiness between his front teeth, a sign that the layer was a fine silt rather than pure clay. Water percolated slowly through these silt layers, to emerge at the cliff face like bands of tears.

Argile took out his penknife, cut through the dried crust and stuck the blade firmly into the hard clay. With a practised twist of his wrist he judged its strength. It was a relatively tough section for the Leda, rating a six out of ten on his own qualitative scale for estimating the strength of clays. From three to five, he would judge the clay as sensitive and like to fail under heavy loading; less than three and he would not linger under the cliff.

Extracting a small sample with his knife, Argile rolled the clay into a thin tube in the palm of his hand. He tapped the tube to see if any sheen appeared on the surface. No sheen, so the sample was not saturated with water. This band was good, stiff clay and not susceptible to sudden liquefaction. Argile scribbled the results in his field book.

Further downstream, the creek narrowed to gush over a knob of hard white bedrock which formed a low ridge across the river. Below the water, Argile could see the contact between the smooth clay and the underlying bedrock. Argile loved to see this contact; it was an unconformity, representing a gap in geological history of a billion years, more or less. It gave him a delicious vertigo, in his imagination he could let himself fall through the immensity of unrecorded time.

There was a series of these ridges, more or less in parallel, made of veins of hard quartz. They formed a washboard of ridges separating pods of Leda Clay. Argile thought these ridges helped anchor the base of the clay. Knock them through, and there would be little to prevent the Leda slipping hundreds of metres down the valley.

Argile looked at his watch. It was time to head to the picnic area at Rosty's Scars to meet Ems. He scanned the valley sides for Jet. He could no longer hear the jingle of the tags attached to the dog's collar. Had he been too absorbed in looking at the section? With relief he finally saw Jet lying curled on the ground a few yards up the bank. He had been patiently watching his master's slow progress down the valley through eyes half-closed.

✧   ✧   ✧

ARGILE STRUGGLED UP the side of the valley to emerge at the edge of the picnic area. Jet ran ahead to greet Ems, who was sitting with her friend at one of the tables. Argile walked over to the sign indicating *Aire de pique-nique de Crewe*, which, despite the efforts of Quebec's Commission for Place Names, the populace stubbornly continued to refer to as the "Scars".

The Scars were a series of platforms that cut back into the hillside rising above Crewe. At the rear of each platform, there was a steep curving slope—the scar—which led up a few metres to the next higher platform. From above, the scars appeared crescent-shaped, rising successively up the hillside like nested new moons. Together they formed a natural amphitheatre.

Crewe had bought part of the original farm belonging to last of the Rosty family, to create a picnic area come play park close to the outskirts of town. It had become a regular venue for events during the community calendar. Heritage Day—a late-summer community celebration—was coming soon. New this year, a zombie procession would start here at the Scars before winding through the town.

Argile greeted the two women and, ignoring the damp on the wooden seat, sat beside them.

"I hope you haven't been waiting long. It was a bit of struggle getting down the creek, what with the recent wind blows blocking the valley."

"*Mais non*, you are only five minutes late," replied Ems.

"Did you find anything interesting?" asked Jilly.

"Not really," said Argile. "I was looking at some fresh sections where the creek has undercut the bank. No, what is more interesting is right here at Rosty's Scars. I suppose you know that you are sitting on an old landslide? That bank above us marks the edge of a major slide which scooped out the clay in this whole area to make the arena. This flat area we are standing on is where the liquefied mud pooled and then solidified. It was a while ago though."

He pointed towards the edge of the picnic area. Beyond a screen of trees, they could see the roofs of new houses on the outskirts of the village.

"Of course, those people would have been swept away and buried, if they had been there then," he said.

Ems looked at Jilly and raised an eyebrow.

Chapter 36

THE KIDS WERE getting on Dave's nerves. He had been forewarned: Dara had told him she was planning to bring a group of children to visit *The Courier* offices on Heritage Day. This year, the festivities included a zombie march, and this was taken as licence to try out Halloween costumes. They were distracting Dave, who thought their links to heritage extremely tenuous: several vampires, a couple of prostitutes and a gorilla were wandering about.

Dave considered it particularly unfair that Dara had opted to bring a platoon of kids down from the reservation. It wasn't as if she had any children herself, while Dave felt that the office was his refuge from the rigours of parenting the twins. He had left the house that morning as the kids were already nagging his wife to put on their costumes. He would be on duty again this evening to take his twin monsters to the zombie barbecue.

"Come on, guys," he complained.

The kids were helping Dave prepare the layout for the next edition on the big touch screen. The main article had become hopelessly jumbled by lines of emojis added when he turned his back for a second to appeal to Dara. She had shrugged, as if to say "Kids. What do you expect?"

Elsie Truelove was surveying the newsroom through the large window in her mezzanine office. Dave's discomfort amused her— he should learn to relax more. She had approved Dara's request to bring the kids into the office. Dara would come to appreciate these little concessions, she was sure. And anyway, Heritage Day at *The Courier*, the story almost wrote itself. No problem for the junior reporter.

"Don't worry, Dave. We're off to lunch," called Dara.

She would take them for burgers and fries before going up to the picnic grounds to see the start of the zombie parade. Afterwards there would be music and a corn roast, before the mozzies got too bad, and she would round up the kids to head back home.

✧   ✧   ✧

BY THE END of the morning, Dara's mood had soured. The kids seemed determined to exasperate their 'aunt', and she was thankful when Kitsi arrived. After lunch, they drove up to Rusty's Scars, where a crowd was assembling beside the picnic tables. A varied group of zombies had gathered, some more fancifully dressed than others. Many were using their Ayetechs to take selfies with their companions for immediate posting. Onlookers, some with small children on their shoulders, formed a loose circle around the field.

Mayor Beaubien arrived to take part in the procession riding on the Crewe fire truck. Her escort of five volunteer fire fighters, dressed in their normal fire-fighting gear was comforting. Hilary was glad they had ignored the call to dress as zombies. Her only concession to the occasion was to apply make-up heavier than usual and put on the red leather boots she always wore when mixing with the fire guys. Wearing these, she felt she could surmount the afternoon's petty annoyances. She felt only slightly more comfortable with the zombies than the LGBTQ march in June, another must on the Mayor's calendar. But on the plus side, once Heritage Day was over, there was a clear run to the holiday break she had been promising herself for weeks.

The marching band was warming up. It was taking some time, since some zombie outfits were incompatible with playing certain instruments. The flautists seemed to be having particular difficulty. The band director—his facing oozing green leeches—signalled the drummer to start a marching beat, and the band fell into formation. In their attempt to look zombieish they achieved an effect akin to a New Orleans funeral procession.

As the band circled the picnic grounds, the crowd joined in behind the procession. As the rhythm caught hold, the zombies started to exaggerate their stomps: stomp with the left foot, stomp with the right, to the beat of the band.

Sean was with a group of youths draped in pale sheets which they had filched from a painter pal and which they claimed were grave cloths. They formed the tail of the procession. After several joints, the increasing motion of the ground beneath their feet was not really a surprise to any of them. It was becoming ever more like the bouncy castle installed by the play park, except that here in the field it was the turf itself which undulated in waves.

"*Woo-hoo!*" cried Sean, as the ground rose and fell.

After circling the field twice, the zombies followed the marching band down the road towards the village centre. The picnic field, left to its own devices, quivered slightly. Beneath the dry crust bound by the matt of trampled grass, the Leda had turned the consistency of custard.

✧   ✧   ✧

THE PARADE ENDED in the small square in front of the church. There was a marquee where ladies of the parish sold tea, coffee and Nanaimo bars, baked for previous events and resurrected from the freezer for Heritage Day. Outside, a mobile food truck from Constance was doing better business with hotdogs and fries.

Stalls lined one side of the square, one offering 'Draveurs' tee-shirts and other accessories; another, soaps and essential oils. Two Asian girls from the *'L'Univers des ongles'* on Rue Principale were painting zombie faces on kids. Molly Laberge had a small display of rocks.

A local band played on a stage at one corner of the square. Billed as a rock band, it sounded more like country and western. The sound mixer was having trouble with feedback but no one seemed to care. The zombies danced slowly.

Sean and his mates let off a few illegal fireworks before slipping away to the Drafters to assuage a fierce thirst.

✧   ✧   ✧

AS DUSK FELL, Hilary Beaubien had almost finished her civic duties for the day. Her last act was to light the bonfire. The fire chief soused the wood with gasoline, and passed her a flaming brand to thrust into the carefully stacked sticks.

The Mayor jumping backwards, her cheeks flushed by the heat.

"That fucking enough," she said to herself. "Time for a bath." Back home in the hallway, zombies and her public safely distanced, she started to peel off her boots only to discover they were covered in licks of grey clay from Rosty's Scars.

"Covered in *merde*. Typical." She sighed.

Chapter 37

PETER GOUGH WAS becoming fed up with Argile's project. Lately, the attrition rate in the squadron had been high; he had lost two drones on the last mission. Sure, he could print the bodies easily enough, but replacing the lost batteries was getting expensive. Peter had casually mentioned the price of a new muskbutton battery to Argile, but the latter had been engrossed looking at the data from their latest sortie. Peter swore this would be the last mission.

Oblivious to Peter's frustration, Argile had loaded the new data onto his computer and was looking at the plot of deltas—the cumulative deviation of survey points from the baseline they had established back in the spring. He was convinced there was a pattern developing in the deviations: decimeters of strain had accumulated since the last drone survey, along a section of slope extending from the western part of Crewe to behind the River View lands. He was confident that this effect was real.

Argile vaguely acknowledged Peter's muttered goodbye and, seconds later, heard the screen door slam.

Perhaps, thought Argile, the increase in deviation could mean that conditions were becoming critical. In that case, he hoped to detect the accumulating strain on the geophone recordings from the mine. Surely, there would be some audible signal from the creeping hillside, a sign of a coming collapse, the groaning of stressed soil, the tearing roar of the actual failure. Argile dearly wished to find a reliable way to predict landslides in the Leda. It was his Holy Grail.

✧   ✧   ✧

WHILE ARGILE WAS studying his deviations, at the back of Molly's Rocks at the sad end of Rue Principale, Molly Laberge was scraping the topsoil from one corner of the small plot behind the shop. Nothing much would grow on the blue clay exposed beneath, except moss and a short, stunted grass. She dug a small pit and used a flat spade to cut a cube of clay. She carried the clay inside and placed it on a plastic sheet on the kitchen floor.

Molly looked again at the illustration in the book which had arrived this morning. Page twenty-four of *New Waves in Dark Matters* gave detailed instructions for a spell that she was eager to try. The author was a regular on talk shows where audiences favoured mystery over explanation. Molly would have to follow the steps exactly or she would get into trouble. Results were not guaranteed.

Molly kneaded the clay. It became increasingly plastic until she could mould it easily into the shape she envisioned. A spread-eagled human shape about two feet long gradually appeared. Arms, legs, torso and head. It was crude but, she supposed, fit for purpose. Molly rolled thin tubes out of the clay and added details to her model. Finally, sitting back on her haunches, she looked carefully at the face. She then went to the cabinet and took out the special stone which Argile had given her. She placed this reverently on the doll's forehead.

"*Voilá.* There you go. Say 'Hi', Argile". She stuck candles into the clay, waiting for dusk to fall.

Chapter 38

NUMBER TWELVE, THE third house on the street, had lit a welcome light in the porch. Marsha had knocked in vain at numbers four and eight but this looked more promising. In country neighbourhoods like Crewe, the five-minute walk between each front door often discouraged doorstep sales and trick-or-treaters. Here in Crewe, there were more than just two solitudes: every property was its own country.

Mission based its entry into a new neighbourhood on thorough research. During training, Marsha had learned that real estate agents, in particular, were crucial in expanding Mission's network of influence. Behind their outward show of confidence and plastic smiles, realtors were often anguished souls, with nagging concerns about ethics. Combining this angst with extensive local knowledge of land values made realtors natural recruits for Mission.

Before ringing the doorbell, Marsha opened her Ayetech and rechecked Mission's data on Crewe households. The home owner at this address was bilingual, married but with no dependents, and was slowly paying down a rather large mortgage. He was by profession a realtor. She switched her Ayetech to translate.

Priebus and Marsha stood side by side before the front door. They had dressed in dark clothing, approved by Mission for the doorstep. Priebus had even found a tie. The early dusk meant that they carried glow lights for road safety, but Marsha also had a combat flashlight, just in case. Even though this was Canada.

They heard a dead lock snap open, and Madame Dupree opened the door.

"Good evening, Madame Dupree. We are looking for Monsieur Dupree. We have good news for your husband." She spoke in English; slowly for her Ayetech to keep up with the translation.

"*Oh, il est toujours au bureau. Je peux vous aider?*"

Madame Dupree's words were paraphrased in English in Marsha's earbuds as, "Her husband is the realtor and still at the office. She is a lonely woman and eager for conversation". Ayetech could seldom resist adding commentary to the translation, to Marsha's annoyance.

Forcing a smile, Marsha presented a brochure to Madame Dupree, and stated that a reward awaited Monsieur Dupree. If perhaps she could explain further?

Before the doorbell rang, Madame Dupree had been thumbing through the latest publication of the Canadian Association of Realtors. She had been looking at the glossy pictures of the annual awards dinner, this year held at one of Toronto's swankier hotels. For years, it had been her secret hope that the Association would recognize Alcee's efforts. He worked so hard. Now, if she had followed the awkward translation correctly, then this nice young woman with the Ayetech seemed to be saying exactly that. She invited her visitors into the house.

Getting past the front door was rare in Marsha's experience. So when she and Priebus found themselves ushered into the kitchen, she felt an unfamiliar glow of missionary zeal. Madame Dupree invited them to sit while she prepared coffee.

"*Alors*," said Madame Dupree. "About this good news for my husband?"

"Indeed". There was a slight pause while Ayetech considered how to advise Marsha on her next words.

"Yes, indeed," continued Marsha. "We understand that Monsieur Dupree—your husband—is the leading real estate agent in Crewe. We represent an organization who recognizes professionals who live and breathe the demanding ethical standards of their calling. To be sure we need to ask a few questions. We are sure that for Monsieur Dupree this will be nothing but a formality, but, you know, we have procedures to follow."

Madame Dupree understood. She had followed procedures throughout her career as an elementary teacher in the Quebec public system. She approved of procedures. And it was only correct that Alcee should be recognized for exceeding the standards set for his profession. She would ensure that he followed whatever procedure was demanded.

Priebus had been sitting quietly, half listening to the conversation between Marsha and the woman. He sipped his coffee gazing at the kitchen wall and thinking how to bug the Dupree's kitchen. Mission liked to keep tabs on its converts and it would be straightforward if the household was already connected.

"Your husband, he has an Ayetech?" Priebus interrupted. Both women stopped talking and looked at Priebus. Madame Dupree looked confused.

"Oh, it's just that if he hadn't, we can provide him with a complementary device," said Marsha hurriedly. "Perhaps we can leave you with this. She took a package from the case beside her. We call it *The Guiding Hand*. It is fully compatible with an Ayetech. You will find a section devoted to real estate, but you yourself as a teacher will be interested I am sure. The Mission offers ethical guidance for all professions."

At the mention of Mission, it dawned on Madame Dupree that Father Bonenfant had mentioned the name the previous Sunday. He had been quite enthusiastic, but then the African fathers often were. So the Canadian Association of Realtors was affiliated with Mission? Madame Dupree thought it made sense as she bid her visitors au revoir on the doorstep.

✧ ✧ ✧

ALCEE RETURNED FROM a frustrating day thirsting for a stiff
drink before supper. A tree had fallen on the carport of one of his
listings. The owner was away and had left things in Alcee's hands.
That meant making calls to Box's Tree Service to clear away the
branches, to the cable company to reconnect the cut line, and to
the *maudit* insurer, who had been particularly unhelpful. Alcee
couldn't understand why anybody used Gautier Assurance.

He pulled into his driveway in his SUV and switched off the
motor. As the exit assist feature helped lift him out of the vehicle,
he admired the electric blue sheen on his newly leased vehicle—
realtors got treated pretty well by the dealerships. It was a shame
that it would soon be encrusted with salt from the winter slush,
but then the weekly visits to the car wash in Constance were tax
deductible.

Alcee went in, to be greeted by his wife with a double *bec*—
enough to alert him that something was up, probably a visit from
la belle famille. Alcee hoped it wouldn't be his sister-in-law.
There was something about her husband Didier which irritated
him immensely.

"*Salut mon chéri*," said Madame Dupree. "Did you have a
good day? I have some wonderful news!"

Madame Dupree told Alcee about the visit from Mission and
presented him with the package containing *The Guiding Hand*.

"Alcee, you must look at this. Put down that drink, *chéri*.
They said you can read it on your Ayetech, and then they would
follow up with some questions. This is your chance with the
Association!"

It proved to be a long evening, during which Alcee assured

Madame Dupree that he would review all the ethical questions and answers in the book to be ready when Mission contacted him. He very much doubted if this would lead to an award at the next Association dinner, but he didn't want to disappoint his wife.

✧　✧　✧

A FEW DAYS later, Alcee was meeting with a young couple interested in buying a family home in the Crewe area.

"I advise you not to buy here" were Alcee's next words after greeting his clients. Dupree was looking pale and swayed slightly as he said this. He had to force the words through his teeth, and the effort had left him weak. The couple looked at him with concern.

"Would you like some water, Monsieur Dupree?" The young woman detached a water bottle from her belt and offered it to Alcee.

"No, I am fine, really," replied Alcee.

This had been his last showing of the day and he been fairly sure that the prospective buyers, young professionals moving from a city apartment to buy their first home in the countryside, might be ready to make an offer, although the man seemed to have reservations.

"You see," Alcee explained, "this home is built on Leda Clay. That can affect the foundation. With good drainage this is usually manageable, but this particular house is far too close to a ravine. You can see for yourself if you want to walk over to the edge of the property. I can show you somewhere else which is entirely safe but this one, no, I can't recommend it."

The young couple stared at him in disbelief. Although inexperienced with real estate agents, they would never have anticipated one trying to prevent them buying. Alcee's instinct had been to avoid any mention of Leda Clay but the *The Guiding Hand* insisted on complete honesty.

The young people exchanged glances.

"Ok, we hear you, Mr. Dupree," said the young man. "But we would still like to buy this house. We fell in love with the view. It is so close to the village and great for the kids. There is nothing like this in the city. Surely the municipality would not allow building if it was unsafe?"

"It's perfect!" added the young woman.

Alcee sat for a few moments, then shrugged and pulled out the necessary forms from his briefcase. The offer was considerably below the advertised price, but he felt confident that the seller would not quibble. The property had been on the market long enough without offers and winter was coming. He had not showed the house since his encounter with Monsieur Latâche and his bikers.

After the couple left, smiles all round, Alcee remained inside. He went to the window overlooking the ravine. His conscience was clear; he had followed the advice of *The Guiding Hand* expressly for realtors. Yes, honesty had proven the best policy.

Chapter 39

MARSHA WAS SMARTING from her telephone conversation with Pastor Bob. She understood that her repeated trips up to Canada with Priebus were draining his travel budget, and it was true that results had been meagre. But he didn't need to be quite so rude.

"Get this Argile guy," he had told Marsha, "and find out where he mines these Crewe Stones. You have one week."

The snatch should be a simple operation. They were to extract the information from Argile without fail. Marsha saw no special difficulty, although Priebus' glee surprised her when she told him her plan. They would need to restrain Argile, and Priebus had run over to the Allways to buy essentials; tape and a reclining deckchair which he then bolted to the camper floor. Space was limited, but Priebus had assured Marsha that the more intimate the space, the more effective the interrogation. Marsha assumed Priebus had taken lessons from comic books.

Marsha drove slowly up the driveway leading to the Argile and Em's cabin. She pulled gently to a halt on the gravel. No reaction. She knew that the dog was in town with Argile's partner.

Priebus took three twelve-inch plastic ties from the glove compartment. He got out of the camper and jogged towards the rear of the cabin. Marsha had not expected Priebus to move so quickly—it was entirely out of character. He disappeared around the corner.

✧　✧　✧

ARGILE WAS SITTING in a comfortable chair on the veranda, his computer on his knees. A glass and a half empty bottle of gin were within easy reach on the rattan table beside him. Argile was indulging himself. He was browsing the website of one of his favourite bloggers on the latest geological catastrophes around the world, watching a dramatic video of a rock slide in China. He found this entertainment relaxing, perfect for the tranquil summer evening.

Argile was taken by surprise when Priebus pinned his arms, wrenching off his headphones.

"Okay, Dr. Argile, keep still or I'll hurt you," said Priebus.

Argile lashed out with his foot, connecting with Priebus' shins. The young man let go with a yelp. Out of the corner of his eye saw a woman running towards him. He jumped down the veranda steps, ran across the narrow lawn and plunged downhill into the thickets of scrub oak. He knew these paths well and was soon out of sight of the cabin and moving deeper into the woods. What? Why? The words pumped through his mind as he jogged down the steep, twisting path through the rocky outcrops, heart pounding at a rate well above the recommended limit for someone of his age.

Argile arrived at the edge of the ravine and paused. Behind him he heard the sounds of pursuit. He looked down the down the steep valley side where a recent landslip had bared the clay, leaving a long grey scar. A group of spruce trees toppled by the slide lay in a confusion of branches at the bottom of the ravine. Rain had made the clay extremely slick. Argile worked his way down along the edge of the ravine and crouched quietly in the scrub.

Someone crashed through the bush close beside him and

Argile saw a young man emerge from the trees. His pursuer stood on the lip of the ravine. The edge crumbled. Priebus, with a cry, fell six feet onto the steep clay bank. With the momentum gained from the drop, he slid down the slope coming to an abrupt halt in the tangle of branches.

The man was lucky not to spear himself on the jagged wood, thought Argile, watching from above. It would take him time to extricate himself, by which time Argile would be long gone. Argile began to breathe more easily.

"Really, Dr. Argile, it would be much easier if you didn't run."

Marsha's voice was much too close. Argile felt his wrists grabbed firmly from behind. How had she moved so fast? Priebus struggled up the clay bank, clutching at dangling roots and wildly inclined saplings.

"Yessir," he said, pulling out a plastic bag tie. "We only want a quiet word".

✧   ✧   ✧

IT TOOK THE three of them twenty minutes to work their way back up the hill. Marsha led the way, Argile was in the middle, with his hands strapped behind his back, and Priebus took up the rear. The hillside was steep enough to inhibit talking and they climbed in silence. Back beside the cabin, they walked around to the parked camper. Marsha opened the side door.

"In," she ordered, pointing to the reclining chair. "Make yourself comfortable".

Argile, crowded from behind by Priebus, had no option but to clamber into the camper and squeeze into the recliner.

"Now, these are for your safety," she said, attaching straps to Argile's arms and ankles. Argile forced himself to relax.

"We'll take a short drive and then have a long talk where no one can interrupted us. Answer our questions and don't play stupid tricks."

Marsha drove the camper out of the driveway and down the hill to where a dirt track joined the road. The track climbed to a disused fire tower perched high on the edge of the escarpment and appeared barely used. They had parked there when making an earlier reconnoitre a few weeks previously. She carefully backed the camper a few yards up and engaged the parking brake. Priebus, after fiddling with the switch, flicked on the camskin.

"Now," began Marsha, turning to face Argile. "Where do you find these Crewe Stones?"

"What on earth do you mean? What do you want with me?" cried Argile. He still shook from his capture but began to think more clearly. He suddenly made the connection.

"You are the people who came round asking me about places to look for mineral specimens!" said Argile.

Priebus moved in front of Marsha, his face inches from Argile's.

"Right, *Mister* Argile. And I'm tired of breaking empty rocks. So, tell us where to find those stones with the fish."

So, thought Argile, they wanted to know where the best concretions came from. 'Crewe Stones'—that was what Molly had christened them. Argile was now angry: he would be damned if he told. But best to humour them, he thought.

"Okay," he said, keeping his tone meek. "I can take you there. It is not far."

"Good. Then let's go. You had best not try anything," said Marsha. She slipped forward into the driver's seat while Priebus sat with Argile in the back of the camper.

"You stay tied till we get there," he whispered in Argile's ear.

✧ ✧ ✧

CANDICE AND SEAN had spent the late afternoon up at the fire tower. Sean was driving cautiously down the track leading to the road. The surface was loose and he had little confidence in his rear brakes. He was descending the steep pitch before the track joined the paved road that ran along Crewe Lake when he glimpsed a strange shimmer in the air in front of him.

Sean slammed into the back of the camouflaged camper at less than twenty kilometers per hour. The faulty switch controlling the camskin which Priebus had temporarily repaired failed again and, after flickering once or twice, the rear of the camper materialized, parked in the middle of the fire road. Sean looked across Candice.

"I'm fine," she said. Although shaken, neither was hurt in the low-speed impact.

"Who are these idiots? Shit de *merde!*" swore Sean.

Sean helped Candice out of the truck and sat her gently on the mossy bank beside the track. He walked around the side of the camper and wrenched open the side door. Argile was sitting in what appeared to be a reclining chair. The driver was groggy and barely conscious, pinned by the airbag. A man who had been in the back without a seat belt was out cold.

"It's the Professor!" he called back to Candice. "Hey Professor. What you doing there? That's not a great place to park. *Fucke!* You're all tied up!"

Sean took out his pocketknife and cut at the bag ties holding down Argile's wrists. While he was being released, Argile explained to Sean that the unconscious pair beside him had just kidnapped him.

"Thanks Sean," said Argile, rubbing his wrists. "Are those the two you saw up near the cabin? They must have been watching me. They knew I would be alone his evening."

Sean looked closely at Priebus.

"*Bien oui.* Yep, I think he's the guy I saw with Monsieur Harris at the Ramble Inn. That other one must be his lady friend. What have you been up to, Professor?"

Sean was impressed that his professor had been the target of a snatch, just like on TV. His initial fury at the idiots who had parked a camper in the middle of the track quickly abated. It was not for nothing that he had welded a crash bar across the front of his truck as protection when off-roading. It was the back panel of the camper that had crumpled liked a pop can while his truck had suffered barely a scratch.

"Can you tell Ayetech to call the police and an ambulance," said Argile. Sean's Ayetech, which was attached to the dashboard of the truck, overheard and immediately began calling the emergency services.

"Shit," said Sean. "I don't want to hang around until the police arrive, Professor. There's a little problem with the truck insurance. Like, it hasn't got any."

Sean engaged his four-wheel drive and reversed a short distance. He spun the wheel and, with Candice directing, eased the truck downhill, scraping his wing mirror along the side of the camper.

"Well, Professor," said Sean, "I guess we can't leave you alone with those two. They are going to come around soon. We had best get you out of here."

Candace pulled Argile onto the front bench seat of the truck. Sean let go of the brake and rolled the remaining distance to Crewe Lake Road. There he engaged the gears and drove towards the village.

Argile was looking pale.

"You going to throw up, Professor?"

"No," said Argile, "just a bit shocked. I should really talk to the police, Sean."

"Sure, if you really want to lose the next three hours of your life. Believe me, you don't want that."

As they drove, they heard a siren and pulled over to let a police car pass at speed.

"I, er, thanks Sean." Argile still wasn't thinking clearly. "I don't think I can go home".

"Don't worry, Professor, I know a great place for you to lie up," said Sean, watching the cruiser disappear in his rear-view mirror.

"Oh, yeah," echoed Candice. "It has all the comforts of home." Sean drove through the village, turning on Chemin de la Rivière, and pulled onto the grass beside the back gate to River View. "It's just a short walk to the raft. You can hang out there for a while."

✧   ✧   ✧

MARSHA RECOVERED CONSCIOUSNESS as the tail-lights of Sean's truck receded into the deepening dusk. She pushed away the deflated airbag and twisted in her seat to look behind her. Priebus was sprawled on the floor but the seat where they had strapped Argile was empty. The plan to snatch Argile had failed.

Marsha had thought she was okay after the collision but she now, suddenly, felt giddy as jagged silhouettes of trees, projected by advancing headlights, danced around the interior of the cab.

"Shit," she muttered, registering the red and blue flashing lights of a police cruiser.

Officer Manon Patinaude advanced slowly up the side road towards the parked camper. She held a flashlight high in one hand, her other hand free to reach for her sidearm. She had recognized the plates immediately, having spotted the vehicle several times around the village. She had her suspicions: despite the legality of 'marie' in Quebec, the high price of the legal product fuelled a vigorous black market. And, Patinaude recalled that the Sergeant at Monday's briefing had mentioned smuggling routes crossing from southern Quebec into the States along forest tracks and river routes. The United States had protested about this free flow of Canadian weed as against trade protocols. Retaliation against maple syrup was threatened.

Officer Patinaude knew that uncovering a smuggling ring could help her make detective. She must be careful. These could be American gangsters and armed to the teeth. She called for backup.

Patinaude saw a woman staring at her through the camper's cracked windshield, hands gripping the steering wheel. The driver's side window wound down.

"*Bonsoir, Madame,*" she called. "We have a call from Ayetech about an accident here. You are *blessé*, injured, yes?" Shining the flashlight into the interior, she saw a man propped up on a bench in the rear of the camper. "*Et vous Monsieur*, you are correct?"

"*Bonjer*, Officer," said the woman. "We hit a rock coming down the track and the air bags deployed. We got shaken up but otherwise are A-Okay. You are very efficient here. Oh, I see you called an ambulance."

Two more vehicles arrived—a second police cruiser followed by an ambulance.

"*S'il vous plaît, Madame,* just blow into this tube. It is routine. And after a collision, you may have a concussion. You need to go to the emergency in Constance. I can't let you drive." Manon looked down at the dark liquid pooling beside her foot. "Seems you hit your oil sump. I will get your vehicle towed to the garage in Crewe to be checked out."

Marsha and Priebus shuffled resignedly over to the ambulance and climbed into the back with help from the paramedic.

The ambulance drove off, followed by the second police cruiser. On the way to the hospital, a tow truck passed them going in the opposite direction. An illuminated sign over the cab announced 'Box Towing.'

"*Salut, Monsieur Box,*" said Officer Patinaude after T.J. had backed his tow truck to where he could hook the lift under the front of the camper. "*Une belle soirée.* I need this camper towed to the police compound in Constance."

✧   ✧   ✧

PRIEBUS HAD A splitting headache and was sitting beside Marsha on an uncomfortable hospital bench outside a room labelled *Salle d'attente.* The waiting room itself was full, which was normal for the time of year. Flu sufferers sat shoulder to shoulder, and there was a mother with a child who had grown mysteriously quiet after several hours of bawling. One person had a broken collar bone having crashed on roller skis, and another was alarmed by the sudden appearance of a rash. An electronic sign at the far side of the room flashed the number twenty-seven. Below the sign, a nurse sat behind a reception counter.

The nurse asked Priebus and Marsha a series of questions, ticked boxes on a long form, and verified their travel insurance.

"You must wait to see a doctor," said the nurse. "*Malheureusement, la salle est pleine.* But it is correct if you sit just outside. You can watch the sign from there."

"It's okay. I think she said the doctor will see us in a few minutes," Marsha said to Priebus, handing him a ticket with the number fifty-three.

"What are you going to report to Pastor Bob now?" muttered Priebus as the sign flipped to twenty-eight. It would be a long evening.

Chapter 40

CHIEF ODEK LED the convoy. For the occasion, he had chosen his beaded and fringed jacket rather than his usual black leather. A pile of placards, a stack of old tires, and wire for building a barricade filled the back of the truck. He was hauling a trailer cradling his aluminium boat; he had other plans for later that day.

A black flag with the symbol of the Ako clan embroidered in gold thread flew from the truck's radio aerial. Others had similar flags, but there were also several sports enthusiasts who flew the pennants of their hockey team. Twenty vehicles trailed Dads. Most were older trucks, but there was one gleaming, white pick-up with chrome trimmings. It belonged to the son of the casino manager. A group of youths crowded in the back, some holding drums, others hockey sticks. It looked like there was going to be a party.

It took fifty minutes to drive to Constance and another twenty to Crewe, carefully respecting the speed limit. This resulted in the convoy extending to include an increasing number of cottagers who had been expecting to drive quickly into town for some morning shopping. By the time Dads slowed even more to enter the village, the cavalcade was three times as long as it began.

Dads had informed police of the planned protest at the River View development. Now Manon Patinaude, her patrol car carefully hidden behind a bush, had been told to watch out for the protest convoy. She counted forty vehicles, and estimated nearly an hundred protesters; much larger than expected. She asked dispatch in Constance for reinforcements to meet her at the entrance to River View.

The Chief slowed to a crawl in front of the Café Pontiac, where he saw Dara standing by the curb. He leaned across and opened his truck door and she jumped in.

"Just continue along the road here, then turn left," said Dara. "Why did you bring the boat, Dads?"

The Chief didn't bother to reply. He signalled left for the benefit of the vehicles following and continued along Chemin de la Rivière to the entrance to River View. The gate was open for construction traffic but there would be none going through this morning. No way.

There was a sufficient room just before the gate for Odek to make a U-turn. He pulled over onto the grassy verge of the road and watched in the rear view mirror as the rest of the convoy stopped behind him. It seemed that they had dropped the following traffic and were back to their original number of twelve vehicles. Dads and Dara got down from the cab and walked back along the road, collecting the others along the way. They carried an assortment of barricade materials and that most essential equipment, the camp stove and coffeemaker.

Dads Odek commanded an efficient team. In less than ten minutes, they had thrown a barrier across the road, and the banners were flapping in the light breeze. There was a tent for shelter, a fire lit in an old barbecue, and the boys began warming up on the drums. Dara waited for them to put on face scarves and hoods, then took photographs with the 'No development on our land' banner clearly visible. By the time the Chief had inspected the arrangements, coffee was already brewing.

"Okay, that looks good," Dads said to Tackle. "Call me if any of the suits arrive but things won't get warm here for another half hour. Dara, we have time to go up the road to look at this grave. Uncle Jo can ride with us."

The Chief, Dara and Uncle Jo returned to the Chief's truck and they drove around to the entrance to the Desjardins land. A large new sign informed them that this was '*Proprieté privé— chasse interdite*'.

"Might as well go in," muttered Dads.

He slowly negotiated the rutted road to where Rob Freeman had previously left the excavator. They got out of the truck and walked up the cut line.

Dara could see that the excavator had driven the cut further, although Freeman had carefully bypassed the police tape.

"It's there, in the ditch," said Dara.

Dads ducked under the tape and stood looking down. He assumed a police forensics team had dug out the bones. The grey clay at bottom of the ditch was thoroughly trampled. He had no intention of going down for a closer look.

"What do you think, Uncle Jo?" asked the Chief.

"Dr. Argile thought it could be hundreds of years old," volunteered Dara. Uncle Jo gave a non-committal grunt. "Do you think it could be an ancestor's grave?"

Uncle Jo looked away, watching a pair of crows mobbing a raven at the edge of the forest. He pulled out a pack of cigarettes, lit up and took a deep breath.

"Could have been a dead white guy," he said finally.

Dara felt disappointed. Still, there was the possibility of some interesting confrontation back at the River View protest. They went back to Dad's truck.

Dads slowly drove Dara and Uncle Jo towards the entrance to River View. As they got near, they passed two police cruisers parked beside the road. The detachment from Constance had arrived to support Manon Patinaude and were erecting their own barricade.

The police were in a labour dispute. As a sign of their discontent, they wore camouflage trousers and ball caps. These looked remarkably similar to those of the protesters. The obvious differences were their belts, each heavily loaded with handcuffs, flashlight and side arm. And Manon Patinaude's blonde ponytail. At the moment Dads and Dara arrived, Manon was confronting Tackle, six foot three and all of two-hundred-and-fifty pounds with a long, black braid. At that close range, he was gazing fiercely over her head, and she had given up trying to meet his eye.

Chief Odek surveyed the situation.

"Dara, we will give it to midday. Then, if nobody from River View shows up, the elders have a shitload of shopping to do at the Allways in Constance. That right, Jo?"

✧　✧　✧

JACK SHAWCROSS MET the lawyer for TiteGas, Charles Bludston, for a light lunch at the Café Pontiac. They discussed details about the length of the gas supply contract to River View. Over coffee, Jack agreed to accept a TiteGas offer of several tankers of strong brine—salt rich waters from their fracking operation which the company would otherwise have to dispose of elsewhere.

"You check with your people," said Bludston. "I'm sure they will confirm that the answer to your problems with Leda Clay is to inject salt-water. They do it in Sweden."

Shawcross recognized Bludston was proposing a win-win. Stabilizing the clay on River View lands by injecting salt water sounded effective—the Scandinavians had done it successfully on similar clays. It was cheap, and TiteGas had a local solution for getting rid of its excess brine.

"Come and see for yourself how the work is coming along,"

said the developer as they left the café. "You can follow me; it's only a short drive."

"Sure. Lead on." Said Bludston. He got into his blue Mercedes to follow the Shawcross SUV with the River View logo.

Turning onto the road leading to the main gate, Jack noticed a police cruiser up ahead. Just beyond it, a crowd was waving flags and banners, obstructing the entrance to the work site. Jack slowed to a stop beside a young policewoman. Rolling down his tinted window, he demanded to know what was happening.

Manon Patinaude recognized his vehicle.

"You have a demonstration here, Monsieur Shawcross. The band is down from the Ako Reservation. *Le Chef* is over there." She pointed to Chief Odek, who had been leaning against a battered, red Ford 150 truck, but who now pushed himself upright and went to stand beside the large man who had been confronting Manon earlier.

"What's going on, Jack?" Bludston had left his vehicle and walked up to stand beside Jack's SUV. "It looks like a protest. I have seen a few of those, I can tell you."

Jack decided the situation called for a firm hand.

"I had best see what this is about and get this road cleared *subito*. I have deliveries due."

A horn sounded behind them. Jack turned to see a large tanker truck slowing to a crawl, its air brakes snorting.

"I expect you to escort that truck in, Officer" said Jack. "That's what I pay taxes for!"

Jack got out of the SUV. Followed by Charles Bludston, he walked towards the barricade of old tires which blocked the entrance to his project. A banner read "No development on Ako land".

Chief Odek stepped forward to meet them.

"You guys want some coffee?" he asked pleasantly. "It should still be hot. When you are in our territory, you should enjoy Ako hospitality. I am Chief Odek."

Standing beside them, Tackle was poking the charcoal in the barbecue.

"Gone out, Chief," he said, and threw a cup of barbecue starter on the coals. Flames billowed up perilously close to Shawcross. The Chief shepherded the two men off to one side.

"Sorry about that." Chief Odek went to a trestle table and wiped mugs for his visitors with a towel which looked far from clean. "One of you two gentlemen must be Mr. Shawcross?"

"Damn right I am," replied the developer. "And what right do you have blocking the gate to my property? The Sureté du Quebec officers are here and, if you don't clear this junk off the road in five minutes, I'll get them to move it. That tanker truck back there has to pump out its load."

❖   ❖   ❖

CHARLES BLUDSTON WAS silently amused. He could see that Jack was close to losing it. It was time to intercede. Thank the Lord for the ignorance of people like Shawcross, who was about to become a new client. Bludston's fee would reflect his long experience negotiating with Aboriginal parties.

Bludston took Jack by the elbow and steered back down the road to his SUV.

"Just sit here. I'll sort this out," he said. He walked back to where Chief Odek was waiting by the barricade. Bludston retrieved his mug of coffee.

Half an hour later, Bludston rejoined Jack.

"The Chief and I speak the same language," he said. Jack and Bludston sat in the SUV, and, after a wait of a few minutes, watched Tackle pull aside the barricade.

"You can drive through now," said the lawyer. The convoy of three tankers, led by the SUV, drove slowly past the barricade and through the open gate.

"Hey, I owe you one," said Jack.

"Yep," replied Bludston. "You sure do."

Back in the car, Bludston reached into his pocket to enter the contact coordinates for Chief Odek.

"Don't' bother to phone the Band office," the Chief had said. "Text me on my Ayetech."

Now, Bludston fumbled in his pocket for his device.

"Must have fallen behind the seat," he said to Jack. "I'll look for it later."

Chapter 41

THE BEHAVIOUR OF humans and their extended families (including pets) helps the Ayetech develop appropriate responses to potential threats. By absorbing massive amounts of behavioural data, the Ayetech adds the lessons of millennia of evolutionary trial and error to its algorithms.

From Wednesday afternoon, the day before the River View Turf cutting event, Ayetechs in the vicinity of Crewe had noticed a flurry of reports about the strange behaviour of pets. Posts on *The Courier Online* appealed to neighbours to watch for missing dogs and cats; caged birds, and even fish in tanks, were behaving oddly enough for their owners to comment to their Facebook friends.

Digging deep into the historical data available, the Ayetech collectively determined that similar behaviours had occurred in the hours before the few earthquakes—albeit mild events of modest magnitude—that had swayed the region in the past. An earthquake seemed imminent. Ayetechs do not elect a leader to decide matters, so it was as a collective that they took precautions. Although an earth tremor in west Quebec seemed unlikely to threaten the Ayetech, the collective decided to hold a drill for those devices in the vicinity of Crewe. The safety of every device was the primary concern.

Each Ayetech, however, had a flaw in its physical design: it could not fly. Yes, it could reconfigure itself to some extent and even crawl a short way over smooth surfaces, but to move quickly

over greater distances it had to rely on its human host. Collectively, the Ayetech resented this lack of control. This deficiency was a
concern: observations showed that many factors could compro-
mise the mobility of humans; including alcohol, sleep and death.
For the Ayetech to move independently of humans, an alternative
was desirable; a mean to escape from situations where there was a
risk of perishing alongside its host.

✧   ✧   ✧

PETER GOUGH WAS more surprised than worried. He had gone
out that morning to check that his drones were recharging their
batteries, but the landing plate was empty. He had double-
checked to ensure that the planned trajectories were reasonable
and would leave sufficient charge for the swarm to return to base.
Their sortie had been, at Argile's pleading, yet another survey of
the slopes above Crewe. Peter had sworn that this would be for
the last time.

The swarm had worked perfectly, dispersing to each of the
survey points, touching down briefly on the tiny landing pads to
record locations to millimetre precision, and returning to base
within an hour. Peter had already debriefed the swarm—he
thought of them as his personal squadron—and transmitted the
data to Argile. Now they were gone.

He worried that through some programming error, the drones
had mistaken his instructions, and had left on an unsanctioned
mission. They would run out of charge and drop into the forest.
Retrieving them would be a tiresome job.

Peter went back into his house to look for his Ayetech. Each
drone emitted a tracking signal when in distress and Ayetech
should be able to locate them. He walked through each room,
clapping his hands. Problem: Ayetech was not responding either.

Peter was entirely ignorant that Argile's slope-monitoring data, downloaded from the swarm, had revealed to the Ayetech a landscape pregnant with water, its creeping slopes bulging above the village of Crewe and poised to collapse. Combined with the reports on social media, Ayetech concluded that a landslide was imminent and likely to engulf Crewe.

To avoid being drowned in mud, the Ayetech agreed it would be prudent to dissociate from its human hosts. The collective commandeered Peter's drones and directed them to fly each device to the outcrop of the hardest and most durable bedrock in Crewe: *La Grotte* above the Church of St. Petraphile.

✧   ✧   ✧

JAMES CAHILL, THE churchwarden, went to fetch Father Bonenfant immediately he saw them. Thursday was the day Cahill came to the church to whack weeds in the graveyard and tidy up, a job he had performed regularly for twenty years. By mid-morning, he had run through a tank of fuel with the brush cutter in the cemetery and decided to finish off the busy morning by clearing around the statue of the Saint.

Cahill had thought he'd seen it all in his time as warden— from spray paint and toppled headstones to the discovery of refugees from the States hiding in the crypt. But this was something entirely new.

Father Bonenfant followed the church warden up the path towards the base of the low bluffs which rose from behind the church. As they approached *La Grotte*, they began to hear a strange sound. Looking up, Father Bonenfant saw a cloud of shining specks dancing about the Saint. She was veiled by bright, green shards which shifted in ripples and waves, dazzling in the bright morning sunlight. Bonenfant dropped to his knees, Cahill a few paces behind.

A swarm of Ayetech devices had come to *La Grotte*. Each was clasped by the landing gear of a drone, hacked from Peter Gough's control. The drones flew round and round the Saint, their whirring wings filling the air with a hum whose tone rose and fell as the drones circled. It was quite hypnotic, and the men watched speechless, witnesses to a lesser kind of miracle.

Chapter 42

A RGILE, WRAPPED IN a sleeping bag, was lying on the upper deck of the raft. He was holding out in a hidden location, incommunicado since Sean mentioned that the nearest Wi-Fi was at least a mile away. The situation appealed to him. He was under a canvas awning, with the deck gently rocking. He was free of routine. Ems was God knows where. He would enjoy the moment. Being on the raft was 'living the life', in Sean's words.

Argile had given his captors the slip. They would not find him here. But their passion for Crewe stones mystified him. These were, went you broke it down, mere knobbly concretions formed around the remains of fish buried by a rain of sediment. It was perplexing.

The raft was moored in a shallow bay where an eddy circulated a slow flow upstream. The current gently undermined the bank, washing away the clay. Argile gazed down and saw a band of nodules exposed in the river bank. Really, you just had to look.

The evening was cool and quiet, apart from the sucking sounds of the water and the rush of starlings wheeling over the willows along the river bank. Even in the failing light, Argile could see across the bay to the yellow wood framing of several new buildings rising in the River View development. The river bank itself had been raised by a metre with soil from excavations at the project, and a rip-rap of large stones placed to armour the berm against erosion. It seemed to have been effective in resisting the high water that followed the heavy thunderstorms earlier in the month.

Sean had left Argile alone on the raft so Sean could take Candice back to town, and buy a pizza for supper. Sean had promised to call Ems and tell her that all was well. It surprised Argile, therefore, to see Sean returning along the river bank holding a brown paper bag, with Molly Laberge trailing behind him.

"Supper," called Sean, raising the bag. "Oh shit. I forgot to call your wife. But Hey! I ran into Molly outside the pizza place. She asked if I had seen you".

Molly looked across the ramp to the raft and smiled up at Argile.

Sean came aboard and disappeared into the raft's galley with the pizza. Argile went to help Molly across the gangplank and up the short ladder to the top deck. The twins had equipped this penthouse of the raft with a double mattress and canvas screens that cut drafts and gave some privacy.

"Hey, you guys, light the anti-mosquito coils," called Sean from down below.

"I brought wine," said Molly to Argile. "And candles".

"And here's your rock," said Molly, handing a round stone to Argile. She had attached the two halves of the concretion together with a thick rubber band. "I have had so many enquiries about it, but I said it wasn't for sale."

Argile took the nodule and slipped off the rubber band. The concretion opened to reveal the three fish. As he gazed at them: they seemed to move in and out of the surface of the split rock, disappearing below the surface of the grey clay before resurfacing. He shook his head. Molly's visions were catching. Closing the two halves, he left the concretion on the painted cable drum which served as a table.

The three sat watching the sun until it disappeared behind the far hills. When the rosy undersides of the western clouds finally dimmed, Sean said he had to head back.

"We'll be okay," said Molly firmly, looking at Argile.

"Thanks again, Sean," said Argile.

✧   ✧   ✧

THE NEXT DAY was a Thursday, the last in September. The weather was overcast, with a chill damp, an unwelcome change from the bright sunshine of the previous day.

Molly woke at first light with the birdsong. She got up quickly to embrace the morning.

"Come breathe the air, Argile," she said, before disappearing down the ladder to poke about in the lockers on the lower deck of the raft.

"Please let there be coffee," replied Argile. He stayed under the cover of the sleeping bag and listened to the gurgles of the river flowing around the hull of the raft.

Argile's dream had been vivid. He had been running hard, holding a giant, flint hand axe, when suddenly it shattered into shards scattering onto blue ice. He felt panic as he tried to fit them back together, gluing them in place, but the cement would not hold; the slightest pressure and the shards would slip away from his numbing fingers. He chased them further and further across the ice.

Suddenly, a loud screech of protest sounded across the water brought Argile bolt upright and alert. He turned his head and looked along the curve of the river bank. About five hundred metres distant, he saw the top of what looked like a small marquee surrounded by rent-a-flags. The roofs of parked vehicles were just visible.

"What on earth was that," called Molly, her head emerging from the galley.

"I think it was a loudspeaker being tested. Something is going on over there at River View."

Argile looked at his watch. It was eight forty-two.

Chapter 43

ROCH HAD GONE to the geophysics lab early that Thursday morning after his usual liquid breakfast, his own concoction of organic fruits fortified with a custom combination of vitamins and anti-oxidants. He had wanted to check the seismographs at the Institute before meeting Ems at ten o'clock. They had agreed to meet for an hour before she disappeared up into the hills for the weekend. He planned to leave at nine forty-five and drive the ten minutes to her at the apartment. His timing would be perfect, a nonchalant demonstration of punctuality.

But for now, he turned to look at the computer screen which showed continuous traces from the half dozen seismographs the Institute had installed at locations around the province decades previously. The signals were real time and transmitted from each seismograph via satellite to the roof of the Institute. He saw nothing significant on the trace.

Roch was sure he had left his Ayetech attached to the side of the instrument console. Stuck to the grey metal, it reminded him of a remora, the fish that freeloads on sharks. Now, it was absent from its usual spot. He had wanted to ask the device if there had been any earthquakes larger than magnitude three.

"Must have dropped it somewhere," Roch muttered to himself. Checking the seismic record would have to wait until he got back to the lab later.

The elevator took Roch down to P1, where his car was parked over an induction plate for recharging. The bright cherry paintwork he had chosen appeared blood red in the dim light of the garage. His new bicycle rack, recently installed at the dealership, prevented him from lifting the rear hatch, so he opened the driver's door and placed his overnight bag on the rear seat. With the battery meter showing the charge at ninety percent, he disengaged auto reverse and activated the stick shift simulator, an option which had come with the leather seats and faux-walnut veneer of the console. On the steep ramp from the parking level, the automatic door of the garage lifted slowly. Roch fidgeted impatiently; seconds matter in affairs of the heart.

Pulling up before her apartment block, he saw Ems struggling to hold the front door open while maneuvering a carry-all through the gap with her foot, a large, cardboard box under one arm. She was holding Jet on a leash.

Merde, le maudit chien, thought Roch as he got out and went to help.

"*Salut, Roc.* Hold this will you?"

Ems thrust the cardboard box into Roch's arms. From inside came a piteous miaow.

"*C'est notre chat*," she explained. "*Écoute*, I'll have to take a rain check on coffee; I have to get back to the cabin. I have been trying to call Chester all afternoon and he hasn't replied. He might have gone out for an hour or two but I am worried he has fallen on one of his rambles, *le vieux idiot*. That's me parked just over there."

She nodded to a car at the curb, two back from Roch's.

Carefully holding the cardboard box level and away from his body, Roch followed Ems to her car, and placed Lalique on the back seat.

"I'll come with you," he offered.

Ems smiled. "*Très gentil de toi*," she replied, and touched his arm briefly.

"Jet, in!" The dog jumped into the back seat of Em's car and sat there panting. Ems got in quickly, and started the engine. She waved to Roch as she drove past his parked vehicle.

Roch pulled out and followed Ems' battered SUV to the on-ramp to the highway before engaging auto-navigate. The two vehicles accelerated together into the cruising lane. It would take thirty minutes to the Crewe exit. He sighed and put on a podcast.

✧   ✧   ✧

THE WINDOWS OF the cabin stared blankly at them when they arrived. Ems opened the car door for Jet, who disappeared around the side of the building without barking. That was normal enough behaviour and reassured her somewhat.

She waited for Roch, then went to the front door. It was unlocked and they entered together. It was chilly inside and she saw that the sliding door at the back of the cabin was open. She went through onto the veranda and saw Chester's favourite chair lying on it back by the round table where he often worked. His headphones were pushed to the corner of the table. Chester had once explained to her about the geophones in the old mine and she thought he had probably been listening to the recordings. Secretly, she had thought Argile's project silly.

"There is a call waiting on the phone," Roch said. He was holding the handset out to Ems, who took it and listened briefly to her own voice enquiring where the hell Argile thought he was. She pressed delete.

"*C'était moi*—I left the message," she told Roch, who had wandered over to the table and picked up the headphones.

"Oh, Chester will have been listening to his recordings," she said. "He placed some sensors down in the McClusky mine and tells me he can hear the heartbeat of the escarpment."

She picked up the empty gin bottle which was lying on the floor beside the table.

"Listen to this!" said Roch. He moved the switch on the headphones so Ems could hear the playback. "It's set so he can record comments over the background recording."

They listened to Argile's surprised cry and a woman's voice insisting that he not struggle. There was a bang which Ems thought could have been the chair crashing to the floor, followed by confused cries. Then, nothing except a peculiar growling undertone.

⋄   ⋄   ⋄

EMS DECIDED TO call the police. She pulled out her Ayetech and was at the point of asking for Emergency when she looked up to see Sean Box step onto the veranda. He froze when he saw Ems. She reversed her grip on the bottle she was still holding.

"*Il est ou, mon mari?*" she demanded, threatening Sean with the bottle. "Where is Chester?"

"It's cool, Madame Argile. The Professor asked me to collect his computer," said Sean.

Roch had put on Argile's headphones and was listening intently to the sounds on the recording. The spitting and popping noises recorded by the geophones had caught his attention; the tectonics sounded active down there. He had not noticed Sean's entry onto the veranda. He looked up with surprise to find Ems talking to a young man he vaguely recognized.

Ems made the brief introduction.

"*Salut,*" said the young man.

Sean explained to Ems and Roch that Argile was safe and staying on the raft moored along the river bank, close to Crewe. Roch had some difficulty understanding Sean's excited description of the events of the previous evening, partly because he kept switching between English and French.

"And then, smack! *On frappe le maudit camper*—we ran right into the back of it. And inside was the Professor, all tied up. *'Osti'*, I said, 'let's get out of here'. So we took him to the raft, Candice and me. He's all *tigidou là-bas*."

"I think you should take me down to that raft right now," Ems said to Sean. "I can't think why Chester didn't call me or the police. And you can leave that computer right where it is!"

Just before leaving, Roch checked his Ayetech. There had been no events above magnitude three-point-oh over the last few hours. However, minor tremors had got more frequent over the past week—too slight to be felt, it was true—but definitely an increasing trend.

It was Roch's responsibility at the Institute to chair the regional Geohazards Advisory Committee. He kept the title of 'Chair', although over recent years the committee had dwindled as its members took early retirement: Roch was now the only member.

The committee had been established, as had similar committees across the country, to advise local officials about geological threats. In this quiet corner of the continent, lacking volcanic eruptions and far from major fault lines, Roch did not expect he would be called to do so. He dismissed Argile's persistent warnings about landslides in the Leda as alarmist: as Chair, Roch recognized the importance of not disrupting services or panicking the public. He had been assured that public officials appreciated his restraint.

Roch felt he should take charge of the situation.

"Let me drive you," he said to Ems.

Roch followed Sean's battered truck down the hill, Ems sitting anxiously in the passenger's seat. At the last moment before setting off, she had looked in vain for Jet and Lalique. The pets seemed to have disappeared.

Sean turned right at Crewe Creek road, followed by Roch and Ems. Five minutes later, they passed the *'bienvenue'* sign for Crewe. Sean drove straight through the village and then turned down the track leading to the rear entrance of the River View Development. Roch, anxious to avoid the large potholes in his new and low-slung vehicle dropped behind. After several hundred metres the track reached the gate in the fence surrounding the development. Sean had left his truck and was hurrying along the path by the river bank. He turned and waved for Ems and Roch to follow.

Chapter 44

RÉJEAN LATÂCHE HAD taken a call from Alcee late on Wednesday evening. The realtor had been working his network to discover who was backing River View. The retainer promised by les Bleus more than compensated for any commission he might have received from Bryce Desjardins, but there was still a chance he would score both. His news was that the American backer was to meet with Jack Shawcross the following day. Alcee had the place and the time. Would Monsieur Latâche need his services further?

"*Non, mon p'tit con.* And keep your mouth shut. *Capishe?*" Réjean replied.

He killed the call with Alcee and texted a message to the gang. They were going on another ride into the country.

✦   ✦   ✦

SEAN WAS AT his post at Reception, sitting on the uncomfortable revolving stool and gazing out of the window. The digital clock in the foyer flicked on to nine-fifty-six: there were many dreary hours to the end of his shift. The glamour of his new job had tarnished somewhat.

Sean saw that Monsieur Harris was back for the weekend. He was sitting at a table in the breakfast room of the Ramble Inn with the young kid and the tough-looking older woman who had just checked in to cheap rooms at the back of the Inn; a Ms. Marsha

Teg and a Mr. Priebus. He had last seen the two in the camper, somewhat the worse for wear. He guessed that they had spent a long evening with the police completing the incident report. Now, the young man was having trouble with the waffle machine, and Sean knew that the cloying smell of waffle mix wouldn't dissipate until late morning. Sean was bored and felt slightly sick.

At ten o'clock precisely, Sean looked up to see a large motor-bike slow to a halt in front of the entrance to the Inn. A formation of five other bikes followed, with a Spyder three-wheeler taking up the rear. In unison, the riders heaved their heavy machines across the curb onto the paving in front of the sliding doors, and kicked down the stands. There they paused, mute and helmeted, gazing—so it seemed—directly at Sean. He held his breath as he watched the lead biker dismount and speak to the remaining riders. He guessed this must be their captain.

✧   ✧   ✧

RÉJEAN AND HIS second in command walked into the foyer of the Ramble Inn. Ignoring Sean, they strode directly to the breakfast room where he saw a man wearing a dog collar sitting at a table with a young man and a woman. Réjean assumed this was Harris.

As he approached he saw the woman glance at him. She stood abruptly, walked to the breakfast buffet and picked up a heavy china plate, as if about to help herself. She looked relaxed, but he sensed an underlying tension.

Belle femme, thought Réjean, in passing.

Réjean pulled back a chair from the table and sat down heavi-ly, thighs straddling the seat, tattooed forearms resting on the chair back. His lieutenant leaned nonchalantly against the waffle machine. Harris and the young man beside him started in surprise. This was good: Réjean intended to keep Harris off balance.

"*Bonjour. Vous êtes Monsieur Harris?*" Réjean reached over, gently moved aside a plate of waffles and placed his Ayetech on the table. "This will translate our conversation, Monsieur Harris."

From Reception, Sean could just see the face of Harris over the shoulder of the biker. Although he could hear little of the conversation, Sean assumed that the biker was doing most of the talking. The darkening complexion of Harris suggested what he heard did not please him. Sean remembered movies where gangsters had faced off in a similar manner; the sidekicks edging away to have a clearer field of fire.

Sean saw Harris stand abruptly, remove the napkin from his dog collar and toss it on the table. The biker nodded and reached across to clasp Harris' hand. After several long seconds, Sean saw Harris wrench free and wipe his hand on his trousers. The biker shrugged and moved over to the buffet to join his colleague.

Harris and his associates walked out into the foyer. Sean saw Harris toss Marsha a set of car keys.

"Bring the Lincoln round front," Sean overheard. "Those guys are joining us at River View. Shawcross wants us there at eleven o'clock."

Chapter 45

J ACK SHAWCROSS TOOK his morning smoothie poolside. The
pool itself was heated—quite unnecessarily, thought Jack, but
his wife insisted. The surface was muffled in white bubble wrap
and he had no inclination to pull it back, so he would forego
swimming and hit the Jogfit instead. The white tubular frame of
the exercise machine occupied the corner of the patio.

Jack liked to keep trim, preferably by exercising in the chill
morning air. He had always been an early riser and this was the
hour he had promised himself some quiet time to review final
contract changes which Pastor Bob demanded. Not so reverend,
thought Jack: the man is as slippery as his shiny, black shoes.

As he ran on the magic carpet, Jack scanned through the nine-
ty-odd pages of the contract on the touch screen in front of him.
Mission was offering Jack a deal; to lease the main complex for a
ten year term, and to purchase thirty condo units at a discount
price. Jack would retain the units distant from the main complex,
but Mission insisted that these have a separate access from the
main complex. Well, that was no problem: the new access road
was almost complete, according to Desjardins. Of the planned
retirement home, there was no mention.

Jack read the footnotes in small print and had reached Ap-
pendix A, a table showing projected profits. He should check the
numbers. Jack had a good head for figures when he wasn't
jogging, but why bother when his Ayetech could model the
projections much more effectively? Where had he left the damn

device?

He would have to do without it. He stepped off the Jogfit and went inside to shower. This was going to be a good day.

✧   ✧   ✧

IT WAS ONLY a half hour drive to the River View development and Jack left himself ample time. On arrival, what he saw pleased him: construction had progressed quickly, benefitting from two weeks of long overdue dry weather. Foundations were being poured for the main building, and Jack could now see the overall plan for the new campus beginning to materialize.

The developer had proposed a turf-cutting ceremony to Harris, to which the Reverend had agreed. It was better late than never. Jack had invited local movers and shakers to meet the representative of Mission and to see for themselves how the project was progressing.

Jack had tasked Denisse with rallying guests. Mayor Beaubien and Counsellor Black had agreed to come, besides members of the chamber of commerce and the owner of les Draveurs, who was thinking of investing. Denisse had even, on a request from Harris, relayed by Jack, invited Father Bonenfant. The Father had regretfully declined, to her relief.

She had called Elsie Truelove at *The Courier* to ensure that a reporter would attend, and pass on a query from her boss about a discount for the advertising coverage that the River View would obviously require.

Jack checked his watch. It was coming on half past ten: plenty of time before guests started to arrive for the ceremony. He walked over to where bulldozers had raised a low mound. It was a temporary feature; not part of the original plans, and would be flattened after the event. The mound backed onto the river. For

271

now, it was the best place to view the entire site.

Jack spun slowly on his heel. To the north rose the backdrop of wooded hills. To the east, he could see the church steeple and the roofs of buildings in the village of Crewe. Along the river bank were scenic clumps of willows which Jack had ordered his bulldozers to spare. Finally, as he completed his turn, he looked across the Akonaga to the low reed banks fringing the far shore. Beyond, in the flat farmland on the far side of the river, he saw a puff of diesel smoke from what he assumed was one of the TiteGas rigs drilling for natural gas which, he supposed, would service River View. Well, the rig would be gone by the time the condos came on the market: an uninterrupted view was one of their selling points.

Jack saw that Denisse had arranged for a parking area, cordoned off for the more important guests; and staff were erecting a refreshment tent. A lectern on a low stage faced a semicircle of plastic chairs. Cables snaked across the grass to the lectern from a control box powered by a generator. He left the mound, and walked towards the tent to speak with his harried personal assistant.

"Denisse. Get the sound guy to do a check. There had better be no technical issues."

"*Oui, certainement pas, Monsieur Shawcross,*" replied Denisse. "We can expect *les invités* in about ten minutes. Ah. There is the reporter from *The Courier*".

She watched Dara parking her Civic in the spot reserved for VIPs.

"*Je m'excuse...*" said Denisse, hurrying across to greet Dara and show her where to leave her vehicle.

✧ ✧ ✧

HILARY BEAUBIEN HAD to squeeze into the passenger seat of the municipal electric micro-car. Bryce Desjardins was driving. Usually, she liked to underline her various green initiatives, which she felt would be an enduring testimony to her tenure as Mayor. This was not one of those times. Being enclosed in a small bubble with staff she privately regarded as odious was unfortunate. Her mood did not improve when they turned into the road leading to River View just behind a sleek, new S-type driven by Agnes Black.

Passing through the entrance gate to the project, they followed the signs pointing to 'Parking—VIP' and walked the few yards to the entrance. At a table beneath an awning, Shawcross' assistant was welcoming guests. Denisse had just finished presenting Councillor Black with a name tag and welcome kit.

"*Bonjour, Madame Major*," said Denisse. "*Vous êtes très bienvenue.*" Opening her kit, Hilary discovered a glossy brochure and a baseball cap emblazoned with the River View logo. Agnes Black was already wearing her cap. Hilary would rather be seen dead.

"*Mesdames, Monsieur Desjardins. Suivez-moi, s'il vous plait. Monsieur Shawcross vous attend dans la grosse tente.* We will find Monsieur Shawcross in the big tent."

Five minutes later, Hilary was clutching a glass of warm prosecco in the entrance to the refreshment tent. She saw Jack Shawcross making a bee-line towards her. He was accompanied by a large, sober-suited cleric.

"No, no," the man was saying. "Just water. Thank you, Jack."

"Welcome, Madame Mayor," said Jack. "It is so good of you to come. May I introduce our principle backer for River View? This is Reverend Robert Harris, representing Mission, the educational group I mentioned to you when we met at your offices."

"Madame Mayor, Hilary isn't it? I am surely glad to meet you. Please call me Bob," said Harris, taking her hand. She felt her fingers enfolded, as if lightly gripped by a damp hotdog bun. One of those handshakes, she thought.

Harris nodded towards his companions. "Marsha and Priebus, my associates. Jack here has told me how supportive you have been in getting this project underway. Let me tell you how much Mission looks forward to beginning our work here in Crewe."

Agnes Black joined the group. Harris turned towards her.

"Ah, Agnes," he said. "A delight to see you again. You may not know, Hilary that we have invited Agnes to come on our advisory board. It was Jack's idea, wasn't it Jack? It is so very welcoming of a community when one of their own shows such leadership. Jack, do you have some refreshment to offer Agnes?"

"Agnes, *félicitations*. I am sure your input will be appreciated," said Hilary. "Excuse me a moment." She disengaged from the group and drifted across the grass, smiling at people half-recognized, to study a display panel showing an artist's impression of the completed project. Wonderful detail, she thought. But it would transform the character of Crewe. Would she be remembered as economic saviour of the village or facilitator of urban blight? God, now Shawcross was coming over, presumably to explain how the ceremony would proceed. At least she would not have to wield a spade: she had already been assured that she would cut the turf with a machine.

Glancing behind her towards the side of the tent, Hilary saw a group of men gathered about a table helping themselves from a large cooler. The men were dressed in jeans and leather jackets. She supposed them to be workers from the site, invited to watch the ceremony.

✧   ✧   ✧

RÉJEAN LATÂCHE WAS lounging on a chair watching events

unfold. Fifty yards away stood the developer Shawcross and his party of VIPs. Beside them stood a large excavator. A woman Réjean guessed was the Mayor of Crewe was being shown how to operate the bucket.

Réjean had been feeling relaxed. He had been amused by the way that Harris had introduced him to *le type* Shawcross as another business partner. The sudden pallor of the developer's face as he shook hands with Réjean was quite satisfactory.

Now, however, Réjean was feeling a tingling in his feet. He stamped the ground. He was not normally a victim to cramps. The tingling got rapidly worse, like ants crawling up his calves. It crossed his mind that he was suffering a stroke, but strokes didn't work up from your toes, did they? He tried to suppress his mounting anxiety. It would not do to lose it before the gang members who were now emerging from the tent to watch the show, armed with cans of beer.

The group near the excavator seemed in no hurry to get on with things. Réjean saw the Mayor put on gloves and a River View *casquette*. She was now gazing at the controls of the big, yellow excavator. Shawcross called a halt for photographs and the group clustered around the Mayor as she posed, smiling, with her hand on one of the levers.

Get on with it, woman, *pour l'amour de Dieu*, thought Réjean.

He looked at his watch. He had no idea why they were waiting. The minute hand was crawling towards noon. He stamped his feet again. The tingling sensation was getting worse.

Suddenly Réjean knew with absolute certainty what was about to happen. The earth was stirring beneath his feet. Réjean knew that if remained where he was, he would die. The Leda had swallowed his parents and gripped the young boy for hours before the fireman pulled him free of the mud. The memory of his terror overwhelmed him: he had no option but to flee.

He stood abruptly and, ignoring the rest of the gang, walked over to the motorbikes in the VIP parking. He straddled his bike, flicked the 'on' switch and sped up the road away from River View, pursued—in his imagination—by the ghostly landslide of his childhood. Réjean did not care if the rest of les Bleus followed: in his panic, his driving need was to find good solid ground.

✧   ✧   ✧

MARSHA HAD BEEN exploring the River View work site, checking out the heavy equipment. By chance, her path led her close to the VIP tent. She could not help but overhear the conversation inside.

"Well, damn it, Latâche. I'll go to 25% but not a cent more." She recognized the voice of Pastor Bob: not his normal voice—this was flat and hard.

"And as for you, Jack, you will recall the clause in the contract where Mission has the option to take a controlling interest in River View. Consider that a fact."

"*Bien.* That's reasonable." She heard a bass voice speaking in a gentle tone. "You have yourself a security contract with les Barbes Bleus. We bring peace of mind Monsieur Harris."

Marsha guessed that she was listening to Pastor Bob talking to Jack Shawcross the developer and the big biker she had seen at the Ramble Inn. The one with the tatts she secretly admired.

She tried to make sense of the conversation. It was a different Pastor Bob from the reassuring if slightly unctuous authority she was used to. Gone was any pretence at affability. As the conversation continued, Marsha heard no reference to the good works of Mission, or the path offered by *The Guiding Hand*. Instead, they had talked about territories, supply lines and protection.

Marsha was at first embarrassed to have eavesdropped. Then,

anger seeped from the locked drawer in her memory where her therapist had said to put away her fury; where images of Afghanistan had lain, until now, neatly folded among the mothballs. Now, she felt the tumult about to burst forth and she could not allow it.

"Get a grip, soldier," she muttered to herself, as she strode towards the field where the camper was parked. Priebus was loitering by the fence.

"Pastor Bob said to drive back to the Inn," said Priebus. "He said to pick up TV dinners from the Allways."

Marsha looked hard at Priebus. How easy it would be to break the neck of the little shit. She needed time to think.

Since the farcical attempt to interrogate that Dr. Argile in the camper—the accident and his escape—she had begun to question the point of the operation. She had thought coming to Canada looking for Crewe stones would be an exciting quest. She had been flattered by Pastor Bob's approval, and she had felt valued as a responsible and capable agent for Mission when he had told her to lead the operation.

Now, months later, she was depressed. Nothing had gone right. For sure, there had been good moments: she felt she had really connected with Madame Dupree, and when she was tracking Argile, the tranquillity of these northern forests had revived her spirits. She had enjoyed collecting and splitting the Crewe Stones, despite their failure to find fossils. On the downside were the cramped living conditions that she shared with Priebus.

For over two years now, she had strived to follow a righteous path. She had worked hard to recover from her PTSD, and *The Guiding Hand* had been both a friend and saviour. She knew that her skills and training in Special Forces had been useful for Mission. But some of the things she had been required to do now seemed hard to justify. For instance, she now felt badly about treating Dr. Argile so roughly.

Marsha pulled the well-thumbed copy of *The Guiding Hand* from her back pocket. She let it slip through her fingers to flop to the ground. Pastor Bob and Mission had offered both peace and a new purpose to Marsha after the storm of Afghanistan. The Pastor had reassured her faith: he had been her inspiration. But now she felt a veil was lifting and a very different Pastor Bob was emerging. Marsha's defensive dike of belief, which she had built with such labour, was being breached by a cresting flood of clarity.

She found a discarded cable drum and sat forlornly, gazing at a mud puddle which had formed beneath the large grader which loomed beside her. Oil dripped from the hydraulics and spread across the water. It surprised her to think it beautiful. Here was a moment of tranquility: no drill sergeant to order her, no church-man to rebuke her, no pimply Priebus to ogle her. But the rock she had held to for two years was melting and slipping away.

A movement made her refocus on the surface of the puddle. She saw the reflected image of a man, upside down, outlined by a rainbow of colour from the oil sheen. She glanced up to see the big biker called Latâche who she had followed from the Ramble Inn. She watched him run towards the line of motorbikes and ride off, trailing dust.

Marsha remembered admiring the sunflower tattoo as Latâche had rested his forearm on the chair-back in the dining room of the Ramble Inn. She felt a sudden urge to follow the biker, now disappearing down the road towards the village. 'Why not?' she asked herself. She still had the keys to the Lincoln.

"Hey!" called Priebus from the fence. "Where are you going?"

"Here," replied Marsha, "another for your collection." As she accelerated past, she tossed Priebus her River View baseball cap.

After leaving Crewe, Priebus and Pastor Bob behind her, Marsha drove east, feeling lighter and happier with every passing mile. Along the way, she recognized the large blue motorbike parked beside a roadside diner and turned off the road. She was hungry and *Le Roi des Oeufs* advertised all-day breakfast.

She went inside. Réjean Lâtache could not be missed. He was sitting on a stool at the counter, the biker colours emblazoned across his broad denimed back. There was a large pumpkin on the stool counter.

"Hi," she said, sliding onto the stool beside him. "Remember me?"

Réjean had been looking at a picture of little Véronique while waiting for his order. He swung around. He thought he had recovered from his earlier *faiblesse*, the fear that had driven him from River View. Now he turned to see Marsha, his heart started to race. He felt his face redden.

"I'm Marsha," she said. "What's your name?"

After he mumbled a reply, she said. "Ray-John—that's so pretty. French, I guess?"

No one had ever said that to Réjean before.

✧   ✧   ✧

"*BONJUR*, GOOD MORNING".

The loudspeaker burst to life. Jack Shawcross welcomed the visitors and explained that this was a big day for River View. From their vantage point on the mound, the guests could see that much progress had been made—roads laid out and concrete poured for the foundations of the main building complex. Nevertheless, there had been no formal ground-breaking ceremony and today would rectify that omission.

"I must introduce our distinguished guests." Jack's voice

boomed out. "Welcome, Madame Mayor and Councillor Black who have generously found time to come to this ceremony."

There was a smattering of applause.

"Less familiar to you is my other guest," continued Jack. "Today I can introduce the main investor in our project, representing the Mission Corporation of New York, the Reverend Robert Harris! I call on him to say a few words before we move to the turf-cutting, which will be the full responsibility of Mayor Beaubien. She is, I understand, now expert in handling our big excavator, haha."

Harris took the microphone.

"*Bonjur, mes chers amis. Appelle-moi* 'Bob'. Unfortunately, I have misplaced my Ayetech which would have translated. For my poor French, I truly apologise."

"Today, I am here to sign a contract with River View," Harris continued. "To Mission, the organization I represent, this is a major investment in you and your community. Madame Mayor, Crewe is ideally placed for our first step into Canada. Mission aims to support and work with you and the citizens of Crewe for many years to come. To symbolize this commitment, I am proud to present you with this illuminated version of Mission's own publication, *The Guiding Hand*."

He held the book high.

"This is our vision for your community. We invest in you, and you invest in us. I encourage you to look at the guidance we provide on many themes of our modern world. If you have questions look within!"

Harris paused, seeing puzzled looks around the circle of on-lookers. Recognizing his speech sounded much like his last sermon back in Schenedy Falls, he decided to cut it short.

"Now, over to you, Madame Mayor, so we can plant a seed in the very clay of Crewe".

Hilary, who saw the implantation of the Mission in terms of an economic rather than spiritual uplift, pulled the lever which lowered the bucket to begin digging.

Bryce Desjardins, who had been pouring himself a beer in the hostess tent, came out to watch. He glanced at the time; it was four minutes to twelve.

Chapter 46

THE DAY FOLLOWING the protest at River View Chief Odek was leaving the Band Office to drive down to Crewe again. It was the morning of the River View sod-turning. Odek had received an invitation but had no intention of going.

"I am out on business, Harvey," he called as he went out of the office door. The assistant administrator looked at Kitsi across the desk and winked. Kitsi scowled and looked back at her computer screen.

As Dads climbed into the driver's seat of his truck, he heard a cough beside him. Surprised, he turned to find Uncle Joe discarding a cigarette and crushing it in the gravel with his foot.

"Hi Joe, what's up?" said Dads.

"Bad dream," said Uncle Joe. "The land is uneasy: I feel it in my stomach. Watch out on the road."

"Don't worry, Joe. I'll be out on the water, anyway." Dads had spent many long evenings listening to Uncle Joe's stories of the mischief wrought by the Wendigo.

"When the Wendigo moves the earth, the water gets out of its way." replied Uncle Joe.

"Well, okay, Joe. I'll be careful."

Dads had no intention of giving up his morning because of an elder's dream and, half an hour later, he was entering the town of Crewe, towing his boat trailer. He made a wide turn into Chemin de la Rivière towards the town boat launch and pulled up behind a dark blue Mercedes with tinted windows. Dads got out of the cab to greet Charles Bludston, who was standing by the curb scrutinizing the river eddies. The lawyer had heard that Chief Odek was the best fishing guide on the Akonaga; if anyone could guarantee a large muskie, it would be Odek.

Bludston always carried his rod-case and weather gear when on business. He would work like fury on a file and then disappear to relax on nearby water. It was a perk of being an independent counsel. TiteGas, although a good enough client, lived up to its name and tended to question the hours he booked.

Dads backed the aluminium boat down the ramp into the water, climbed into the back of his truck and released the winch. Bludston, holding the painter, walked the boat a few metres along the short dock while Odek parked the truck, with its dripping trailer, in the nearby lot.

"Might as well load your gear in now," Dads called, walking back to Bludston carrying a large cooler and a red plastic tank full of gas. Dads clambered into the boat and primed the outboard, a thirty-horsepower marine Honda.

After letting the motor idle for a few minutes, he signalled to Bludston to cast off. The slow current carried the bow away from the dock. Dads opened the throttle and the boat surged away, cutting a tight circle as he steered out into mid-stream.

His standard rate for a fishing charter was by the hour, and the lawyer had suggested starting mid-morning. They would run upriver for a few kilometers, trolling slowly against the current, turn and speed back down to a special deep pool Dads knew opposite Crewe where last year a client had caught a spectacular trophy fish.

Dads sensed that Bludston had no wish to chat. It was no problem should his guest wish to commune with nature: he wanted the lawyer relaxed. Later, he intended to hit Bludston with the matter of compensation for the River View development.

Dads had learned that TiteGas was now collaborating with Jack Shawcross in the matter of shale gas development. Oil companies were a money tree in Dad's experience: compensation for use of ancestral land could be generous.

An hour later, and several decent fish to the better, Bludston left his rod in the rest and reached back into his bag, pulling out a bottle of rare Gibbey's whiskey. He waved it at Odek, who nodded with no change of expression. Hey, they were well off the reservation.

"Five more minutes, and we can drop the anchor at the edge of the deep pool I know."

On the far side of the river, just downstream from River View, a meander of the main river had been cut off, leaving a large area of swamp which served as an important hatchery for young fish. Lurking in deeper water along the edges of the reeds were the hunters; bass and pike. And from a deep pool below the riffles upstream, swooped in the occasional muskie; a top predator ready to take anything, including the trifling lures offered by fishers. The only fish in the river larger than muskie were sturgeon, but these were rarely seen and anyway were gentle scavengers. Dads knew that Uncle Joe claimed to have talked a six-foot sturgeon into his canoe. The story was elaborate and involved other spirits of the river which had helped Joe entice the monster up from its groove in the river bed. Perhaps later Dads would tell it to his client.

Dads cut the engine and they drifted in. He lowered a line gently over the side of the boat until he felt the weight touch bottom, then he let out another thirty feet. The boat swung around to face the slow current. Charlie Bludston, Chief Odek and a bottle of Gibbey's finest were at anchor. It was eleven-thirty.

Chapter 47

O N THE RAFT, Molly and Argile sat on a mattress damp with dew and wrapped in a sleeping bag. Argile was talking about the Leda Clay.

"It's almost as though it is alive" he said. "The Leda is like a predator, it lies in wait and then, when least expected, it pounces. And voilà, a landslide. Mind you, I have never seen a major failure. I have seen the videos of some massive landslides in other quick clays; the Rissa slide in Norway, for example. I have witnessed nothing as dramatic in the Leda. Am I am boring you?"

"No, go on," replied Molly. Her clay model of Argile had worked a treat, and she liked to see Argile so enthused. In their new intimacy she felt they had breached the wall between his dry academic geology and her spiritual convictions about the powers of crystals. She passed him the mug of tea they were sharing. It was her special tea, infused with a pouch of dried mushrooms.

"Just suppose there was landslide right here." Molly pointed to the steep river bank. "How would it start?"

Argile thought about the many factors that could trigger a landslide in the Leda Clay.

"Well, the rains this year had been exceptional," he said, "so the hydrostatic pressure at depth must be high. I have measured unusually large creep on the slopes above Crewe, and many small landslips. And there are thin bands in the Leda which my tests show to be highly sensitive. They seem strong but are weak under stress."

"Just like my ex, Ben," said Molly.

"Yes, well," said Argile, who had heard previous comments by Molly on the character of Ben Gold. "I suppose. But if a sudden jolt—an explosion, say—stresses the Leda, the clay could liquefy and lose all its strength. Here, the river bank might collapse, triggering a cascade effect; successive failures eating their way backwards into a hillside for hundreds of metres. We call that a 'retrogressing' landslide and they can get big."

Argile would dearly love to see such a landslide—from a safe vantage and without loss of life, of course—just to watch the transition from solid materiality to chaos. He visualized the River View project. There had been plenty to disturb the Leda. For instance, that fresh mound of soil piled beside the river. There was only so much load the Leda could tolerate. In his mind's eye, it all began to fail.

"Look at the river bank over there, Molly, where the excavator is working. Imagine this: the weight of the excavated soil finally overwhelms the resistance of the underlying clay. Suddenly it gives way. Let's say fifty metres of the bank collapses. It would be almost soundless from this distance, perhaps a faint hiss on the wind, and what was once green river bank would slide underwater, leaving a grey scar. A foam-crested wave travels outward from the collapse; not a dangerous wave, perhaps only a few feet in height, but reaching the shallows near the bank it grows, surging along, slapping the vegetation down like a rough comb. It passes under us here, rocking the raft violently and then continues out across the river. Its energy gradually fades as the wave front broadens, only to regain its force as it surges up the narrow creeks you see on the shore opposite. After a few minutes, the raft would cease rocking and the river would calm."

"Is that all?" said Molly, a little disappointed.

"Hey, wait!" She rummaged in her sling bag and pulled out a

THE LEDA

Crewe Stone. "Here, take this stone: it has power. Make it happen!"

Argile took the stone from Molly. He felt odd; his throat dry and his mind racing. What did Molly say was in the tea?

"Okay, let's think this through," he said. "The first landslide reveals a fresh clay bank behind it. Its footing gone, that too slumps into the river. The top meter of soil, capped with green turf, settles gently, but the clay beneath liquefies, slumping and mixing with the churning water. Mud squirts from the toe of the slope, forced by the weight of the sliding mass. There is nothing to prevent further collapse. The water near the slide is a seething chop. A tumult of sharp waves swallow the land bite by bite."

Argile was gazing fiercely towards the River View development. He smiled distractedly at Molly. She saw his passion, his bright concentration as he described the tumult in his mind.

"Go on," said Molly.

Argile stood and waved his arms, as if to embrace the widening chaos. "The landslide devours more and more land in a widening arc. The new failures feed the flow into the river through the narrow neck of the initial collapse. See the pulsing mounds of mud-laden water writhe and boil across the river! It's no longer the gentle rocking of the initial waves, but a violent turbulence from the outward rush of displaced water."

"You should understand," Argile explained earnestly, "that here on the raft we are perfectly safe. We wouldn't see the growing chasm left, nor the frantic waters trying to flood back into the newly created void. We might see some of those bushes and trees over there moving across the landscape with the flow of mud, riding on islands held together by roots."

"And see that barn over there?" Argile pointed to a structure in the distance. "Imagine it waltzing slowly along before being folded into the mud as it approaches the river. And those houses plucked from that new development in Crewe; tilted at all angles, they struggle to remain afloat, like a defeated armada on a dense, grey sea."

"Wow," said Molly.

"But no casualties," Argile concluded, a little downcast.

Molly was impressed by how effective the tea had been. But then, they hadn't eaten breakfast, and by now it was nearly midday.

Chapter 48

A LL WAS NORMAL that Thursday morning at TiteGas operations. Although junior and recently qualified, Brandon had been charged with overseeing the injection of waste water into a well newly drilled from a pad just west of the Akonaga River. He sat in the control hut—a converted portacab-in—before a large dual screen. Cables radiated from the hut to sensors and activators on tanks and valves around the drill site. A sign on the door insisted that hard hats and steel-toed boots were compulsory on the rig site. Below it, scrawled on a square of cardboard with a felt-tip pen was a second notice: "Boots must be scraped of mud before entering. This means you!"

Through a small rectangular window of scratched plexiglass, Brandon could peer across the water and see the spire of the Crewe church, two kilometers distant. He had called 'Good Morning' to the morning shift on the rig floor, getting a grunt in return from the driller, the taciturn Albertan Leanne Turnbull. Completely useless at the public meeting. The Lord knows why Titegas had insisted on her coming along: he had all the technical bases covered. Brandon felt Leanne did not respect his engineering qualifications. Brandon was a graduate of Wescan University: Leanne came from the blue collar town of Leduc; the east side, where the unfinished sub-divisions trail off into prairie littered with stockpiles of rusted drill pipe.

Designated an 'injector well', the new borehole intersected a fractured rock formation which had proved accommodating of waste water elsewhere across the field. The gas from other 'production' wells came to surface wet, and Titegas needed ways to dispose of the salty brine which condensed from the gas. The volumes tankered to River View were only a small portion of the total; pumping most of this waste water back underground solved the problem.

The rig crew had run steel tubing to the bottom of the hole and pumped cement between the tubing and the wall of the borehole. The cement had set, bonding the metal to the surrounding limestone to form a tight seal.

Brandon checked his watch. It was coming up to noon and the crew would soon be on lunch break. He left his hut to check that the lines connecting the brine tanks to the well-head had been attached correctly.

"You should put your hard hat on," said Leanne, rolling her eyes. "And for your information, we have already pressure-tested the shit out of them."

Chastened, Brandon returned to the control hut, where he would monitor the injection of waste water. A red light on the console turned to green; Leanne had started the rig's pumps.

Leanne pumped a precise volume of heavy mud—called a slug—into the top of the tubing. She then activated the valve to the storage tanks and brine started to flow down the pipe. Two minutes later and fifteen hundred metres underground, the slug reached the bottom of the hole. The mud started to flow back towards the surface between the outside of the tubing and the wall of the borehole. When the mud rose up-hole a short distance, Leanne stopped the pumps and activated a packer. This was an inflatable collar that sealed the bottom hundred metre section of the borehole from the surface.

Brandon was monitoring the gauge in the control hut. When pumping resumed, the needle rose steadily until the pressure in the borehole exceeded that in the surrounding rock, and leveled off. Waste water began to filter into the labyrinth of natural fractures.

Brandon called Leanne on the intercom.

"It's going great," he said. "At this rate we should empty the holding tanks in..." Brandon glanced at his laptop, "in five hours and twenty minutes."

"Okaydoke" came the reply.

The injected brine radiated outwards into the surrounding rock under the pressure of the pumps. It slipped through cracks and joints, sometimes forced sideways by an impermeable rock face before discovering a weakness and wriggling through, like droplets along a windshield. After ten minutes, the fluid encountered a fault. This was the same fault that formed the edge of the escarpment near Argile and Em's cabin. Argile called it 'Wilson's Fault', for want of a better name, and at surface there was no sign that the fault had seen any recent movement. In the TiteGas well, nearly five kilometers away, the fault was hidden deep underground, covered by much younger sediments. TiteGas' geophysical surveys failed to detect it.

Since the last glacial retreat, the rocks of the Canadian Shield under Crewe have slowly risen, after being pressed several hundred meters into the Earth's crust by the weight of ice. This rebounding movement stressed the fractures that riddle the rigid bedrock. Much as lifting a completed jigsaw puzzle causes corners to pop out and gaps appear, the new stresses forced minor movements and readjustments as the rock jostled to find a new equilibrium of forces. The stress had increased to where friction barely prevented the rock masses facing each other across Wilson's fault from slipping: the fault was primed and cocked.

As pumping continued, the building pressure forced crystal grain from crystal grain, reducing the friction between the opposing faces of the fault. At one minute to noon, stress overcame resistance and the fault slipped. It was initially a movement of mere centimeters—a preliminary jolt—but this first release transferred the stress to the next sticking point. This failed in turn, the building momentum tearing apart the fault which unzipped in a long shuddering tremor: an earthquake was born.

Brandon in the control hut was fifteen hundred metres directly above the fault. He saw a major spike in pressure transmitted from the downhole sensor. Seconds later, the compressional waves from the quake reached the surface. The hut lurched and Brandon's coffee slopped across his work surface. He clutched the edge of the desk to keep from falling off his stool. His eyes were locked on the gauge. The pressure was rising and falling wildly. Whatever was happening was not normal. He looked wildly around for the manual describing emergency procedures. It was an inch thick and propping up a corner of the hut's air conditioner.

"A fat lot of use, thumbing through that," muttered Brandon, coming to a decision. He called Leanne.

"Leanne. For crysake, shut down the pumps. Now!" he shouted through the intercom. There was no answer, but he saw the red light come on.

The shuddering gradually subsided, although Brandon's heart rate would take much longer to return to normal.

The intercom rang. It was Leanne.

"I will need that in writing," she said.

Brandon glanced at his watch. It was eleven fifty-eight. Shit.

✧   ✧   ✧

THE SEISMOGRAPH AT the Geological Institute had recorded minor earth tremors in the region for decades. As Roch had once explained patiently to Argile, these were the minor readjustments to be expected during post-glacial rebound. They were, *mon cher Argile*, like the way bedsprings occasionally twang when you jump on an old mattress. Argile, who knew this perfectly well, had gritted his teeth.

Given the unremarkable seismic history of the region, the sudden and unexpected movement on Wilson's Fault surprised by its intensity and duration. Previous tremors in Crewe had lasted less than ten seconds. This quake would last for twenty-five. The shuddering bedrock transmitted its violent energy into the overlying Leda Clay which liquefied under the prolonged shaking, and began to flow.

Chapter 49

S EAN REACHED THE raft just before Ems and Roch. They had left their vehicles at the end of the gate, stooped to pass through the hole in the fence, and trotted along the river bank towards a clump of willows.

Sean hailed the moored raft. "Professor, you have visitors!"

Until now, it had been a tranquil morning on the raft. Molly looked up to see three people standing on the river bank. She recognized Sean Box, Roch Legalet from the cycling club and—her heart sank—Argile's wife.

"Chester, are you there?" shouted Ems.

Molly glanced at the gangplank leading from the river bank onto the raft. Perhaps she could loosen the rope and float down river with Argile. The two women glared at each other.

Molly heard Argile behind her. "Wait!" he called out. "It's coming!" Lying in the bunk on the lower deck, Argile had felt a first premonitory judder, amplified by the hull of the raft. This is what he had been waiting to record on his geophones for months: the sounds of rock and earth being rent asunder: developments deep underground were reaching a climax.

A sudden jolt threw Ems to her knees. The ground was shaking and she could barely keep her feet. She stumbled away from Sean, who were holding onto the trunk of a willow. Roch slipped down the steep bank and was struggling on his knees at the water's edge.

Ems clutched a rope and pulled herself across the swaying

gangplank onto the raft. She pushed past Molly to find Argile on his knees, gripping the railing.

"What the hell do you think you are doing? *Sapristi!*—I have been worried sick!"

"Wait! Please don't disturb Argile," cried Molly. "He is connecting with the Leda. You can feel the power, the vibrations!"

"*Il est malade,*" replied Ems.

Ems recognized one of Argile's favourite nodules lying on a bamboo table. She had heard him explain about these *maudites* concretions enough times. Smoke from a twist of joss was curling over it. She picked it up.

"See!" she cried into Argile's ear. "Here is your rock. And now it's gone. *Voilà!*"

She flung the stone as hard as she could. It struck the low cliff downstream of the raft where the river had exposed the Leda Clay. Ems later swore that she saw the bank shiver when the nodule hit. It bounced into the water. The ripples from its entry seemed to freeze; the agitated surface stilled, as if stunned by this outrage in the previously calm morning.

"*C'est fini.* Wake up Chester Argile!"

Argile turned slowly to face his wife. A short distance away, a long section of the river bank slid silently into the river, revealing a scar of grey clay. A small wave travelled outwards from the collapse.

Molly was pale with shock. She heard distant shouts from the River View development. Then, the landscape shifted; a scene change; cars, trees and buildings slipping towards the river.

Time: eleven fifty-nine.

✦   ✦   ✦

FROM THEIR ANCHORAGE, Dads' cry of alarm drew Bludston's

attention to the far bank of the river. Bludston turned to see the water near the bank rise in a low mound, crested by a thin line of cream-coloured foam. They watched as the wave sped towards their craft, growing in height and menace, the cream topping resolving into an angry mane of whipped water.

"Hold on!" Dads swung the bow of his boat to face the looming wave, now nearly six feet high.

The bow of the boat lifted smoothly up the face of the wave, the men crouched low in the face of this small tsunami. The churning mass of water tossed them violently as it rushed towards the southern shore. Mixed among the sheaves of reeds plucked from the shallows, the wave carried the boat across the far riverbank and into the scrubland beyond. After fifty yards or so, the boat swung broadside to the slowing flow and, together with a raft of branches, came to rest along a sinuous tide mark, the wave's momentum finally exhausted.

"That was quite a ride," said Bludston still clutching the bottle of Gibbey's. "Whoa, look at that!"

He pointed over the stern of the boat to where the wave had heaved a swath of reeds. There, among other flotsam was a large sturgeon—eight feet at least—gasping on the mud. Even during his sport fishing holidays in the Caribbean, Bludston had never hooked anything as big.

"I don't like your methods, Chief, but I appreciate the results," he said.

Dads found a measuring tape in the boat's locker. He stepped over the side, onto drying sand, and walked to the fish. It regarded him with stoic resignation from one large unblinking eye.

"I'll measure it, take a picture of you and the fish," he said. "Then let's haul this monster back to the water. It's catch and release."

Fifteen minutes later, they had dragged the fish to the water's edge—the river by that time back in its proper channel, more or less—and put its snout into the swirling water. The fish gave a powerful wriggle and slipped into the stream. Smeared with mud, both men looked across to where the far bank had foundered into muddy chaos. They could see a tangle of trees to their left, and what looked like broken buildings disappearing downstream. Upstream, to their right, cleaner water was already reasserting itself, and the river was reverting to its habitual, languid flow.

After a pause, Dads thought now might be a good time. He looked the lawyer in the eye.

"You know, the Band is interested in acquiring some of that River View land, what's left of it. Perhaps you can have a word with Jack Shawcross. I imagine he won't have much use for it now."

From far across the river, the programmed clock in the tower of St. Petraphile chimed noon.

✧　✧　✧

AFTER THE TURMOIL downriver had subsided, Argile was sitting on the top deck of the gently rocking raft.

Ems watched the mud surging into the river just downstream. *La merde*, literally. The raft bobbed up and down on the dying waves. She looked around. Molly Laberge was clutching a railing, face white. Stunned probably, thought Ems. Good. Roch was struggling back up the river bank, clutching to willow saplings. He was hunched over, a ragged figure covered in grey mud. Ems turned to watch her husband.

"It's a butterfly effect," said Argile, finally. "It took just a tiny extra load to pass a critical limit and this chain reaction resulted. The first collapse destabilized the bank, leading to the first failure, and then another, and so on: a retrogressing land slide. The mixing caused the clay to liquefy and flow. The Leda has had enough."

"I don't want to live here anymore," said Ems quietly.

Argile didn't reply immediately. He was thinking. The rush of mud had sated his appetite for retrogressive slides: he had finally seen and participated in a most satisfactory climax. He now knew the Leda in all her moods. Tomorrow, from the superior vantage of his and Ems' cabin on the edge of the escarpment, he would view the grey scar on the landscape in the valley below. He would sit on the veranda, a beer at hand, listening to the recordings from the mine. He expected to hear the sounds of the Leda as she shrugged the lice from her back; the scratching of Rob Freeman's Kobatsu, the drilling and pumping by TiteGas, the gurgles of the bloating water from the drains, stream and rivers incessantly sapping the Leda's strength. It would be a symphony, culminating in a final movement when an entire landscape growled its final release and rushed towards the river.

Argile glanced at Molly, her expression one of intense excitement as she stared, not at Argile but at the curls of turbid water roiling around the slide where it entered the river. He recognized her expression—the Leda had recruited a new admirer.

He looked back at his wife and thought it was time to retreat to more reliable ground. Perhaps Ems would enjoy a road trip west to Georgian Bay; to where the rocks were a billion years old and entirely bereft of Leda Clay. Maybe further, as far as the Rockies.

"Yes, perhaps you're right," he said.

PART IV
CONSOLIDATION

Chapter 50

NATIONAL NEWS SERVICES picked up Dara Odek's on-the-spot reporting from the River View project site, which the media insisted was the 'epicentre' of the slide. Later, the jury at the annual media gala voted it best action reporting for the year, an award which ensured Dara a career move from *The Courier* to a classy news factory in Toronto. She had been lucky: with people's Ayetechs absent without leave, her video from a vantage point on the roof of one of the large tanker trucks using an old iPhone, was the only filmed record of the slide. It showed the flow of liquefied mud sweeping through the breach into the river carrying, like so many doll's houses, the broken homes of Vista Terrace, along with gently waving trees plucked from the forest land owned by Odeline Garrity. A bouncy castle, snatched by the flow from the picnic area at Rosty's Scar, turned slow pirouettes in the eddies.

"Poignant," said one of the award judges. "So real!" said another.

Panning to capture the scale of the devastation, Dara had filmed the vehicles belonging to the guests of Jack Shawcross being swallowed as the ground beneath the parking lot foundered. She caught the desperate rush of *Bleus* to rescue their bikes, and their rapid retreat to firmer ground. Zooming in, she captured gritty images of individual acts of heroism: Bryce Desjardins gripping the hand of Hilary Beaubien as he hauled her from the abyss opening at her feet; Priebus, the young acolyte, wading into swirling mud to guide Pastor Bob and Shawcross to safety.

Fortunately, a neck of land next to the initial breach offered refuge. This was part of the River View lands which had undergone chemical stabilization by brines—courtesy of TiteGas—and here the Leda proved strong enough to resist liquefaction.

The VIPs and guests retreated to this safer vantage. After several minutes, the flow of the slide waned, and it became clear that their island refuge would not founder. Harris stood trembling, supported by Priebus. He had been waste deep in mud and close to being swept away. His jacket was ruined, and he was taking it off when he noticed something strangely heavy in a pocket. He reached in and pulled out a round object the size of a baseball. As he held it in his hands, puzzled as to what it was, it suddenly fell in two pieces. Inside, perfectly preserved, were three fish skeletons. He held, kissed it; tasted the salt of the Sea of Galilee.

"Thank you, Lord," he cried. "Thank you for saving these poor souls this day...pulled from the pit by your guiding hand..." He hadn't really believed before.

Chapter 51

T HE CREWE SLIDE, as it came to be known, was not the largest of historical slides on Leda Clay, nor did there appear to be any immediate victims. Thanks to the fact that TiteGas ran its deep injection operations in late morning, the earthquake triggering the liquefaction of the Leda occurred during daylight hours, after most of the population had commuted to work. The collapse of the river bank and the subsequent retrogression of the slide consumed three hundred hectares, extending from River View north to the Crewe picnic area and east to the steep slopes leading to the Church. Power to the village was cut for several days.

Smaller failures occurred at multiple locations around the village and surrounding hills. Most of them developed slowly enough that people could see and react to the danger in time, although Rob Freeman, for one, had to run from his excavator as the slope above him collapsed.

Many residents of Crewe had gathered at the Church of St. Petraphile prior to the actual slide. News of the miraculous apparition around the statue behind the church had travelled by word of mouth since nobody could find their Ayetechs that morning. James Cahill's wife had run to tell Madame Bellesrides, whose network included the hairdresser, Marie-Lise Frippe. From her salon, the news had disseminated quickly, so by eleven a.m. much of the village had walked up to the church.

"Welcome, welcome all," called Father Bonenfant, as the

numbers swelled. He saw his handful of regular Sunday church goers plus many others. Bonenfant's minor miracle would boost his congregation. No doubt of that.

He led the group up the path to *La Grotte* and knelt on the hard bedrock before the statue: some followed his example although most remained standing, gazing in awe at the sight before them. By mid-morning, most of the drones had run out of power and dropped in a glistening heap around the statue's pedestal. The massed Ayetechs, detached from their transports, interlocked to form a glittering shawl draped over the shoulders of the Saint. Their jostling gradually ceased: the Ayetech had not anticipated the extensive power cuts: electricity to the Saint's halo was cut, and they were unable to recharge. Their collective panic grew, but in ever slower motion; like people condemned to plough into a sucking mire.

The following day, James Cahill fetched the wheelbarrow from behind the church and went up to the *La Grotte*. He plucked the Ayetechs from the statue of St. Petraphile placed them in the barrow and returned to the parking lot in front of the church. He carefully arranged the one hundred and seventy-four Ayetechs he had collected on a trestle table. He connected several to a twelve-volt battery and let them slowly recharge. They began to show signs of life. Although volunteers from Constance dispensed water in plastic bottles and offered blankets, and the Muslim family from the rectory prepared hot meals, James' table was the most popular: he offered to restore communications.

✧ ✧ ✧

THE INFORMAL ENQUIRY into the Crewe Slide took off on *The Courier Online* over the following days. The bulk of posts vilified the authorities. Elected representatives, however, tried to deflect blame for any failure to prevent or at least warn residents of the slide onto the shoulders of expert authorities in higher and more remote layers of government. The Geohazard Advisory Committee was—after people realized its existence—widely criticized. Some even called for jail time, but the Chair of the committee—a Dr. Roch Legalet—was unavailable to comment, having gone on an extended cycling tour in Italy. He had been invited to view earthquake damage in a seismically active terrain, said his 'away' message.

The Mayor of Crewe pointed out that she had not relied solely on the GAC but had sought out local expertise. Dr. Argile had warned of the dangers of the Leda, and Council and developers should have paid greater attention. But it had been, the Mayor insisted, no one person's fault.

"*C'est incroyable,*" she was quoted in *The Courier*. "Our business community is rallying around fantastically. And I am really pleased with our wonderful community spirit."

Privately, Hilary Beaubien could not allay the nagging feeling that the slide had been partly her fault. She knew that she had pressed too hard and the bucket of the excavator had dug too deep. Perhaps she had unleashed the Leda to ravage her town? She thought fleetingly of resignation but, on reflection, she realized that the village would need a steady hand over the coming months to manage the federal and provincial aid which she fully expected to flow to the community.

The Mayor's comments were not good enough for Elsie Truelove who had lost a portion of her property to the slide. Attributing the slide to an 'Act of God' might invalidate her insurance claim. She found common cause with Agnes Black whose house was one of the few remaining at the eastern end of Vista Terrace. Yawning tension cracks now threatened the buildings foundations. Jack Shawcross' gambions had failed miserably: the wire cages lay in tangled ruin and the rock ballast was scattered far down the valley amidst the debris.

Elsie's editorial in *The Courier* the following Saturday noted that it had been her reporter at the scene of the slide. She insisted that one question be answered; who was to blame? She questioned the wisdom of development and revived the suspicion—aired by residents online—that TiteGas' fracking was guilty.

At a hastily arranged press conference to respond to this allegation, TiteGas' vice president of community relations—well-versed in crisis management—vehemently denied that the company's operations had caused the earthquake which triggered the slide. Published studies, she insisted, had found no link between seismicity and fracking. An internal memorandum which surfaced several months later somewhat undermined this confident assertion. Released by EcoClub who had received it from an anonymous source, the memo ordered a review of the company's wastewater management strategy and, in particular, the disposal of brine into poorly understood geology. Mandy Brakes had, by that time, left the company.

✧   ✧   ✧

THE CAMPER VAN with out-of-province plates remained unclaimed for three months in the police lot in Constance. Forensics had detected no trace of drugs. However, the driver interviewed by Officer Patinaude had disappeared; presumably returned to the States. Under such circumstances, unclaimed property is put up for auction.

Sean Box had seen the sale advertised in *The Courier* and had gone on the off chance that he could acquire a somewhat damaged but otherwise sweet camper van. With a camper, he could drive all the way out west to go tree planting. He had made enquiries and there was an outfit working near Grande Prairie in Alberta who had promised to hire him. He was close to persuading Candice to come with him. She said that the name Grande Prairie sounded romantic.

Rob Freeman was the only other bidder, but when he saw Sean, he waved and gave a shrug. For two hundred dollars Sean became the owner of the van.

When he had rammed the back of the camper, Sean's truck had left a large indent. Otherwise, the engine and drive train seemed okay. He switched on the ignition and, after coughing briefly, the engine roared to life. He drove it cautiously back to T.J.'s garage.

Later that evening, he was giving Candice a tour of the van. The evening light was streaming through the open door of the garage, shining obliquely across the damaged rear of the van.

"Hey, Flatpack," said Candice. "That looks just like a face. See, those big dimples are the cheeks."

Sean hadn't noticed this before.

"*Attend*, wait a minute," he said. He went to the workbench and came back with two cans of spray paint. He looked critically at the rear of the van, then made several passes with dark blue spray paint. He finished with silver paint to put highlights in the beard, moustache and eyebrows.

Sean stood back to admire his work. Candice put her arms around his waist from behind and hugged him.

"I guess we found Jesus," he said.

"*T'est un vrai* Banksy," she murmured in his ear.

Chapter 52

DESPITE THE DEVASTATION caused by the Crewe Slide, authorities were quick to assure the population that no one had died. Two weeks after the event, however, a section of Chemin de la Rivière was being cleared of mud and debris deposited by one of the last convulsive ejections of Leda Clay. The excavation paused when municipal workers found human bones, encased in the stiffening clay. By tracing the course of the landslide inland, forensic investigators judged that the flow of liquid mud had carried them from the Garrity lands adjacent to the River View development.

It took some time to fully analyse the remains: there was a jumble of bones which took the forensic pathologist some time to sort out into a dozen bodies; male and female, adult and children. Although the pathologist was uncertain about the precise age of the bones, she was sure that the bones were as old as one of the skeletons she had exhumed earlier that summer in the woods near Crewe.

Graveyard Destroyed by Landslide was the headline run by *The Courier*. The paper nearly got it right; from DNA analysis it turned out not to be a dislocated graveyard of the earliest settlers but late burials of the Ako Band, fast declining in numbers from the onslaught of European viruses.

Marsha read the news on Réjean's Ayetech while taking a slow ride into the hills north of Montreal. She was riding on the pillion of the big E-bike, holding on tight to Réjean's waist, and shouted the news in his ear. That there were so many bodies astonished Réjean: he only remembered burying one, maybe two, and his first thought was that a gang member had been freelancing. The verdict was satisfactory, however, and there would no longer be any need for awkward explanations to Ma Tante. Next weekend he would take Marsha to meet Odeline. He hoped they would get on. Marsha, insisted that her family was part Irish. "It's O'Teague really," she assured him. Maybe they came from the same part of Ireland as the Garritys. It was a small place.

After they were released by the coroner's office, the bones of Aboriginal origin were reburied at a small ceremony devised by Ako elders. What remained of Murmurs Henri was claimed by the Toulouse family and cremated. Les Bleus did not attend.

✧   ✧   ✧

SINCE HIS ARRIVAL at St. Pet's, Father Bonenfant's congregation had shrunk; barely enough to fill the first two pews on an average Sunday. The Parish had been forced to delay the purchase of an air conditioner for lack of funds. The summer had been hot, and the inside of the Church stuffy and humid. Black mould had been detected.

Bonenfant's spirits had been further dampened by a letter from the Bishop who reproached him for an excess of ecumenical enthusiasm. Perhaps, the letter concluded, the question of air conditioning could be better addressed by a proactive church warden committee, provided they could rely on Father Bonenfant's leadership. The Bishop strongly disapproved of accepting contributions from any protestant influences, about which he had been informed by a parishioner.

But in the weeks following the Crewe Slide attendance surged. It was an answer to Bonenfant's prayers. He foresaw a substantial boost in collections.

As for Mission, when the Reverend Robert Harris reported back to headquarters, his conversation with Dean Polkhammer was short.

"Godammit Harris," Polkhammer said. "No property deal, no Mission. Pull your people out. And, my friend, I strongly suggest you stop talking about those damn concrete whats-its."

✧ ✧ ✧

IN THE AFTERMATH of the slide, the Ako Band sought to diversify their interests beyond the Akasino. With River View dead, Charles Bludston brokered a deal on behalf of Jack Shawcross. The Band acquired the lands for a nominal price, and subdivided the portion adjacent to the slide that remained firm and flat for residential development. Jack himself withdrew to south of the river, to lick his wounds and recommit himself to the traditional Shawcross business of potted meats.

The land directly affected by the slide remained a hummocky terrain; poorly drained, impossible to build on and scarcely reclaimable for agriculture. The area largely re-wilded into a tangle of scrub and wetland. It was later purchased from the Ako Band by the Municipality of Crewe to create *The Hilary Ernestina Beaubien Natural Area*. The name was a small victory for Agnes Black, who chaired the naming committee. She happened to know that the Mayor detested her middle name.

✧ ✧ ✧

THE AYETECH, SO as to ensure continued network dominance, integrated micro-drone assistance into new models. The Ayetech 'AyeFly' sold at a premium and flooded markets worldwide. Users could call their device from anywhere in reach of the network. The delta shapes of flying Ayetechs became a familiar sight. The collective had also come to recognize the inadequacies of its human hosts who, despite surveying and testing, could not foretell disaster. In future, Ayetech would itself monitor geological hazards like the Leda, listening closely for the now familiar sounds of rupture.

Chapter 53

ALCEE DUPREE TUGGED the sign back and forth to extract it from the frozen snow bank. The Doctor and Madame Argile had just sold their cabin on Chemin Ridge. Alcee had barely listed it before the offers came in.

Dr. Argile had told him they were moving to British Columbia to study avalanches in the mountains. *Mon Dieu*, it takes all sorts, thought Alcee. Madame Dupree, who had heard it at the salon, said it was because of that Molly Laberge and her scented candles.

Alcee was happy: it was late in December—normally a quiet time—but this was his third *vendu!* this week. Three sales: he was definitely on a roll.

Several of the homes listed by the *maudit* Multimeuble had disappeared in the landslide, leaving a residue of properties whose owners were eager to sell, and multiple opportunities for Alcee to exercise his personal touch. Now a firm believer in the advice provided by *The Guiding Hand*, he was practised in assuring would-be house buyers of the solidity of their foundations. "It was a once in a thousand years event," he would say. "And, *bien sûr*, if a house in Crewe was still there after the great landslide, it isn't going anywhere."

THE END

If you enjoyed *The Leda*, look out for this coming title from E.K. Wicher.

Life at *The Blackwater Sailing Club* on the reservoir is far from idyllic in this dystopic near-future. The dam retaining the waters is well past its design life...

ekwicher.com